Ransom
Redeemed

The Deverells
Book Four

Jayne Fresina

A TWISTED E PUBLISHING BOOK

Ransom Redeemed
The Deverells, Book Four
Copyright © 2016 by Jayne Fresina

Cover design by K Designs
All cover art and logo copyright © 2016, Twisted E-Publishing, LLC

ISBN-13: 978-1536840711
ISBN-10: 1536840718

"Well, he had brought this being to life. It was up to him now to teach the child how to live. Fortunately, he knew something about survival. But he could not coddle the child when it cried. That he could not do, for he had no knowledge of how. As if the babe knew this, its wailing petered out. Man and boy studied each other.

"I'll do what I can," True muttered gruffly. "I make no promises."

It was all new to him. To them both.

The babe raised a fist toward his face and shook it.

"Just like your mother," he sighed.

It was some time before he realized his son was trying to reach his nose, not blacken his eye. They would be at similar cross purposes for many years to come."
— **From the Memoirs of True Deverell.**

"Children are an extraordinary inconvenience, always wanting attention. At least Ransom was a quiet baby. Although, I suppose I would not have heard him crying from my suite at the other end of the house, in any case. Thankfully." — **Lady Charlotte Rothsey Deverell.**

"Brat will end his days swinging from a gibbet. And good riddance." — **Evelyn Bond, Nanny.**

"The upstart put me face down in the privy and ruined a very good cravat. Now that I am minded of it, I shouldn't be a bit surprised if the blackguard stole my pater's gold watch. It seems they'll let anyone into Oxford these days." — **The Honorable Cedric "Drippy" Pennington-Whittmore.**

"Infidele! Sans coeur! L'homme impossible!"— **Belle Saint Claire (Mademoiselle), Stage Artiste of Popular Renown.**

"He is worse even than his father; a despicable scoundrel, a sybarite without conscience."— *Anon. of Mayfair.*

"One (1) Brovver For Sale: Free to good howme. Or any howme."— **Raven Deverell, (seven and three quarters), in a note left on park railings.**

"Who?" — **Miss Mary Ashford, proprietress of** *Beloved Books*, **Trinity Place, London.**

Part One
The Determined Malefactor

Chapter One

Brimstone and Treacle
1844

Hell was considerably colder than he'd expected. Somebody must have let the fire go out.

In that dream-like moment, while his soul escaped for a wander and left his body falling through the air uninhabited, young Ransom Deverell felt quite certain the end was upon him.

Some would say, "Not before time considering the way he lived his life." But there was no one there to say it just then. The last human sound he heard that night was the excited shriek of a woman's laughter, just before it was abruptly silenced.

And her name was Sally. *Sally White*.

Yes, he finally remembered the name of his recently acquired traveling companion. Like shot, clumsily discharged from an old blunderbuss, his mind fired off little sparks of thought and memory as he watched her body and his, tossed through the air.

Sally White, barmaid at The Fisherman's Rest, was also the former mistress of his older half-brother. She hadn't seemed to notice that Ransom couldn't recall her name all evening. Now, only when it was too late, he remembered.

The sudden silence felt ominous, for although he

knew little about her he did know that Sally was not a quiet woman. With terrible certainty, therefore, Ransom could arrive at only one conclusion. She, like him, was dead when she hit the cold, hard ground. And although her hands were the last to hold the reins, folk would assume he had killed her with his well-known recklessness. There would be no one left alive to tell what had really happened.

But after a while— he had no idea how long— he felt his drifting spirit slip reluctantly back inside the familiar body. It moved very slowly, making great objection, like a little boy who, while longing to stay outside playing cricket in the last glimmer of summer daylight, was forced indoors by Nanny for a supper of tasteless, gelatinous dumplings and lukewarm, greasy mutton broth.

"This will chase those wicked, restless demons out of you, brat. And the bowl will be clean, young sir, before you leave that table. However long it takes and however many curses you mutter at me under your breath."

Nanny Bond. How unfortunate that in his last moments he should think of that mean-tempered old harridan. There had been a lot of nannies, but he remembered Evelyn Bond as the worst because of her obsession with forced feedings, followed by the liberal dosing of brimstone and treacle. And her favorite torment for the sick child— senna and prunes.

Perhaps Evelyn Bond was now an Imp of Satan come to fetch him. Would it be his punishment to spend eternity abandoned to her company again?

There was still no sign of Hell's fire. In fact, he was colder than ever.

Although his brain gave them no command, he knew his fingers clawed mechanically at rough grass. Brisk night air fluttered against his wide-open eyes, yet they saw nothing. His mind continued firing sparks of memory from the flared muzzle of that imaginary flintlock blunderbuss.

If only he had not encountered Sally White in need of rescue that afternoon and offered her a ride in his smart, new curricle. But when he saw her flashing money about, boasting loudly of a win on the horses, attracting the attention of unsavory characters, he knew somebody had to help her get home. Meanwhile, Ransom was meant to be travelling to his father's wedding, and it just so happened that any delay, any distraction from that journey, was a welcome relief. So he bought her dinner before they set off, and a great deal of wine was consumed.

Alternately laughing and screaming, Sally had begged for the reins and he, in a moment of drunken foolishness, had let her take them. He recalled a flash of her wheaten curls bouncing under a cheap straw bonnet, and her plump, wine-stained lips opened as if they were mid-summer petals on a blousy rose, almost past its peak. She wore cheap scent, so pungent that it became sickening.

There was an instant when the rare commodity of doubt had shimmered and fluttered out of the blackness, like an anxious moth tapping against a window, drawn to the light of a candle.

Perhaps he ought to get the reins back from her, he'd thought in that sliver of clarity. This was, after all, a brand new curricle and had cost him a pretty penny.

Too late. She would not relinquish control and when he no longer heard hooves on stone, Ransom realized she must have steered the horses off the road. Far from town then, they hurtled forward into the thickest, wildest darkness of the moor.

Suddenly the wheels had encountered a rough dip and then a boulder. As he lunged for the reins again, there was an almighty crack and he flew out of his seat. It felt as if his spine had just been rammed up through the back of his skull.

So there he was, his fingertips digging into cold earth, blood in his mouth, and a horse pushing at his foot as if to jolly him along, reminding him of their destination.

"Good of you to get here at all, I suppose." The horse took on his father's voice. "Might have known you'd be late for your own funeral!"

Would anybody mourn for him? No. He was an "unwanted, unlovable boy". Where had he heard that? He didn't know. The sparks would not fire for that one; instead there was a dull thud. Powder must be damp or the flintlock jammed.

Was it odd that he felt no sense of terror, merely anger and frustration? Probably not. Deverells were known for their audacity, a fighting bravado that never backed down or gave in. Amongst other, less admirable, things for which they were known.

The crumpled, dour face of an Oxford professor loomed out of the dark to lecture, "I am sad to say, Master Deverell, that despite your apparently vast, provocative, inventive and colorful command of the English language, you have no understanding of the word 'fear'. Like any other moneyed, twenty-one-year-old, determined malefactor, you have no limits. The world is yours to plunder. Women are plentiful, pleasures so abundant that they surpass your own ability to consume them all— certainly exceed your patience to fully appreciate each one— and youth, in your eyes, will last forever."

At the time this speech was uttered, it had floated into Ransom's ears only to be escorted out again with the mental foot-to-the-breeches alacrity he preserved for any such cautions and sermons. But on this darkest of all nights, three years later, he quite suddenly remembered every syllable.

The ease with which he had sailed through his studies, without seeming to put much effort into them, had been a great irritation to those university tutors. They'd viewed his success with skepticism, as

11

if it were a conjurer's trick. After all, his father was nothing more than a self-educated foundling, who made his fortune from gambling, and who might be— so the rumor went— American, of all things. Although the staid, hallowed halls of Oxford University were occasionally forced to accept other young men of the "noveau riche" class, there were none quite so new, nor so filthy rich as a Deverell.

"I merely advise caution," that grim professor had continued gravely. "Luck and youth are not infinite, nor do they come without cost. Eventually you will find yourself presented with a bill. One your father cannot pay for you."

On the moor that night Ransom suspected the account had just come due.

Something evil hovered nearby. Was it spiteful, cruel Nanny Bond with her brimstone and treacle? He would fight her. He was bigger and stronger now, and if she tried to put that bloody spoon near his or his little sister's lips again, he would fight the bitch with everything he had. Suddenly his spirit was fully re-awoken, inhabiting his veins, muscles, and sinews with renewed vigor, his tongue ready to spit and curse.

And so he didn't die that night after all. The thought of Nanny Bond waiting for him on the other side made Ransom even more determined to live. Which, as it turned out, was another form of punishment.

Just as he knew they would, many folk believed Sally White's death to be his fault. Even when it was later discovered that she had survived the accident and wandered away from the curricle, only to stumble upon another man who took advantage of her wounded state, stole that money from her purse, beat her and left her face down in a stream, people still held Ransom accountable for her even being there on the moor that night. His name was forever linked to the tragedy of Miss White's demise— to such an extent that many doubted the official verdict in the case and "knew" he should have gone to the gallows. For something. Anything.

He had probably used and abused poor Sally, they said. Although, in life she had few friends, and many critics who called her a slattern— and worse— in death she became the girl they all pitied, a lost, ill-used creature. An angel for the downtrodden. Those who once joined in the scornful chorus of sanctimonious jeers and would never have lifted a finger to help her while she lived, now cried the loudest about how so much more should have been done for her. The angry mob looked around for reasons why their "Own Dear Sally" had suffered such a tragic end, and Ransom Deverell, an outsider, was the perfect target for their self-righteous anger. It didn't matter that he'd been one of the very few who ever tried to help her.

One only had to look at him, they said. Just like

his notorious father, he was a cocksure, irreverent fellow of indeterminate pedigree or class. On the surface he appeared indifferent, cold, while on the inside there were, according to rumor, unplumbed depths of sin and depravity.

No, they didn't like him, never trusted him, never thought he'd amount to anything. He'd even shot at his own father once, so who knew what he could be capable of next? Ransom Deverell, they were sure, had got away with murder. He was wicked, irredeemable.

He heard it so often that he too believed it.

Chapter Two

Six years later
London, 1850

She was coming for him again. He heard her bones creaking and clattering as she crawled along like a disjointed spider. His lips broke apart, fighting to get her name out, but a gust of wailing wind filled his mouth. He choked, suffocating, and then, at last,

"*Sally!*"

Ransom jerked upright and cracked his knee on the side of the hipbath. Slowly he came back to reality.

It was a dream. Only a dream. Again.

At least three times a week for the past six years he'd endured a similar nightmare— the bloody, rotting image of Sally White, creeping across the moor, with her broken limbs and twisted neck, just to find him and wreak her vengeance.

That thick, sickly-sweet perfume she wore, although excessive, was not enough to mask the odor of putrid flesh.

His hand trembled as he wiped a damp palm swiftly across his equally moist brow. Beneath a sweat-saturated shirt, his heart pounded like a fist trying to punch its way out of his chest.

He leaned back against the chill metal— a welcome coolant for his hot, throbbing head— and

15

cautiously lowered his gaze, taking inventory of his parts. Still wore his boots and breeches, surprisingly, although his shirt hung loose, as if he was in the process of undressing when he climbed into the dry tub and fell unconscious. An empty wine decanter and a large candelabra rested on the floor nearby. The candles were all burned down to the brass, wax tears frozen into lumpy stalactites, suspended with an eerie sort of grace from the charred wicks.

Ransom took a few deep breaths, letting his pulse fall to a calmer rhythm.

What he really needed was some toast, coffee, and headache powders. He'd feel better then, get on with his day and the art of evading Sally's ghost. Until the next time he could no longer avoid falling asleep.

Holding his head as still as he could, he climbed out of the tub and then halted in surprise as a soft snore from the room beyond told him he was not alone. Oh, lord, he was in no mood to face anybody yet this morning, and he couldn't, for the life of him, remember who he might have brought to his bedchamber last night during the party.

But he could hardly hide in the bathtub any longer, could he?

Christ, he was stiff! Must be getting too old for this.

With a lurching step, leaning slightly off kilter, because he suddenly felt too tall for the house, he made his way from the dressing room to face his day and whoever lay in his bed.

A ghostly, bluish-grey haze meandered through half-closed curtains and fumbled over the wreckage of his bedchamber. Apparently he'd enjoyed quite an evening. Or might have, if he hadn't ended up in the empty bath alone and almost fully dressed. The three naked women on his bed were clear evidence of a missed opportunity.

Ransom's lips began to bend in a wry smirk, until their progress was interrupted by a wide yawn as he sagged against the doorframe. Maintaining the infamous Deverell reputation was exhausting. Nobody, of course, would believe that he hadn't laid a finger on any of those women. They would take one look at the scene and assume he'd been living up to profligate expectations.

The nearest female was a gloriously rumpled redhead. Didn't recall her name, if he had ever known it, but she possessed the shape of a Rubens muse. On her left a slender brunette stretched out, face down, one arm curved around a pillow, while a harvest-gold blonde sprawled across the end of the bed.

He now had a vague memory of inviting them in and sloppily pouring wine into four glasses— an action delayed by hands running through his hair, pulling on the knot of his cravat, fingers wriggling into button holes, removing his waistcoat. Excited giggles and gasps blowing in his ear. He remembered suddenly needing to do... something, heading for the dressing room and bumping his shoulder into the doorframe so hard it spun him one hundred and eighty degrees.

But then ... nothing.

His pretty sirens must have grown bored waiting for his return from the dressing room, and finally drifted into sound sleep. Perhaps he should check that they too weren't dead. He could see the lurid newspaper story already.

Deverell's Son Found With Three More Dead Women.

They'd hang him for sure this time.

But the contented rhythm of their snores assured him they still breathed. Thank goodness.

One shoulder propped against the doorframe, he pondered the debauchery those four walls must have witnessed. This was once his father's bedchamber, but True Deverell rarely came up to London now and had given the town house to Ransom with only the following proviso— "Don't wreck the place and don't tumble the maids. I pay the staff to keep the house clean and maintained, not to polish your newel post."

As if Ransom couldn't keep his hands off any attractive petticoat he saw. Well, he thought with a grim smile, his father probably knew him better than he knew himself, for almost everything Ransom did, True Deverell had done before him.

"Father, you're being a hypocrite," he would say.

To which his father replied, "I try to save you from the mistakes I made with women, but I see it's a

18

fruitless, thankless task."

Yes, it was. He didn't understand why his father even made the effort at this late stage.

"So do as you will. Just don't shoot at me again the next time a female betrays you, boy. Because I might not be able to convince the Justice of the Peace that it was an accident another time."

His father always brought up that shooting sooner or later, and Ransom would reply, "Well, perhaps you shouldn't have bedded my fiancée." Of course, it hadn't quite happened that way, but he still went through the motions of accusing his father, and True, likewise, would repeat, yet again, his version of events.

"I did not invite that woman into my bed. She tried to seduce me and when my rejection wounded her pride, she told me she was engaged to you and had the gall to suggest I pay for her silence, otherwise she would tell you a pretty tale. She knew, it seems, that her word would hold more weight with you than mine. Since I refused to entertain this clumsy attempt at blackmail she ran to you with her filthy lie and you, being a hothead like your mother, instantly came after me with a dueling pistol. And very bad aim. Next time you shoot at a man, sober up first."

Ah, yes: Miss Flora Pridemore, failed blackmailer. At the age of only nineteen Ransom had made a lucky escape, and learned a very good lesson about the mercenary intentions of females.

"Pity you had to scrape my shoulder with a bullet before you came to your senses about that one," his father would add with a dour chuckle.

These days, Ransom managed his personal affairs with only three rules: avoid promises, remember to leave a window open for timely escape, and always keep one's boots close by.

"Why do I constantly feel as if we're caught in the midst of a house fire?" a lover once whined to him.

But he always made it plain, from the beginning of an affair, that pleasure was his only pursuit and nothing was to be taken seriously. Ransom Deverell had no interest in marriage and there were, he was certain, rats scuttling around the east end of London that would make better fathers. He did not like children even when he was one. He was a man with something damaged inside, and he suspected it was so at birth.

Born of a loveless marriage and then blamed for every discomfort and discontent his parents suffered as if he directly caused it, Ransom grew up under a dark cloud of animosity. Left often to the "care" of detached, bureaucratic nannies, the first two things he'd ever learned were the art of self-preservation and how to make his own entertainment. When his sister was born even less attention came his way. Unless, of course, he was in trouble for some misdeed.

"You're a horrid child," Nanny Bond had hissed

at him once, because he spat out some foul-tasting soup she'd tried to force down his throat. "God is watching you!"

At ten years of age, Ransom already had a smart tongue. "But He forgives. Isn't that the way it works? If God didn't forgive sinners there'd be no one in Heaven."

"He won't let you in, boy. There's a part missing from you and the Devil took it, so you're his creature," she'd assured him. "You have no conscience, and you'll go straight to Hell."

"Good," he'd replied stoically. "Because I've seen some of the high and mighty folk who go to church on a Sunday and call themselves Christians, and I'd rather not go where they're going, thank you very much."

That got him a beating about the ears.

Now he thought of the space where his conscience should be as an untenable moor. Nothing was allowed to dwell there long. If anything tried, he chased it off with his wild pursuit of pleasure — a bacchanalian force that, in his imagination, took the form of a large, ever-hungry falcon. From its perch in the stark branches of a dead tree on hardscrabble land, this bird swooped down on any pitiful, lost creature that wandered into its sharp-eyed view. Thus Ransom patrolled his mind during waking hours, fed his imaginary bird of prey with sinful delights at night and, by never being still, kept Sally White's ghost at bay. Or tried, for as long as he could.

Last night's party, like all others he held at the London house, had been a bright and noisy event that helped keep him awake and active well into the late hours. Ransom was a generous host who asked for nothing from his guests except to be entertained and kept awake. Nobody left until dawn had spread her petticoats across the sky, and sometimes they remained even longer. Like the trio of sirens on his bed.

So this was how he kept up the brazen image expected of True Deverell's eldest legitimate son and hell-raiser. He gave the "punters"— to use one of his father's gambling terms— what they anticipated, nothing more or less. He was firmly entrenched as the worst of men, the Determined Malefactor, as that old Oxford professor had once labeled him.

For most women, so he'd found, that description appeared to be a fascinating lure rather than a warning.

There was one young lady, however, who was not drawn in. And Ransom caught her eye now, as he sleepily surveyed the untidy room. Like the crack of a whip, her gaze, staring coolly down at him from an oil painting on the far wall, brought him sharply upright. He pushed himself away from the doorframe and brushed down his shirt sleeves.

"Yes, yes," he muttered, wincing up at her, "I know I must be a pitiful sight this morning. But if I lived in a painting and never actually collided with real people, I could stay as pristine and self-satisfied as you, Contessa."

A woman of mystery and eternal distance, she remained mildly scornful, of course. She did not need words to communicate her opinion of him and the various problems he got himself into.

When he first moved into the house, Ransom had found her portrait hanging downstairs in the hall, but he'd moved her to his bedchamber because there was something about her countenance that made him think she read all his secrets, all his sins. Such an intimate confidant ought to be kept in a less public area of the house, he'd quickly decided.

Occasionally his female guests complained that they felt her disapproving gaze even in the dark. He knew what they meant, but he never got around to moving her elsewhere.

He called her "La Contessa" because, although he knew nothing about her, she had a very noble mien. Her complexion was olive, the hair very dark, tightly framing an oval face, and she posed beside an arched window, through which some medieval town could be seen, a cluster of rounded bell towers and tall, narrow houses of bleached stone, with terracotta roofs jumbled against a coppery, almost sinister sky.

But Ransom's gaze always went to her hands, which were gloveless and held a long-stemmed thorny rose. The proximity of her small fingers to those vicious-looking thorns troubled him every time he looked at the picture.

"Think you're so clever, don't you?" he grumbled. "You look down on me for my mistakes, but clearly you don't even know the first thing about thorns." Had nobody warned her? Perhaps, by the time the portrait was completed, she had learned her lesson about pricks, he mused.

Her eyes—pale and clear—observed his antics with guarded amusement. Her mouth was softly curved in an almost-but-not-quite smirk.

Look at yourself, Deverell, she seemed to chide softly. *For pity's sake, pull yourself together. Don't you know what today is?*

No. Should I?

She seemed to think he should know. Something important was supposed to happen, but she would give no further clue. Her smug lips were sealed.

Catching sight of his scowling reflection in a mirrored wall panel, Ransom finally realized that his shirt was badly stained with red wine. Like a large bloodstain. He tore it off over his head and returned to his dressing room. There he splashed his face and chest with water from the washbasin, drew fingers hastily through his hair, and looked around for a clean shirt.

But his head hurt too much, his mouth was dry, and the need for sustenance was so overwhelming he felt certain he'd lose his stomach any minute if he didn't soon fill it with something. Driven by a new burst of urgent steam, he grabbed an evening jacket instead of a shirt. That was good enough for a quick visit to the kitchen, and while there he'd put a tray of food together for his companions too. They must need replenishment.

But he was only half way down the stairs, when a clattering of the front door bell halted all thoughts of breakfast. Tripping to a halt, he looked down through the window at the landing.

A Hansom cab waited in the street below and when he opened the window to peer farther out, he saw a young woman in a chartreuse silk coat and bonnet, waiting patiently at his door. Ah, it must be Wednesday.

He called out a hasty "Good morning", and his visitor glanced upward. At once he recognized the pretty, doe eyes and warm brown skin of the woman he should be expecting today for their standing appointment. Before he could complete his course to the front hall and let her in, however, a second Hansom cab rattled to a halt behind the other and amid a great deal of clucking and fussing yet another woman appeared— this one far less inclined to wait patiently at his door. She marched up the steps in an extremely large, extravagantly trimmed bonnet that could only belong to a woman with both a bold fashion sense and the greedy desire for attention.

Belle Saint Clair.

He had forgotten her return to England today. But why was she there so early?

Perhaps it was not as early as it felt.

Even while pulling on the bell rope, she embarked upon a screaming interrogation of the girl in chartreuse silk, but her efforts were wasted for the first young lady knew only a handful of English words and Belle, being French and in a temper, spoke a mixture of languages that would confuse anybody.

Barely waiting for the last ring to finish echoing through the house, she pulled on the bell cord again, before thumping hard with her knuckles and shouting his name at the door like a landlord looking for overdue rent.

Uh oh.

Ransom had never led her to believe he promised exclusivity, yet today he heard a tenor of possessiveness in her voice, and in the way she abused the poor girl on his steps, that suggested she might have formed dangerous expectations of their affair.

That wouldn't do at all.

Ransom swore softly and glanced upward to the ceiling, on the other side of which his lovely trio still slept peacefully. It was most unfortunate for Belle if she had assumed their relationship to be exclusive, but, should that be the case, the tableau upstairs would immediately assure her otherwise. Nothing he could say would persuade her that he had spent his night alone in a hipbath, but the last thing he needed anyway was a woman foolishly thinking he had any capacity, or desire, to be monogamous. Better she get that straight in her pretty head at once.

He heard the footman opening the front door, then her voice.

"Why do you take so long, imbecile? Where is 'e? Je vais ecraser ses noix!"

Something about his nuts.

For the past few weeks Belle had been away, performing in her home land, but today the delicate, darling flower of the music hall stage returned. She must have dashed to his house directly after arriving on the train from Southampton. And her ribald declarations of what she meant to do with his various body parts suggested that it was not a loving eagerness for his company that brought her there so swiftly.

Oh, yes, she had definitely formed the wrong expectations for their relationship, despite the fact that he thought he'd made himself clear. He'd assumed, in fact, that they both wanted the same thing from their affair and nothing more. She was as little suited to monogamy as he.

Ransom was in no fit state to confront her this morning without losing his own temper. Two people in a rage at the same time was never a good thing, as he had witnessed too often in youth when his parents fought. Indeed, the idea of facing Belle this morning was about as appetizing as a bowlful of Nanny Bond's dumplings and broth.

Alas, he had no choice. Her voice—usually so melodious, but today raucous enough to render cracks in the plaster— echoed through his walls.

"Deverell! Where are you? Sors du lit! Get up! 'Ere I come to find you, Monsieur Infidele!"

The sound of her little feet clip-clopping up the stairs quickly followed. If any servant tried to stop her, they would be unsuccessful. Belle might be small in stature, but she could be very forceful when in the mood. She was also remarkably inventive when it came to expressing her wrath, for which anything sharp would be put to use. That large hat she wore looked as if it required several pins to keep in place, and Ransom was not keen to discover how many.

Putting on his most cheerful, amiable expression, he met her on the small landing between flights. "Bonjour, my sweet. I wish I knew to expect you so early! You should have sent a message. As you see I was just on my way out."

"Donnez-moi un couteau. Je vais lui couper fier coq!"

Ah. Cockerel. Cut off. And knife.

That was plain enough.

He attempted to grip her by the arms and deliver a kiss to her cheek, but she was having none of it. Slapping his hands away and stamping on his booted foot, she started up the second flight of stairs toward his bedchamber.

"I know you 'ave a woman 'ere, you pig!"

"Belle, why don't you come down to breakfast and we'll discuss—"

"Non!"

He followed her. "Is it necessary to make such a fuss, my sweet?"

"Oui!

"But Belle, we did not promise exclusivity. I ought to warn you—"

She swung open his bedchamber door and marched in. The three women on the bed were in various stages of awakening at that point, and the state of the room— wreckage of last night's indulgences— looked much worse now that more daylight crept in.

Immediately Belle launched into a stream of French curses and tried to drag the women off his bed. They, however, fought back. His threesome of lusty beauties were capable of looking after themselves, full of vigorous cockney spirit and with lungs just as robust as those of Mademoiselle Saint Clair.

"Ladies, please!" he attempted to intervene while dodging a swinging pillow. "Belle! For pity's sake—" He received a sharp elbow to the stomach that left him momentarily winded. As he bent forward, wheezing, another pillow flung savagely at his head, split open to release a snowy cloud of goose-feathers.

And so his day had begun. Not that much different to any other, truth be told.

But he found himself detached from it all, as if he viewed the spinning feathers and flying limbs from a distance, like 'La Contessa' who watched complacently from the wall, waiting for him to figure it all out.

Just one more annoying bloody woman who couldn't say what she meant and expected him to understand her expression, he thought angrily.

Finally he gave up trying to make anybody listen to him. They seemed to have forgotten he was even there. In fact, he began to suspect they were all rather enjoying themselves.

Ducking a flying vase and brushing feathers from his shoulder, he left them to it and went down to the kitchen, where he hoped to find his groom at breakfast. But the staff had already eaten and gone about their business. Only the cook remained.

"Mr. Deverell, sir? Is anything amiss?"

"I'm afraid it's much the same as usual, Mrs. Clay. Where's Ben?"

"He took your horse to the smithy first thing, sir, to be fresh shod."

Damn. He'd have to go out on foot.

"Shouldn't Smith go upstairs, sir, and stop the fight?" his cook asked tentatively, turning her gaze upward as another loud crash shook the house.

"I wouldn't want him to put himself out... or get

30

stabbed in the arbor vitae by a hatpin. Let them get it out of their system, Mrs. Clay. Let them exhaust themselves. Far be it for me to try and speak sense into any woman."

"No, sir. I don't suppose you can speak sense."

He shot her a sideways glance, but she got on with her pastry, not looking at him. "Ah, I almost forgot. There is a young, polite, probably very confused, Indian lady in the hall, Mrs. Clay. Please provide her with a cup of tea, and tell Smith he will find some coins within the inner pocket of my old, dark green cutaway, some bank notes under the Tantalus in the library and, I believe," he scratched his head, trying to remember, "there should be a small amount tucked behind the reclining nude with the ugly babies. If not, definitely a few notes inside the Wedgewood urn. Make sure Smith gives it all to the Indian lady. Her rent is due today."

"Yes, sir. I'll see to it."

This duty discharged, Ransom left via the tradesman's entrance behind the kitchen and leapt up the steps, into the street.

Above him, through that window he'd left open on the landing, the ruckus could still be heard, causing several passing pedestrians to glance upward in wonder.

Belle's face appeared, and she looked down. "Deverell! Ou allez-vous?"

"I told you I was on my way out, my dainty

flower. Simply can't stay, but lovely to see you as always."

"Reviens! T'es rien qu'un petit connard!"

Although tempted to shout back that he was, in fact, one of the few children sired by his father within wedlock and therefore legitimate— most definitely *not* a bastard— he thought this might not be the ideal time to worry about correcting her. Women could be completely unreasonable at moments like these. They simply didn't have a sense of humor. So he merely waved. "Au revoir, mon ami!"

"I will pluck out your eyes and feed them to your own donkey!"

Curious. He was quite sure he didn't own a donkey, so she had clearly got her English mixed up again.

Nevertheless, probably best not to hang about and find out what she meant.

He took off across the street on foot, seeking a narrow alley down which he might escape— somewhere Belle, in a Hansom cab, would not be able to follow. Unfortunately, Ransom had fewer navigational skills in sober daylight. Nothing seemed familiar.

But then, while hurrying along and looking back over his shoulder at the same time, he slipped on the wet pavement and collided, like a blundering idiot, with a gas lamp that stood beside an arched entrance in the wall. Beyond this there appeared to be a small, cobble-stone passage, leading to an arcade of shops and offices. He would not otherwise have noticed the alley, had he not cracked his head on the lantern and been forced to stop, but there it was, the sooty brick brightened by a painted advertisement for laundry soap.

So it was that Ransom Deverell discovered a new path, down which he'd never before ventured. Just when he thought there were none left.

Chapter Three

Mary stared at the hard, stale muffin, trying to reassure herself that the black dots really were raisins. Sometimes the mind could play tricks with the alternate possibilities and quite put a person off. Even a very hungry person.

She poked it with her finger and marveled at the cork-like texture. One thing was certain, if this muffin were thrown with force in a crowded place it would probably blacken an eye or two. Might have its uses after all, she thought wryly, if not the one for which it was made.

But what she really desired was a large, fluffy Parisian pastry, bursting with whipped cream and dripping with sweet chocolate glaze. Oh, what was it called? *Pain a la Duchesse*. Yes, that was it! She saw one once, some years ago at a very fine garden party, and now she bitterly regretted passing the cake platter, forfeiting her chance to experience that delicious confection. At the time she gave it up for two reasons— the fortitude of her corset laces and the puzzling problem of how to consume such a creation in public without making an unsightly mess. It was the sort of delight one could only enjoy to the fullest in private, and she could not very well sneak away with it concealed in her reticule.

Back then, of course, she couldn't have known

that such gourmet opportunities would one day be nothing more than a memory and that she ought to make the most of it, regardless of who watched her eat the pastry. Let them be forever scarred by the sight of her wicked, unladylike greed and chocolate-stained cheeks. What did she care? Well, she'd know next time.

Alas, there was no *Pain a la Duchesse* on her horizon. Not for the foreseeable future.

"Mary, my dear! Dr. Woodley is here to collect his special order. Can you bring it from the back room?"

She hastily set the dry muffin back on her plate and looked for the book she'd been perusing all night. "Yes, Mr. Speedwell. Just a moment. I...I was making the tea."

But as she lifted the heavy book from a chair in which she'd earlier left it, Mary paused again, her fingertips tracing over the gilt letters on that thick leather spine. It was a very ancient manuscript with vellum pages, the text and pictures produced by monks in a scriptorium, probably overlooking a peaceful cloister, hundreds of years ago.

Her father used to keep books like these in his library. When he was alive and had a library in which to keep them. Illustrated books on botany were one of his favorites. Dear Papa. He might have been one of the most frustrating, narrow-minded, old-fashioned gentlemen she ever knew, but she loved him for all his faults. If only he had been able to do the same for others. If only he had been a little less inflexible in his opinions.

Ugh. What was wrong with her today that she should become so dreary and full of mopey-eyed nostalgia? Perhaps it was the grim weather, the skies being a dowdy shade of grey, heavy and low. And she missed her dear friend, Raven, who was spending the winter away in Oxfordshire. Without Raven she had no one of a like mind to share a devious chuckle. Although lately there had been very little at which to laugh, in any case. No doubt all this had combined to affect her spirits.

Shaking her head, Mary briskly pushed these mournful thoughts aside, along with the fantasy of a large French pastry. There was never anything to be achieved by dwelling on the past, or on what one didn't have. It was not a practical use of a person's energies, as she would remind her sister. One must look ahead, plow onward.

Now...books...

Mary was supposed to wrap this book in brown paper and string last night before she went to bed, but instead had become enthralled looking through the colorful pages, and eventually fell asleep in a chair by the parlor fire. As she often did. It was not the most comfortable of sleeping arrangements, and she invariably woke with a little cramp in her neck, but at least she did not have her sister's cold feet in her back, or a pointy elbow nudging her in the ribs when she turned over. Why fight over blankets and lumpy bits in the mattress upstairs, when she could have the peaceful hearth down here to herself? Mary was always up first anyway, to fetch milk from the dairy cart, make the tea, and open the shop. She also liked to run out, very early, and see what left-over delights from yesterday might be procured at half price from the bakery in the next street. Sometimes the mere smell of freshly baked bread was enough to sustain her for several hours. When there was nothing else to be scavenged, it had to suffice.

On the other hand her sister, Violet, waited until a call of nature forced her out from under the quilt, especially on a bitterly cold morning like this one. Mary often wondered where Violet thought their breakfast came from, for she never asked. Instead she chewed resentfully upon the food Mary managed to procure, and then, willfully defying the rigid boning of her corset, performed a remarkably good impression of a weeping willow. In fact, Mary had begun to suspect her sister of rebelling against corsets altogether, for nothing else could explain her spine's ability to curve so dejectedly.

A sudden gust of wind blew down the chimney and almost flattened the flames in the hearth.

She felt the cold draft around her ankles and even down the back of her neck. Her grandmother used to say that when the wind changed direction something new was coming with it. But Mary couldn't muster much enthusiasm for that idea, since whatever was coming would probably only make things worse. That was the way her luck went lately. *Lately* being the previous eight years of her life.

After one last, hasty glance over the book to be sure she'd left no dirty fingerprints, Mary carried it out to the counter.

A second blast of frosty air blew in from the front door of the shop, accompanied by a loud jangle of the bell above it. That chilly draft seemed to snake its way through the shelves and around the counter, just to find her. She shivered, looking up.

Another customer already, and it was only Wednesday morning! Poor Mr. Speedwell must be beside himself at such a rush of potential buyers. He was always terribly bereft when any of his precious books left the premises in the hands of a customer.

But at that moment he was lost in deep conversation with Dr. Woodley — a friend and long-time patron of the bookshop — and paid no attention to the other arrival, who hovered in shadow by the door. Perhaps, thought Mary, only she had felt that draft. It did appear to have sought her out rather mischievously.

Dr. Woodley broke off their conversation rather abruptly and gave Mary one of his stiffly formal bows, which would have been better suited to the French court of King Louis XIV.

Good thing her sister had not yet emerged from bed, she mused, for Violet could seldom hide her amusement when Dr. Woodley made one of his bows. "*One of these days I expect the seat of his breeches to give way under the extreme strain as he breaks wind,*" she'd whispered once, causing Mary to laugh out loud, which was dreadfully rude and the fifth time it had happened in Dr. Woodley's presence. There were a limited number of times a person could break into unladylike snorts of helpless laughter in one man's company and still blame it on something they'd read earlier.

Besides, he was a well-meaning, learned gentleman and did not deserve ridicule from two silly girls. Well...one silly and one reformed.

As always, he asked after her health and then her sister's, before imparting his advice, which was plentiful. Today he appealed urgently for Mary to wear wool next to her skin, as often as possible, and to venture outdoors only when necessary.

"Sickness, my dear lady," he assured her, "is rife on the streets this season, and you must take care not to risk your health by coming into contact with the seeds of disease carried freely about town by rats and other wretched undesirables."

"I shall indeed take precautions, Dr. Woodley. I am, if nothing else, exceedingly circumspect." She sighed. "According to my sister, I am insufferably so."

"One can never be *too* careful," he continued

with his grave warning. "On my way here today, I saw a feverish-looking hound of monstrous proportions, racing between carriages, salivating at the mouth and ready to bite an unprotected ankle. It is most distressing to think of a young lady like yourself, venturing out into the street here and being accosted by such a beast. You should carry a stout stick, Miss Ashford."

She smiled. "I fear it would not be wise for *me* to carry an instrument of destruction, for when the mood betakes me I might be tempted to wield it with excessive force against a few folk who have angered me in the past."

His greying brows lowered in earnest concern. "You have a temper, Miss Ashford? Oh, dear! It is not good for one's blood to let the temperature rise. Particularly in a lady. Too much excitement can cause an attack of the vapors or even an apoplexy. I once knew of a case—"

"It was a jest, Dr. Woodley." She really must stop doing that, for the poor man, quite lacked a sense of humor and had no understanding of being teased. With a sigh, she muttered, "I don't have to worry about the dangers of too much excitement these days. I am quite safe from that."

"I am very glad to hear it, my dear lady. Next time I come I shall bring you a packet of powders to be sure your blood is calm."

Mary was quite certain she didn't need any

powders to keep her temper tranquil. She was the calmest person she knew. She couldn't be any more calm if she were dead. But to say so would only confuse the good doctor further. Instead, she thanked him for his concern. If it made the overly-solicitous fellow feel better to advise her, so be it. She supposed it was a problem inherent in his occupation, just as falling asleep over a book she shouldn't have opened was one of hers.

"I'll just wrap this for you, Dr. Woodley," she said, searching for paper under the counter.

The two men returned to their conversation, which consisted of Mr. Speedwell eagerly discussing new advancements in the art of medicine— things he'd read about in the pamphlets he collected— while Dr. Woodley promptly flattened all enthusiasm by maintaining that the old, tried and true methods could not be improved upon and were better left alone.

As her hands worked swiftly at the task of wrapping, Mary glanced around the doctor's shoulder, wondering about the other customer. There was little to be gleaned from his silhouette, other than the fact that he was tall and wore no hat. Peering out through the bow window in a furtive manner, he had his back to her now.

Without even looking down at her hands, she quickly and efficiently knotted the string, then slid the parcel across to Dr. Woodley.

"Thank you, Miss Ashford. What a very neat

bow you tie and such crisp, tidy corners to your parcels!"

"Would you excuse me? I must tend to the other customer." Before he could begin offering her more health advice— because he always had more to give no matter how impatient her countenance became or how strained her manners— she moved out from behind the counter and made her way between the overflowing shelves, intent on distancing herself from the temptation of being brusque. The poor fellow's solicitous advice did not warrant one of her sharp replies and yet hunger often made her curt.

Meanwhile, apparently unaware of her approach, the unidentified gentleman ducked below the front window of the shop, then up again.

"May I help you, sir?" she asked politely.

No response.

"Sir? Is there some book in particular for which you search?"

Finally, he flicked his head around, eyes fiercely narrowed, as if he suspected her of trying to slip a hand into his pocket.

When she repeated her question, he turned the rest of his person toward her and Mary saw that the man wore no shirt of any kind beneath his evening jacket. His chest and the dark hair upon it was, to her astonishment, quite exposed to the cold winter's air. And her gaze.

At least he wore breeches, she mused, recovering

slightly from the shock. One must be thankful for small mercies, as she was often telling her younger sister, Violet.

Although *small* mercies, in this case, did not seem an adequate phrase. There was nothing of reduced size about this man whatsoever. Mary wondered if she ought to have brought a weapon to defend herself, after all. Not that anything, she suspected, could have been much use in the circumstances. He didn't look the sort to be easily dented.

"What the deuce do you want?" he snapped. "A book? What damned book are you blithering on about?"

Slowly Mary returned her gaze from his bare chest to his face. Oddly enough there was something familiar about his dark, rumpled features. But how could there be? He had hardly looked at her with his cold, dark, disinterested eyes and then Mary was dismissed swiftly, the back of his shoulder turned to her again.

"This is a bookshop, sir. Perhaps you noticed the sign outside? *Beloved Books*. Since you entered these premises in some urgency I assumed your intention was to purchase one."

"Books?" he said again. Or rather, he snarled the word, while scratching his head and looking through the window.

"Yes, sir. We have all sorts here. New and second-hand. Novels and—"

"Who has time to read a damn novel?" No sooner had he got the words out than a deep burp sputtered forth, for which there was no apology offered.

"Pardon me, I took you for a literate gentleman. I see I was mistaken on both counts. Your mode of dress should have been warning enough, I suppose."

"Well, there you are then. Give up on me and peddle your wares to someone else, wench. I'm a hopeless case, aren't I?" She thought she heard him mutter under his breath, "I assumed everybody knew that."

While he obviously wanted to scare her back to the counter and out of his way, Mary's curiosity was piqued. As was her sense of humor. What *was* he doing there? This wide-shouldered, dark-eyed genie looked as if he belonged in another world entirely and had temporarily escaped his bottle. Or whatever vessel it was in which such a dangerous, mischievous spirit might be kept.

Yes, he was dangerous, she knew at once— felt the prickle of little hairs along her arm as if he had taken forceful custody of her wrist and gently blown a warm breath across her skin to tease.

All of that from one glance.

She cleared her throat. "Perhaps we have something here that could be of use to you nevertheless," she persevered.

"Use to *me*?" he grunted, looking over his

shoulder again, his gaze sweeping her from skirt hem to ear, first with nonchalance and then disdain. "You? I very much doubt it."

The stranger was poised to leave the shop, one hand on the door, until he saw something outside that prevented it. Turning to Mary again he almost bowled her over, and then he gripped her by the arms so tightly that she went unusually floppy. Startled and suddenly warm, she completely forgot to protest.

"Don't give me away and I'll be in your debt," he muttered. "Save me."

With that strange plea he darted behind the nearest shelf, vanishing into the dusty gloom. Although he had released her arms, the echo of his heated touch remained.

A second later the door flew open and the bracing wave of air thrust yet another customer into the shop. This one wore a large hat, over-loaded with lush apricot plumes, and a very fine satin coat, the buttons straining to cover a lavish bosom.

"Where is 'e? The bastard?" she yelled, breathless, long lashes wafting up and down as she assessed her cluttered surroundings. "I 'ave chased 'im 'alf way across London. Did 'e come in 'ere?"

Mary thought quickly. Of course, she could easily give him away; he had not been very nice to her— in fact he'd been downright rude— and she probably ought to take the woman's side. Sisterhood and all that. However...

45

Save me, he'd said, as if it was the most important thing she would ever do. Generally people did not ask Mary for help these days; they— like Dr. Woodley— viewed *her* as the sad creature in need of mercy and guidance.

But this man had asked for her help.

Mary was usually most comfortable as an observer of other people's follies, a figure on the edge of the action, but this stranger had put her in the middle of it.

"Well, girl? Are you mute, deaf? Or just stupid?"

There went sisterhood.

"The bastard, madam?" she asked quietly. "To whom or what do you refer?"

As she spun like a child's top, the little Frenchwoman's wide skirt disturbed a teetering pile of books that tumbled and stirred up another cloud of dust — almost thick enough to obscure her completely. The plumes of her hat reached in all directions, curling sensuously in the churning, dusty air, like the tentacles of a curious octopus. "Did a man come in 'ere, girl? Very tall and 'orribly 'andsome with the eyes of a cold-'earted, savage panther and manners the same?"

"I'm sorry, madam. This is a bookshop, not a refuge for stray circus beasts."

The brightly decorated woman sneezed violently and looked down at herself in horror. "Mon dieu!" When she wiped a hand over the spider's web that

46

now patterned the front of her gown, those sticky gossamer strands clung to her kidskin glove and the satin of her sleeve, which only added to her evident distress.

"Perhaps I can interest you in a book, madam?" said Mary, picking up one that had fallen.

The woman shot her a very fierce little scowl. "No. 'E would not come in 'ere. *You* 'ave nothing 'e would want."

Head high and feather tentacles bouncing, she swept to the door again and gripped the handle. But the door of the shop had a tendency to stick when opened from the inside and there was a particular gentleness required when turning the handle if one wanted to get out again, so Mary stepped forward to help.

"Allow me, madam."

"Madem*oiselle*!" the lady corrected her sharply.

"My apologies, mademoiselle." Mary carefully angled the handle, gave it just the right amount of tug, and the door opened. "Good day."

The other woman pushed her way by and, rather than wait for Mary to close the door, she took the handle from the other side, attempting to jerk it shut. In so doing, she trapped her voluminous skirt in the door twice, until she was finally free. Then the stiff breeze outside took hold of that same troublesome garment, inflated the striped silk as if it were an untethered hot-air balloon, and transported her onward down the street so quickly that her tiny feet could barely keep toes on the ground.

This was certainly turning into a very lively morning, thought Mary as she stood at the window, watching through the grimy glass squares. Frenchwomen and escaped savage panthers on a Wednesday before ten o'clock. Whatever next? She wouldn't be surprised to see an elephant dressed in a jester's cap and bells coming down the passage.

Her sister Violet would be very sorry she'd missed the parade. She might even have stopped complaining about their sadly reduced circumstances for five minutes, had she witnessed all this drama.

Dr. Woodley, also on his way out of the shop then, stopped, took off his hat, and bowed again to Mary. "Good day to you, Miss Ashford. It is a delight to see you looking so well, despite the harsh winter weather, which is usually savage upon a lady's complexion. You have a comely glow about your cheeks today."

"I probably sat too close to the fire this morning."

He shook his head. "A very dangerous custom, young lady. It can take only a matter of moments for an unguarded skirt to catch flame."

Only when Mary had reassured the fellow that she would take every precaution against stray sparks did he turn to depart. Of course the handle stuck fast again, but he, being a gentleman who knew everything, always insisted on trying to get it open himself. Mary waited a polite moment, discreetly pretending not to notice his struggle, and then she went to his aid.

"Thaddeus really should mend this handle," he grumbled. "How many years has it been thus?"

Mary smiled as she opened it for him. "I believe it has been mended several times, Dr. Woodley, but it resists the idea of change and stubbornly clings to its old ways."

He looked askance. "It is a door handle, my dear lady. It cannot have sentient thoughts."

She quickly straightened her lips. "Of course."

Probably concerned for the state of her mental health now too, he finally left, venturing out into those dangerous streets that were filled with flea-ridden beggars, wild dogs, and lurking diseases. Sometimes she wondered how he ever got up the gumption to visit this part of town, but apparently the lure of a good book could not be resisted. Even by the eminently sensible Dr. Woodley.

Once he too was gone, she looked back to see that Mr. Speedwell had retreated to his fire in the parlor, leaving her utterly alone with that French lady's lost panther.

She wondered if he was, in fact, the same beast Dr. Woodley had observed running about the street, salivating at the mouth and ready to bite. More than likely.

"It's safe to come out now, sir."

He sidled into view, stopping before her in a shaft of misty, cool light. "Thank you." Since he wore no hat and had nothing to tip, the escapee was reduced to waving his fingers around his temple in an odd, theatrical flourish. Or did he simply have a headache? Now that she was between him and the window, Mary saw a mark on his brow, a nasty bruise. So he was capable of denting after all. "Thank you," he repeated, "Miss....?"

"Ashford."

"Ashford. Very good," he murmured, as if he'd already forgotten the name. Or, at least, had every intention of doing so. With a long stride he made to pass her, heading for the door.

Quite suddenly she thought of that decadent chocolate-covered pastry again, the sides bulging with fresh cream. A chance she'd once forfeited and regretted ever since.

Before he could take another step, Mary reached out, catching his coat sleeve in her fingers. "On the matter of that debt, sir?"

His progress halted, he looked down at her hand and then at her face. He squinted.

"You said you would be in my debt, if I saved you," she reminded him.

"I did, did I?"

"Oh, yes. I remember it distinctly."

"Well...perhaps another day. I'm busy at this

moment."

She tightened her grip on his sleeve. "I thought, perhaps, you might like to buy a book. Or two. While you're here."

There followed a pause while he assessed her with a more focused gaze. Finally he flung out his arms in a grand gesture of supplication to the heavens, dislodging her fingers at the same time. "How can I buy a book this morning? I'm quite without funds. As you observe, I do not even have a shirt on my back, Miss...what is it again?"

"*Ashford*," she repeated steadily. "And we can send you the bill, if you find yourself currently insolvent." Mary did not believe for a minute that he was one of the poverty-stricken. Even half dressed he exuded an unmistakable air of privilege, and his clothes— the pieces in existence— were well made of very fine material, perfectly fitted. A fact she had tried her hardest not to notice. "It is the least you could do, sir, considering I saved your life this morning."

"Saved my life?"

"*Save me.* Those were your words, sir. Since I'm not in a position to save your soul, I assume you referred to your life. Or, at the very least, some necessary parts of your anatomy."

He exhaled a blustery sigh and folded his arms. Like a tall, slowly falling tree, he tipped to one side, resting a shoulder against the door. "But I don't need any books."

To Mary, that was like saying one did not need air. "Everybody needs books," she exclaimed.

"Had my fill of 'em in the schoolroom and at university." He shuddered and brushed dust from his sleeves. "Ugh. Quite put me off opening another dull tome as long as I live."

"Then you're missing out and I pity you. But I suppose not every man wishes to enlarge his mind to fit the size of his head."

The stranger's eyes sparked, spidery cracks in the ice of their practiced indifference suddenly letting the light through. "Just because you've got a ton of the blasted things you're trying to be rid of—"

"And most men, in my experience, do not keep their promises, so I shouldn't be surprised that you now intend to renege on yours."

"Well, I don't make promises, so if you heard one from me it was a mistake."

"Mine or yours?"

Still leaning against the door, he glowered at her for a long moment.

"Fate can lead a fool to a bookshop," she added with a sigh, hands clasped before her, "but it cannot make him read."

Eventually a low groan rumbled out of his bare chest. "Very well. I'll take some of these dratted books off your hands." But despite this weary tone, a cunning, wicked amusement had come into his eyes and stayed there, slowly thawing the ice. "I'll say this for you, you're determined. Don't give up easily, do you?"

"It's a vexing quality that comes to women in advanced age."

He pushed himself upright and perused her more carefully this time, scouring her person inch by inch. Feet apart and arms still folded he reminded her again of a genie come to grant somebody three wishes. Not hers though. Surely.

"The books, sir?" she prompted.

"You choose them. Something to entertain me, Miss... *Ashford*."

He lingered over her name as if tasting it on his tongue, and Mary felt another shiver the entire length of her body. It was a deliberate attempt to unsettle her and get the upper hand, of course. She remained unimpressed.

There was a time when arrogant, good-looking scoundrels like this one were two or three a penny in Mary's life. They were men who rose late and went to bed even later; they had a never ending supply of vitality and saw no cause to slow down. Back then she was an eligible debutante, someone with whom these men teased and tried to flirt. But that was before her brothers went away to war and never returned, and when the Ashford family still had an estate of their own. Before their fortunes were severely reduced and her bereaved father had to sell it all to settle his debts. Before her uncle died in prison, having confessed to murder by oyster fork. Before the Ashford name was, in the minds of a great many, utterly ruined.

That naive, sheltered youth seemed so long ago now. Another era, a sunshine-glazed past that belonged to somebody else.

Once again the grey wretchedness closed in. It made her angry with everybody and everything, including herself, for Mary did not like to waste her time fussing over events in the past and situations that were unchangeable. Yet she had caught herself doing it too often lately.

"You must give me an idea, sir, of what you like to read," she managed tightly.

"But I don't know what I like, do I? I told you I never read for pleasure. I'm a very busy man." One hand to his bare chest, unshaven chin proudly raised, he added, "My mind is always off in several directions at once."

"Yes," she muttered. "My uncle had a pet monkey like that once."

Immediately his gaze hardened, but didn't lose its heat.

"Your mode of dress is somewhat similar to his too," she added. "The monkey's that is— not Uncle Hugo's."

Quizzical lines deepened across his brow, and he slowly lifted his hand to rasp fingers across the stubble of his jaw. He seemed to be sniffing her out, weighing the danger. His eyelids lowered slyly, but she could still make out the devilish gleam of a beast accustomed to getting his own way— of never being corralled or tamed into doing anything he didn't want to do. A very clever beast. Possibly more intelligent and calculating than he liked people to know.

But he had just walked into that shop and encountered a woman as stubborn as he.

Suddenly he moved those fingers to his temple, where an angry, red mark blossomed. He winced, heaving his shoulders, drawing a quick, pained breath. Although he tried to hide it in the shadow of his palm, the gleam of willful naughtiness was evident in his eyes.

He was looking for her sympathy. Expecting it.

Mary was unmoved. "I suppose that is the handiwork of your French lady." She pointed to the mark on his brow.

"No," he conceded glumly. "A lamp post."

"Combined with that scattered attention of which you are so proud."

He uttered a low groan as his fingers tentatively felt the little bump. "I daresay it's the end of me. I am feeling rather weak and...and dizzy."

"Has it knocked your brain loose?"

From between his fingers another glimmer sparked, those wilting eyelids unable to hide it. "I could be at death's door. I've been there before, and it felt something like this." He grumbled, "There was a fearsome creature like you at my shoulder then too."

As he put his hand down, she stepped forward to inspect the wound. Without getting too close, of course. "Goodness it's a mere scratch. What a lot of fuss, but that is what men do best."

"How do you know it's a mere anything?" he snapped.

"I grew up with brothers, sir. I tended all their wounds, of which there were many. Mostly self-inflicted. But then women are the smarter sex and I have, in my latter years, concluded that men are here solely for our amusement." She paused, swallowing the urge to laugh at his confused expression. "Have your housekeeper prepare a saline wash for your headache, a conserve of red roses and rotten apple for the bruise... and I'm sure she has some Godfrey's Cordial for any other complaint you might suffer."

"Isn't that for colicky babies?"

She shrugged. "Six of one and half a dozen of the other. In any case, you'll live."

His eyes narrowed. "It's bloody well lucky for you that I did hit my head, isn't it, since it lured another customer into your trap?"

"Indeed. I'm sure we'll talk about it for years to come— the curious incident of a man who doesn't read books walking into a bookshop. Shirtless. The start of a wonderful story in itself."

"Yes it is." He advanced a step toward her, his shadow looming over Mary, his eyes darkly devouring her as if he was indeed an escaped panther and she a lost lamb. "If not for that lamp post, we may never have met. We might have dashed by — me and my shirtless chest—and never encountered those saucy lips of yours." He spoke in a low voice, not many tones removed from a growl. Or a very wicked purr. "Those delectable, rosy lips, ready to greet a hard-working fellow when he comes home in the evening. Like two soft, full pillows..."

"Pillows? Is that the best you can do?"

"...waiting on his bed after a long, dreary day."

She sighed. "And where is this hard-working fellow of whom you speak?"

"There is a man somewhere, I assume."

"Why would you assume that? Because every little woman needs a man?"

"Don't you?" He smirked. "*Little woman*?"

"If I need a book from the top shelf I have a wonderfully efficient ladder. What else would I need a man for?"

He was the only man she'd ever seen who could scowl and quirk an eyebrow at the same time. It made him look quizzical, amused and frustrated all at once. "If that's the only thing you imagine I'd be good for," he said, "then it would seem as if those ravishable lips are going to waste, madam."

"And yet, somehow, they endure the neglect."

His eyes darkened even further. Apparently there was a color beyond black and it was very, very hot. He took another stride toward her and Mary, unaware until then of her own backward motion, suddenly felt the edge of a shelf against her shoulder.

"May we return to the subject of books, sir?"

"You're damnably persistent."

"As you are deliberately evasive, an habitual flirt who uses that skill to get out of anything he doesn't want to do."

He exploded with hearty laughter that surrounded Mary in a shockingly intimate embrace. It caused a vibration that seemed to shake up all the dust around her. She imagined the many rows of books rustling their pages, as if they were very stiffly starched matrons who, suddenly aware of their dignified presence being invaded by this dangerous rogue, shook out their skirts and petticoats in ladylike anxiety.

"Make haste then, truculent wench, if you wish for me to purchase these books. I haven't all day to stand about idle." He tugged on the cuffs of his evening jacket. "Like I said, I'm a very busy fellow."

Rather than continue to appreciate exactly how pleasing he was upon the eye— *'orribly 'andsome*, as the French whirlwind had exclaimed— Mary turned sharply and walked toward the back of the shop, stopping only to pluck a few books from the shelf as she went. Without showing him the titles, she took them quickly to the counter and began wrapping them in paper. And while she did all this, the panther prowled along in her wake.

For every three of her steps he required only one and still seemed to be catching up with her. Mary felt every advance he made as if it was the caress of his fingertip along her spine.

How did he do it, she wondered darkly— how did he keep touching her without using his hands?

"To whom should I make out the bill?" she asked, her gaze fixed upon the parcel as she wrapped it.

"Deverell. Ransom Deverell. You can send it to Deverell's Club, St. James Street."

Ah.

So that was why his features seemed familiar. She took a deep breath of relief. It was not some mystical sense of having met him before then, but a reasonable recognition, plain and simple. Because she knew his sister.

Mary had become acquainted with Raven Deverell— the only girl in the notorious Deverell litter— more than ten years ago, when they shared the same tutor for dancing and piano lessons. They had remained close friends ever since, despite the Ashford's reduced circumstances and a necessary financial retrenchment which had meant no further lessons for Mary. When Raven's marriage took her away into Oxfordshire, Mary had also taken on the duty of visiting the matriarch of the Deverell family, Lady Charlotte, on her absent daughter's behalf.

But she had never met any of the Deverell males.

Raven always took care to keep her friend away from those infamous brothers. Now, having met this one, she understood her friend's concern— not that Raven should have worried on her account. Foolish flirting no more impressed her now than it had when she was sixteen, and a thin, hopeful, but terribly sappy young man named Lionel Winchester tried serenading her one evening with a song outside her bedroom window.

Poor Lionel. But was it her fault that she mistook the noise for two cats fighting and tipped her washbasin of cold water over the ledge?

Irritated, she realized that one of her fingers had somehow managed to get caught inside the loop of string. She tugged hard to free herself, but the string only tightened around her finger and threatened the blood supply. The tip began to go numb. Where on earth had she put the scissors? Now she was all at sixes and sevens. Panic mounted.

Suddenly a flash of silver gleamed in the corner of her eye and in the next instant she was freed. Ransom Deverell proudly flourished the small, deadly-looking blade with which he had cut the string and exclaimed, "See how blessed you are that I'm here."

Although released from the parcel, she still had the knot around her finger like a ring. He grabbed her wrist.

"Hold still, woman."

She looked up, ready to tell him it didn't matter, that she could manage by herself, but he was intent on the exceedingly perilous business of sliding that blade between her finger and the merciless tourniquet she'd accidentally made around it. Perhaps not a good idea to argue with him at that moment.

It was said that he'd killed a woman. Although it was never proved. She knew he'd shot at his father, the notorious True Deverell, some years ago. Raven had once mentioned the difficult relationship between her brother and their father, how they were always at war, Ransom being too much like his father in many ways.

And everybody knew that True Deverell was once named the wickedest rake in all England.

"There." The knot dropped away from her finger and yet she had barely felt the cool blade brush her skin. "All done." With a swift flick of his hand he hid the knife away again inside his evening coat.

"Put your pout away, Miss Ashford," he muttered. "I shan't say that we are now equal, one favor for another. I could, of course. But since you're such a persistent creature I wouldn't dare leave without those books. You might tackle me to the ground if I tried."

Mary somehow managed a smile— at least she thought she did, but her mind was spinning and she really had no idea what her face did. Her heartbeat had quickened until it must have rivaled the pace of a fox about to be torn apart by hounds.

She'd never seen a man use a knife in her presence for anything more physical than carving a roasted goose. Certainly no one had ever put a sharp blade against her skin. And this man had taken possession of her hand— and of her for those few seconds— as if it was a mere trivial matter. As if he had no fear of drawing blood. As if she ought to have no fear likewise, but trust him completely.

Hidden among the pleats of her skirt, the rescued finger shyly recovered. The same could not be said for the uneven, giddy thump of her heart.

Ransom Deverell had announced his name a little too grandly, she thought, as if he expected her to slap one hand to her brow and faint at the sound of it.

What a strange, amusing man he was. Infuriating too, no doubt, if one was "blessed" with his company for too long.

In the very beginning his eyes had appeared heartless and savage, just as his French pursuer described them. But when Mary challenged him, stood up to his foolishness, the light came and now, when he looked at Mary, there was so much heat and curiosity in his regard that she feared for her skirt. As Dr. Woodley had reminded her, it was a terribly combustible garment. She'd never felt quite so much truth to the warning, as she did now.

Pity she didn't have a washbasin of cold water at hand, as she did when droopy Lionel Winchester performed his tuneless mating call beneath her window.

Today the cooling splash might have been useful, not only for this wild-eyed panther, but for her too.

Chapter Four

She could blame it on the grey-day malaise she'd suffered earlier, or the fact that she was hungry, but a long-dormant desire for mischief suddenly reared its naughty head.

Reaching under the counter for the ledger of bills due, she asked politely, "*Drivel.* Was that the name? Could you spell that for me, sir?"

He rested his sizeable knuckles on the counter and leaned forward. "Deverell! You must have heard of me."

She glanced upward. "I'm sorry, sir. I don't believe I have. Should I? Are you an actor of some sort? Like Mr. Edmund Kean?"

His expression was priceless. Quickly she looked down again, struggling against the desperate urge to laugh.

"No, I'm not an *actor*," he huffed.

"Oh," she muttered with a quaking sigh. "I always rather regretted the fact that I never got to see Mr. Kean perform."

"Well, I'm not a bloody actor."

"It's just that...your attire is somewhat theatrical."
"Because I left my house in haste this morning."

"And your mistress has a certain manner of the stage about her."

"What makes you think she's my mistress?"

"I meant the term as in... owner or keeper."

At once she felt him stiffen with anger.

She took a breath and continued, "Since she chases after you as if you are a pedigree poodle that slipped his leash in the street, I assumed she had ownership."

"*Nobody* owns me," he grumbled fiercely. "Apparently you do not get out much, Miss Ashford, if you don't know who I am."

She readied her pen in the ink and kept her gaze on the open ledger before her. "I'm sure you must be a very important person. So much in demand, apparently, that you are pursued through the streets and forced to run headlong into lamp posts."

"You've never been chased anywhere? No, I don't suppose anybody ever gets you out of breath, do they?"

"Quite. My world is much less dangerous than yours and far more predictable. I don't need to be chased, because I am usually exactly where I'm supposed to be, and nobody goes to great lengths to seek out my company."

"That's a pity."

"I wasn't lamenting the fact."

"Ah yes, I heard you assuring that humorless doctor fellow that your life is very tedious and unexciting. You might have deceived him into believing you prefer it that way, but you don't fool me."

"Don't I? Oh, dear."

Just as she moved to dip her pen in the ink again, he took the little pot out of her reach and turned it in his fingers, holding it up to the light, before putting it down again. "I can see you must be bored out of your stockings, Miss Ashford. You need a worthy opponent, a man to kindle your temper and your passions. A man to challenge you and make your life less predictable. Not one like that doctor fellow who wants to put you to sleep."

It was somewhat alarming that this man, who'd only known her for a matter of minutes, should, so smoothly, take measure of her situation and read the boredom on her face. Had it been that obvious? Nobody else ever seemed to notice.

Agitated, she muttered, "As you're so busy and in such great demand, you must have little time to sleep."

Something sad and raw passed over his face, but it was brief. Now he ruffled the pages of her ledger, flicking the corner with his thumb, making her writing go all wobbly on the paper. "My world can be thoroughly exhausting, truth be told."

She eyed him dubiously. "The great hardships do not appear to have done you much harm."

"I make the best I can of it," he muttered. "Mostly by remaining my own master, free to come and go as I please, steering clear of traps, staying *off* the leash when a woman tries to put one around my throat. Usually they know better than to try."

Why did he tell her all this, she wondered. It was an intimacy that she should neither welcome nor encourage. And yet Mary suddenly heard herself warning him. "You can't hide from your French pastry— I mean, your French *lady*— forever, you know." She looked down at the ledger, feeling the danger of meeting his eye for too long. "Whatever your dislike of leashes, your companion evidently has a different opinion. The mademoiselle's sense of entitlement and ownership is as palpable as your desire to remain unfettered."

"I should keep you at my side then, Miss Ashford, to protect me. You were remarkably effective just now."

"But you are surely old enough to stand up for yourself, sir. She's one third your size."

"So are you, but you put me in my place."

Mary fought the urge to smile, but those lips he had threatened with ravishment acted like a pair of willful hussies.

"Why don't *you* keep me?" he whispered, a grin evident in his voice. "I promise I'll be very good, as long as you don't try to chain me."

"And why, exactly, would I want to keep you? Do I strike you as a person with so few problems in her life that she is desirous of another?"

"Perhaps you have no choice in the matter.

There is a Chinese proverb, you know, that says once you save a man's life you are responsible for it ever after. That, madam, means you ought to look after me."

Is this how he usually got his way with women, she wondered. Did he trick them into a false sense of familiarity with his easy banter so that they forgot themselves? "I'm afraid I cannot afford a pet, sir. Especially one large enough to eat me out of house and home. Besides, I suspect you require a great deal of attention and I have too much to keep me busy already."

"What keeps you so busy then? What do women ever have to do but make themselves look pretty? It can't take *you* that much time and effort, for your features are passable enough in a natural way."

"Are they indeed?"

"Not when you frown like that, of course. Then you could be a devious gypsy woman ready to lay a curse upon me."

Again the temptation to laugh made it impossible for Mary to stay annoyed. "I am kept busy, sir, by the sheer effort it takes for a small, unimportant woman to survive. Not everybody has the liberty of running away from their problems, just to find more."

She felt the air move as he leaned over her counter, and in the next intake of breath she swallowed a taste of his very masculine scent — sweat combined with citrusy bergamot and leather. It jolted to life a warm memory of her lost brothers, who were once so merrily unruly and loved boisterous sport of any kind. But, in this man's case, there was also a distinctive undertone of flowery feminine fragrance, probably belonging to a woman with whom he'd spent his night. It was not, however, the same lily-of-the-valley perfume worn by his French lady.

Hence the chase this morning, she thought.

Oops, she broke the nib of her pen.

"What would you do then, Miss Ashford, to escape a person who pursues you through the streets in a raging, violent temper? Counsel me, if you will, since you're so very sensible and too brave to run away."

She looked up and found his face much closer than she'd expected. His brow crumpled, his eyes narrowed with amusement. Mary reached for a new pen. "Misunderstandings and confusions of purpose between a man and a woman are much better dealt with at once, rather than put off, sir. It saves everybody a vast deal of trouble."

"Does it?" Feigning great interest, he rested his chin on one fist, his elbow on the counter. "The way you dealt with me, you mean. Putting me in my place with one crack of your tongue, before I could practice my dark arts of enchantment upon you."

"When there are expectations on one side and no possibility of fulfilling them on the other, better to be clear at once."

He seemed attentive, even contemplative. Of course, it might not be genuine.

Mary continued cautiously, "I once knew a man who avoided confrontation, because he did not have the courage to be honest with a lady. So he let her suffer false hope for too long, when a simple conversation might have saved them both undue discomfort and embarrassment."

He leaned even closer, eyes cast down as if deep in thought, both elbows and forearms now planted firmly on the counter in front of her ledger. Apparently each of his nannies— Mary knew that he and his sister had endured many when they were children— had failed to teach him that a gentleman should never slouch. Amongst other things he should never do.

"Sir?"

"Hmm?"

It occurred to her then that he was reading her ledger upside down— probably had been doing so for the last few minutes— and was not listening to her at all.

"You asked me what I would do, sir."

"About what?"

She drew a quick breath and stabbed her pen into the ink pot. "No matter. It was an absurd notion to think that you asked because you were actually curious to know my opinion."

"You're making a proper mess of that ledger,

Miss Ashford," he observed. Again he toyed with her ink pot, moving it, and her pen, out of her reach. "I see my presence makes you nervous. Or else you find me so entertaining, you're reluctant to see the back of me."

"What could possibly make you think that?"

"Because you're making such a wretched mess, first of tying the parcel and then of writing the bill. Hindering my departure. Keeping me trapped in your web."

"Please rest assured it is not deliberate. In fact it is as much your fault as mine."

Wide-eyed he asked, "Is there anything I can do to help?" His grin grew broader.

"Yes. Be still and stop touching my... my things."

"Touching your things, Miss Ashford? What things might I be touching?"

"You are a fidget, sir." She paused, raised an eyebrow, and added smoothly, "Perhaps my presence makes *you* nervous."

His eyes narrowed, his lips parted, but nothing more than a low huff emerged, followed by a belated sniff of scorn.

Just then Mr. Speedwell came out of the parlor and Mary silently thanked the heavens that her employer was hard of hearing.

"Did you need any assistance with this gentleman, Mary dear?" As usual the elderly fellow had a book open in his hands and barely looked up from its pages.

"No, it's quite all right," she said loudly. "Mr. Drivel is purchasing some books."

"Oh." Her employer's jowls sagged at the prospect of losing more of his precious stock.

"Only on approval," their customer growled, standing taller and looking Mr. Speedwell up and down in the same terse, challenging way he had first looked at her.

"I'll finish making the tea then, Mary, since you are delayed." Still reading his book, Mr. Speedwell returned to the parlor.

Again she focused on her writing. Or tried.

"Was that your father?" he whispered.

"No."

"The uncle with the monkey?"

"No."

"Not a sweetheart, surely?"

She rolled her eyes. "Mr. Speedwell is my partner in business. We share ownership of the bookshop."

"I see," said the wretched menace, rubbing his hands together. "You *are* unattached then. I thought you might be fibbing when you said those luscious lips are neglected."

"I do not fib, Mr. Drivel."

"Yes you do. You told my friend that I wasn't here."

"I didn't tell her that. I simply pointed out that this is a bookshop. Which is perfectly true."

He laughed. "You're a sly piece. I'm becoming inordinately fond of you already."

"Lord help us both."

This made him laugh all the harder. "Despite your evident desire to insult me by drawing comparisons first to a monkey and then to a stray mutt—"

"A poodle."

"Despite all that, I find myself fascinated by Miss *Mary* Ashford. Who pretends to disapprove of me, even as she schemes to keep my company, first with her insistence that I purchase books, and now with her inability to concentrate and pen a simple line of ink."

"As I said, if you stopped distracting me—"

"My routine has been set asunder by your dilly dallying, woman, and once things get too far out of hand there is nothing to be done to save them. All my plans for today are blown apart like a blasted bulrush pod, and thanks to you and your quarrelsome lips, I am now left dangling at a loose end this morning."

"Sounds most uncomfortable," she muttered, watching his fingers as they toyed again with the corner of her page. "I regret that my lips had anything to do with your loose ends dangling."

Apparently he found something exceedingly amusing about that and chuckled so heartily he was almost bent double. Mary, disconcerted, made another unsightly blob of ink on the ledger.

Once recovered, he thumped his fist on the counter and exclaimed, "I suppose you want to invite me to stay for tea in that cozy little parlor back there. Especially as I'm suffering a hellish thirst and was obliged to leave my house without breakfast."

His gall apparently knew no bounds, but Mary's sense of humor would not allow her to be deeply annoyed with this man. Again she made the mistake of looking up at him.

"'Tis the season of goodwill to all men, etcetera," he added, blinking his dark eyes as if he might try, like a magician, to hypnotize Mary and bend her to his dastardly will.

She'd heard Ransom Deverell described as the most "ill-mannered, licentious beast" ever to walk the streets of Mayfair, worse even than his notorious father. Her encounter with him this morning had perfectly demonstrated the truth of all that.

But despite everything he was and was not, in that terrible moment, Mary felt tempted to say "yes" and invite the devilish miscreant to stay for a cup of tea. He would make a lively change in the proceedings, certainly. He had already.

It wouldn't do, of course. All they had to offer were stale muffins, and besides that— indeed it ought to have been her first thought—he was everything a moderately sensible woman should avoid, for her impressionable sister's sake, as well as her own. Even her friend Raven knew that and had kept Mary safely out of his way. Men like Ransom Deverell spun through life and through women's hearts like a sharp-edged Aboriginal boomerang.

"I doubt there is room for you in our parlor, Mr. Drivel. It's not nearly grand or big enough, to be sure. You would never fit."

"That's a pity." He paused and then added, "You ought to serve refreshments to your customers. Of which I am one now, since you tricked me into it."

"Our customers are here to buy books, not to consume tea and biscuits."

"But if you encouraged them to linger—"

"Why would I want them to linger?"

"Bloody hell, woman! You may be a determined salesperson, but you have no mind for business clearly."

"I fail to understand—"

"Entice customers into your web with other delights and they will take time to browse your shelves, perhaps buy more than they came in for. You should think forward, madam, not let yourself be stuck with the familiar out of habit."

Mary was appalled. "It will be a sad day, sir, when a person must be lured into a bookshop by anything other than a love of reading and appreciation of a good story. I would fear for the human race if people must be promised food and beverages merely to encourage the purchase of a book."

He shook his head. "I suppose that eager but

deadly dry fellow who worries over your skirt and petticoat going up in flames and yearns to guard you from *undesirables,* would like to have some sort of claim over you, eh? Apparently his advice is worthy of being heeded and mine is not."

"I beg your pardon? Do you refer to Dr. Woodley? That very respectable gentleman, who—"

"Clearly wants to put something more than wool next to your soft skin, Miss Ashford of the *comely glowing cheeks.*"

"How dare you suggest such a —"

"The fellow drooled over you just like that mad dog he warned you about." His lip curled in a knowing smirk. "I shouldn't be surprised if he wants to sink his teeth into your ankles too."

"That's quite enough, Mr. Drivel." This teasing had gone too far. "I will not listen to you debase poor Dr. Woodley, whose kindly nature and well-meaning concern does not deserve your mockery."

"It's Deverell," he said firmly, lowering his voice to a menacing rumble. "That's D. E..." abruptly he reached over and guided her hand, the heavy weight of his fingers covering hers like a greedy spider, "V. E. R—"

This time Mary pulled her hand away, leaving a scratch of ink across the paper.

"E. L. L," he finished, his tongue rolling out the last letter with a languid sensuality. "I daresay you'll know it next time we meet."

"Next time? Could fate be so unkind?"

The sound of his laughter once more shook those old shelves and shattered cobwebs. It must surely wake Violet from her slumber upstairs, if it hadn't already. "It's unfortunate for us both, but inevitable, Miss Mary Ashford."

She hastily resumed business. The quicker he was gone the better. "I'll see to it that you receive a copy of the bill. No need to come in person to pay it, of course."

Now he drummed his fingers on the counter, making more noise. "Just to be clear, Miss Ashford, I buy these books from you, merely because your lips won out over my better sense. Something for you to consider, in future. Make the most of your natural attributes. You could trick some gentlemen into spending a small fortune in this shop, if you knew how to put those lips to better use."

"Sir, if a lady has any care for her dignity, she should limit the use of her lips." Especially around men like him, she mused.

"Madam," he smiled. "There are no limits, only possibilities."

"You are an expert in such matters, I suppose."

"Yes, I am very successful in business, so it would do you no harm to take my advice. "

She had referred to the subject of ladies' lips and their possibilities, not of business matters, but Mary said nothing.

"And, let me tell you, Miss Ashford, I managed to thrive in life without reading a single book for pleasure."

"Just imagine how much more successful you might have been, had you picked up a novel once in a while. A good story can do wonders for enlarging a man's mind, his perspective, and his imagination."

"There's naught amiss with my imagination," he drawled, leaning on one elbow and treating her to a meaningful wink.

"That depends on what you use it for."

"For wickedness, of course. All manner of vice and inequity. Is that not what you would expect from a man like me? You took one look at me and knew everything."

"As you did when you looked at me."

He squinted as if she'd just squirted a lemon in his eye.

Mary thrust the parcel of books at him. "Do be careful, sir, not to catch cold out there in this weather. Dressed as you are for warmer climes. Good day."

"You won't offer me that cup of tea then?"

"I'm afraid not. You must slake your thirst elsewhere." She could well imagine the chaos he would cause in that tiny back parlor, especially if her sister Violet came down. That girl had impractical, romantic ideas enough without encouragement from this partially undressed scapegrace. What Violet needed was a steady, honorable gentlemen with an

78

earnest mind to marry and raise a family, not a handsome, lusty scoundrel who took nothing seriously and kept himself trim by running speedily from commitment.

About to turn away, he stopped. "You ought to..." he grinned, just a little less self-assured than before, "dine with me. I could give you some more business advice."

It took her a moment to answer, her breath taken away by the surprise. "No." She laughed softly, shaking her head. "Thank you."

His grin faded. "I suppose you worry for your reputation, in light of mine."

"Oh? Do you have one?" She blinked innocently. "Is it very bad?"

"It's the worst," he confessed without hesitation.

How curious that he was honest about it, even proud. Mary considered for a moment. "I would not fear for my reputation, because I know myself. When others see fit to judge me and find fault, only they are affected by it. Their opinion of me can have no bearing on my happiness or my convictions. I know who I am."

"Then what—"

"My concern is that you and I would have nothing in common, nothing to talk about."

"Talk?"

"You are a man who admits he seldom has time to read a book. While a handsome face is all well and good to look at, if I must share my dinner with a man, I prefer that he have a brain and interesting conversation to offer."

"I have a brain, madam."

"But your interests are not the same as mine."

"How do you know?"

She smiled. "Just an erudite guess."

With long fingers he scratched his unshaven cheek again, and then paced before the counter. "You, a meek little bookseller, are turning *me* down?"

"It would seem so. I'm sorry, but I'm certain you will survive the disappointment."

"Wench, you have no inkling of the chance you let slip through your fingers."

Now she was a *wench* again. "Oh, I think I do. We've attempted conversation for about a quarter of an hour, and I've been exposed to half your naked person for that entire time. I believe I have a good idea of the sacrifice I'm making."

"Damn it all to blazes, woman." Tucking the package under one arm, he murmured, "You really don't know who I am, do you?"

"I do. You told me your name. You even spelled it for me."

"That's not what I meant."

Her lack of awestruck swooning was apparently killing him.

Mary pretended to consider, tapping her chin with one finger. "Are you in disguise then? You must

80

be the Prince Consort. Or the Duke of Norfolk? Or Isambard Kingdom Brunel?" She widened her eyes. "No...oh, don't tell me. I do love a good riddle... the King of Siam?"

A thunderous scowl swiftly darkened his features and cooled his gaze again. He strode to the door, grumbling, "I've wasted enough time here already."

"Do come back next time you need saving from a lady," she called out. "French or otherwise."

She watched, quietly amused, as he fought with the truculent handle. But he didn't waste much time. No gentlemanly restraint and smothered frustration for him. He kicked the door just once, very hard, and his temper apparently frightened the sticky handle into submission, after which he pulled it open with such violence that a screw went flying across the floor.

As he triumphantly slammed the shop door in his wake, Mary closed her ledger with an equal amount of gusto.

That felt better. Put the artful charmer in his place.

But how quiet it was again now.

All that remained was a half-hearted tickle of rain at the windows, and behind her, in the small parlor, the soft snuffle and wheeze of that coal fire. These were the usual sounds of a cold, dreary winter's morning, but for just a few minutes Ransom Deverell — and the breeze that brought him into the shop—

had shaken up the dust and spun her around, like a drunken dance partner, until she was dizzy. Now he was gone and her pulse could return to its stable, sober pace.

If only it didn't suddenly feel like a funeral dirge. And now the most she had to look forward to was a stale, two-day-old muffin.

Chapter Five

Ransom had never liked the plump-cheeked cherubs cavorting around the plaster medallion on the ceiling of his office. There was something sinister, he always thought, about flying babies looking so pleased with themselves. Today, as the club's chief valet drew a razor across his cheek and Ransom scowled up at those plaster figures, it seemed as if they watched him and giggled together with even greater menace than usual.

His mind wandered to the mysterious contents of that brown paper parcel where it lurked on the corner of his desk. Waiting.

Well, it could continue to wait. Ransom didn't like to think of any woman getting the better of him, but *she* had. He'd been robbed, bamboozled into a purchase he didn't want or need. To punish her for that he would not open her damnable parcel and he'd send it back to her at the first opportunity. He would treat it with as much offhand disdain as she had treated his offer of dinner.

My concern is that you and I would have nothing in common, nothing to talk about...if I must share my dinner with a man, I prefer that he have a brain and interesting conversation to offer.

Bloody cheek.

He thought of her fingers gripping his sleeve so

determinedly, making him stop and look at her.

Mary Ashford. He'd heard that name before somewhere, he was almost certain. But where? Wherever he'd heard it, the name must have been uttered as a warning. She was a woman who hid among dusty, abandoned books and skulked there, lying in wait for unsuspecting gentlemen to pass within her reach. Anyone who wandered into that dark, cluttered bookshop must fall prey to her peculiar charms and soon find their pockets lighter. She was such an unexpected sight emerging from the gloom that a man was instantly knocked off balance. He did not stand a chance. It was like the discovery of a bright daisy growing in a coal mine. With a wasp hidden in the petals.

Having trapped these helpless men in her thrall, she pretended — with wide eyes and pert lips— that she didn't meant to do it.

Only when he was safely outside the shop had Ransom returned to his senses and, out of her spell, realized she had separated him from his money with as much skill as a gypsy dancing girl. He had no doubt she'd sneakily added a few extra pounds to the bill. Who knew what else she might have winkled out of him if he'd stayed longer? Even the shop door had tried to block his escape, no doubt working in mystical alliance with her very strong will.

In short, he felt pushed and pulled about like a child's toy.

So who was this woman? She claimed to have no inkling of his notoriety, but then he'd known nothing of hers either, he mused, and he was sure she must have some. A woman with tempting lips like hers, and more than a spoonful of cunning impudence, definitely had a past littered with conquests.

My concern is that you and I would have nothing to talk about.

No, but she'd take his damn money, wouldn't she?

"You seem out of sorts, sir," the valet remarked as he put away his razor.

Ransom ran a hand over his smooth cheek. "I suffered a long night and an abrupt awakening with little sleep between." But that was nothing unusual.

"You ought to get more rest, sir, if you don't mind me saying. It cannot do your health any good to burn the candle at both ends so often."

Ah, but when he slept, Sally White was waiting.

He gave the valet a tense smile, a very good tip, and then got on with his day.

Miss Ashford's brown paper parcel remained on his desk, in his peripheral vision, something to be circled warily but not approached. Which is what he should have done with her. Never should have stayed to buy her rotten books.

So why did he? Something had drawn him to her, and it wasn't great beauty or charm or any seductive quality. She did not gaze up at him with shy admiration or coy invitation. Her expression, in fact, was akin to that of a woman who had just turned in the street to see a large, muddy, wolf-hound galloping playfully toward her with its eager, slobbering tongue hanging out. She did not know whether to flee or brace herself.

Of all the ways women had ever looked at him, that one was hitherto unknown.

But despite that bemusement and faint horror, her fingers had held his sleeve boldly to stop him leaving— those same fingers that had a knack for opening doors other folk struggled over. Her hands were chapped and in need of some tender care. His father said you could tell a lot about a woman from her hands, but what would he make of this coal mine daisy with her wry humor? She was, in fact, as mysterious as the contents of that tightly wrapped package. Possibly as dangerous too.

He scratched his left eyebrow as he passed the corner of his desk again.

Did he hear the paper whisper? No, must be his imagination. Or the fire in the hob grate. Or rain dashing at the window in a sudden gust.

He turned his attention to the sooty view of London rooftops. On this grim day, plump pigeons kept warm atop the chimney pots, fluffing their chests and letting out the occasional chortle.

Miss Ashford's eyes were grey— at first they had seemed as dull and drab as the color of those pigeons and overcast skies, but by the time he escaped her presence they were a shining, lively silver grey, like mercury in a thermometer. Apparently, he had succeeded in raising her temperature to some degree. Was it that hint of something breaking through, some small success achieved that made him feel as if his business with her remained undone?

She was wretchedly tenacious when she set her mind to something, as proven by that tidy, smug brown parcel of unwanted books on his desk. But she could do even better if she had someone with business sense to encourage her. Currently the shop interior was dim, full of shadows that did a good job at hiding her in the gloom. A dust mop could work wonders, as could some proper organization and a good window cleaner. A new sign outside with brighter paint would draw more attention to the place. It was purely by chance that he'd stumbled upon the entrance, and no doubt it was the same for many of their customers.

But when he tried to give the stubborn woman advice she summarily dismissed it, too proud to take his guidance. Why he even tried to help her was quite beyond Ransom's understanding. There were enough females in his life, and he really did not need one who challenged him the way she did— rejected his guidance with cynical amusement, as if he had nothing to offer her.

Yet she had not given him away to Belle when

she had the chance. She owed him no loyalty.

He supposed it was this that puzzled him most of all.

She was beginning to make his head ache again.

Better let that big, hungry falcon in his mind chase Miss Ashford out of his thoughts and off his moor. But the bird was very slow today. Sluggish.

As he walked back to his desk he heard a sudden ruckus approaching his office. Scuffling footsteps and loud French curses.

Of course, Belle had chased him down here, knowing he would head to the club, sooner or later. As Miss Ashford had said, he couldn't hide from her forever.

The staff made a valiant effort to hold her at bay, and he heard them calling for his strongest "arm" Miggs, a former boxer, fiercely loyal to his employer. If anyone could stop Belle, Miggs would.

But Ransom thought of Miss Ashford's words again. *Problems are better dealt with at once, rather than put off. It saves everybody a vast deal of trouble.*

So he opened his office door and signaled with his hands up in surrender. "Let her through."

At least now he had eaten something— thanks to the club's excellent chef— and was better able to face Belle's fury without losing his own temper. In fact, he felt quite unusually serene and decided, as if his encounter with Miss Mary Ashford had thrown cooling water on his hot head, made him see clearer.

Belle elbowed Miggs aside, marched down the passage, removed her glove and struck Ransom's face with her bare hand. It stung for a moment, then went numb.

"How pleasant to see you again, Belle," he muttered, following her into his office. "You should have—"

"'Ow dare you? The moment my back is turned!"

Ransom closed his door. "Belle, I thought that you and I had an understanding. We never promised each other monogamy." Until he heard the note of possessiveness in her voice that morning he had assumed they were of a shared mind.

"Monogamy? What is this?"

He sighed and scratched the back of his neck. "We did not promise to be exclusive, did we?"

The greatest advantage of an affair with Belle was that she, like Ransom, led a mostly nocturnal life and since she was a popular stage artiste he knew where she would be every night for a certain number of hours. Her career also took her away from London occasionally, which kept their relationship from becoming stagnant.

"Exclusive?" she demanded, her artificially blackened brows arched high.

"We made no promises to each other."

"I did not think we must promise. Why should any man need more than I," she dramatically held a clenched fist to her bosom, "Belle Saint Clair, beauty of the stage?"

"I see I should have made it clear. I am not fit for a permanent relationship of exclusivity, and I assumed you realized that when we met. I thought you felt the same."

"But I 'ave given you weeks of my time! I turned away many offers, because of you."

"It was very good of you to put yourself out for me, but not at all necessary, my sweet." He knew she was lying. Mademoiselle Saint Clair was much too ambitious to throw away any chance of bettering her career on the music hall stage, and she had plenty of gentlemen followers who would give her anything her little heart desired. More than he could. No, she had kept her options open, as indeed a clever woman in her position should.

"I suppose it's a defect in me," he added, "but I find it quite impossible to give up my freedom. Nor would I ask a woman to give up hers just for me. People are far better off not becoming entangled, in my opinion."

She laughed shrilly. "You are a *boy*, Ransom Deverell. You are a spoiled, frightened little boy who runs away when he is in trouble. Run, run, run down the street. He does not stay to face the consequence."

Ransom let her laugh at him. That was better than having her fingernails scratching his face and trying to gouge out his eyeballs. "Yes, you're quite right, of course. I'm a hopeless case. You're better off

without me. I'd only make you miserable in the end."
He fell back into his chair with a gusty sigh.

"No, mon ami, you are the one who will be
miserable *a la fin*! You will never be 'appy, until you
become a grown man. Until you stop this running and
running. Until you are brave enough to risk your 'eart
and *love!*" She raised her fist to the ceiling as if she was
about to storm the barricades in Paris. "To love with
all of yourself, not just the one part. When you can
say— *this is the woman for me.* Until you face the bad,
not only the good. Until you see there is more to life
than your pleasures. Then you will be a man. But I
fear it will not be so until you are on your deathbed.
Only then will you see what you 'ave missed. And too
late!"

This must be a speech from one of her better
roles. It certainly did not sound like something she
would have thought up herself, for her deepest
considerations usually went no deeper than surface
appearances.

"I see," he muttered. "Well, I'm sure you're right,
Belle." He was distracted by that parcel on his desk,
still certain he could hear the paper rustling,
whispering. *You are deliberately evasive, an habitual flirt
who uses that skill to get out of anything he doesn't want to
do...*

Nothing to talk about, indeed! Mary Ashford had
no idea how much pleasure he could give her without
a single word shared between them.

"Oui! Certainement, I am right, Monsieur Deverell! But do not call for me then, when you lay dying. For I," she gestured with her hand, "will twist the knife deeper."

"No doubt." He allowed a little smile. "I'll bear that in mind for my final moments."

"You are impossible."

"And you are as ill-suited to a permanent relationship as I." He paused and then added thoughtfully, "Did you ever think we ought to talk more? Perhaps we should have."

"Talk?" she snapped. "Talk about what?"

Precisely, he mused.

Her little nose wrinkled. "What is there to talk of between us? You are drunk, I think."

"Perhaps." What other explanation could there be? Here before him stood the most beautiful and sought after actress in London, a woman whose company other men would die for. Yet he was willing to let her slip through his fingers.

He could beg for her forgiveness, tell her what she wanted to hear, just to make her content and keep the peace— stopping short of a promise, of course. And she would act as if he was the only man in her solar system again. But it would all be false, nothing more than a temporary bandage to halt the bleeding. He could promise her nothing beyond tonight and before too long they would be here again, with her shouting at him.

The fact that he had forgotten the date of her return from Paris ought to be proof enough for the both of them that it was time to end this affair.

"I have enjoyed our time together and will always remember you fondly," he continued. "But as you said, I won't be ready to settle down until I'm on my deathbed. And I'm not dying today, or any day soon I hope."

"Ha! You do not finish with me! *I* finish with you!" She looked around— possibly for something to wound— and saw the brown paper parcel resting on the corner of his desk. With one swipe of her arm she sent it to the floor, whirled around in a satin flurry, and stormed out.

Ransom got up to retrieve the torn package of books from the floor. Now, through the shredded paper, he finally perused the titles Mary Ashford had selected for him.

Hints on Etiquette and the Uses of Society, with a Glance at Bad Habits.

A Book of Good Manners for Boys and Girls.

A Gentleman's Guide to Proper Decorum.

He laughed so loudly that Miggs came to see what was amiss.

Miss Ashford, like most people, underestimated him. Nothing new there. He liked to be underestimated, especially by women, for it kept him one step ahead of their natural cunning. And it kept an important distance, a buffer between the Deverell of myth and the real man.

But for once in his adult life, Ransom wished he'd left a different impression with a woman. A better one.

Chapter Six

Violet hunched her shoulders beneath a knitted shawl and gloomily surveyed the contents of her chipped tea cup. "I heard a man laughing earlier in the shop. Who was it?"

Mary was folding a letter she'd been reading before her sister came down. "Dr. Woodley came to collect his order."

"He doesn't usually have anything to laugh about. I believe he thinks laughter is akin to hysteria and bad for the digestion." Violet gripped her tea cup with both hands and sniffed. "I suppose he fussed all over you, as usual. I do not know how you can tolerate it."

"The gentleman means well, sister. He is very kind."

"He'd like to make you his next wife and workhorse. I daresay he needs someone to keep his house clean and cook his meals, and he knows he has no competition for your hand." Violet sneezed so violently she almost spilled her tea. "To be sure, he bides his time until you lower your guard, or we become even poorer. If that's possible."

"My guard?" Mary passed her sister a handkerchief. "What guard?"

"You must know how you are, Mary. You keep a barred gate between yourself and any man who shows interest these days. After that despicable cad,

95

Stanbury, broke your heart and married another—"
Violet clutched the handkerchief to her nose just in
time to catch another sneeze. The cup wobbled in her
other hand, tea splashing over the rim.

"Oh, Violet, that was *eight* years ago and I seldom
give George Stanbury a thought now. Must we dig up
this old bone again?" Mary took the cup from her
sister and set it down safely in a saucer. "He made a
wise decision, and I am grateful for it. I daresay he
could have managed the matter a little differently,
but—"

"You found out by reading of his wedding to
another woman in the newspaper. I should say he
could have managed the unsavory business quite a *lot*
differently!" Violet punctuated her angry remark with
a loud blow into the handkerchief.

"Nevertheless, it is done with now and we have
both moved on with our lives. I wish him well. I hold
no resentment."

Violet groaned, deflating against the back of her
chair as if someone had stuck a dagger in her ribs and
left a hole in her lung, "Must you always be so pious?"

"Pious?" Mary chuckled. "I suffer as many sins as
anybody. Indeed, I could curl your toes with some of
the wicked thoughts that plague me from time to
time. But I am not a sad wisp of a thing whose life
was ended by an aborted engagement. I'm sorry,
Violet, but I cannot pretend to be expiring of a
broken heart, just because that better suits your vision

of how things should be." Mary knew her sister would be thrilled if she took to her bed in a paroxysm of maidenly grief, because then Violet could play devoted nurse, bringing her calf's-foot jelly and rice pudding.

Violet was very much the romantic heroine in her own melodramatic play, while Mary had only a supernumerary role. But since Mary preferred that to anything more conspicuous, she rarely complained. The only time she objected to Violet's stage direction was when her sister tried to make her show too much emotion. In her opinion it was gaudy, pretentious — to suppose anybody else cared about her feelings— and completely unnecessary, since it achieved nothing.

"Do sit up straight, Violet. Remember your posture! Granny Ashford may no longer be with us, but she would turn in her grave if she saw you slumping. She might even rise up out of it and come to set you straight."

Her sister, however, had few memories of their formidable grandmother and therefore could not grasp the frightening enormity of that suggestion. Off on one of her grand soliloquies, hands clasped to her bosom, Violet exclaimed, "George Stanbury threw you over just because papa had to sell the estate. Without any apology or even a letter, the villain broke off his engagement to you and quickly married another girl. If you feel no lasting pain from that betrayal then you cannot be human, sister."

Apparently Violet thought she needed a reminder of the details. In case she might have forgotten any.

"Of course, I was hurt when it first occurred, sister. I was a naive, giddy, sheltered girl of eighteen. But I am not that same girl now. My eyes are opened wider."

"And even now," Violet exclaimed in high-pitched frustration, "you do not raise your voice to let his wickedness be known."

"What good would it do to scream about my disappointment? I certainly do not want any more pitying glances sent my way. It will serve us far better if you quietly learn from my unfortunate experience and choose for yourself with a wiser head."

"So here we sit cold, hungry, but oh-so-much *wiser*. Meanwhile, thoroughly stupid George Stanbury gets away with his shocking behavior and leads a charmed life, untroubled by any concern for you, never having to pay any consequences."

Mary shrugged. "Whatever the depth of George's feelings for me eight years ago, apparently they could not withstand the first storm once dark clouds set in. Marriage is not all fair weather, so it is just as well he discovered the limitations of his regard for me when he did."

"Yet he misled you dreadfully for as long as he could. Can you deny that, sister?"

"Perhaps I was just as much to blame for

expecting too much and holding out hope for too long, when the signs should have been obvious. I learned an important lesson."

Violet stirred her tea violently and vowed, "If I ever set eyes on that dreadful, wretched man again, I shall beat him about the head," she paused, searching for a suitable weapon and then raising her foot before the fire, "with my shoe."

Quietly amused by that idea, Mary replied, "I think that muffin might do a better job."

"I wouldn't waste food upon the blackguard."

"But we must remember, Violet, that when his father died, George Stanbury's most pressing need was money to keep the estate thriving. His choice was practical. We know the sadness of losing our home, and surely we would, neither of us, wish that on anybody."

"Yet you *loved* him, Mary. Does love count for nothing in this miserable world? I know I shall never marry without it!"

She sighed. "Was I in love? I cannot be as sure of that as you are, Violet. I can say with confidence that I *love* several things: finding another, unexpected chapter at the end of a book; the shuffle of gravel under horse hooves on a crisp, frosty autumn morning; the satisfaction to be had from bursting a pimple, or beating a month's worth of dust out of a carpet; the smell of a good cigar, or of boot polish, newly applied; the thrill of cracking open a soft-boiled egg and spearing the glistening golden yolk with her spoon—"

"That is not the sort of love I mean." Her sister had drawn back and looked at her as if she might be addled. "I mean passionate love for a man. And I know you did love George Stanbury, even if you won't admit it. I heard papa talking about it once and he said, *'When Mary loves she does so with her whole being'*. He said it very sadly, I suppose because he knew George was your last chance and you would never recover from his betrayal."

Mary said nothing, but rubbed furiously at a small speck she'd just found on her sleeve. *Last chance*, indeed! How could a girl have her last chance at only eighteen? But suddenly her throat was very tight, her corset chafing, and she had the most dreadful sore head.

"Papa should have sued Stanbury for breach of promise," Violet grumbled onward like a cart with wheels that badly required oiling.

"And aired our humiliation in public?" Restless, Mary got up to sweep some fallen coals back into the fire. "We had enough dark cloud over us as it was at the time. Such things are best forgotten, left in the past. It is futile to dwell upon misfortune."

Violet set her cup down in its saucer with a *crack*. "You have become the most horribly sensible woman that ever existed, sister. You claim to hold no resentment and you make that pert face — yes, that

100

one—as if you never felt tempted to curse, never wanted to scream at an injustice, never hated anybody, never *felt* anything. It is not a sin to show passion, you know."

"Perhaps not. It is also not very British."

"Well, I do not feel very British," Violet proclaimed angrily. "I swear I should have been born in the sun-drenched Mediterranean where nobody wears corsets and people are not afraid to express their feelings. Somewhere with fig trees, afternoon siestas and cicadas singing."

"Your skin is much too fair for such a climate and since you are rigid with fear if so much as a meek ladybird lands upon your arm, I dread to think how you would form any companionship with the larger, bolder insects of the tropics." Sitting down again at the table, Mary looked at her stale muffin, but still could not muster much enthusiasm for it. She pushed her plate away. "Besides, I'm certain the ladies there wear corsets too, even in that heat. They are accustomed to it, I suppose. People do adapt to their lot. We all must."

There followed a lengthy pause until Violet felt the need to express more discontent. It bubbled within her pot all day long and occasionally overflowed when the lid could no longer hold it in. "Oh, lord! It's so miserably cold!" She rubbed the tip of her nose with the bundled handkerchief. "I hate winter, and I hate this place."

"Hush! Mr. Speedwell might hear. If not for this bookshop and Uncle Hugo leaving me his shares in it, I do not know what we would have done. The portion father was able to leave for us is very small."

"Mr. Speedwell won't hear anything we say. He's deaf as the rag-and-bone man's old shire horse."

Yes, thought Mary, and how glad she was that he had not overheard her conversation with Ransom Deverell that morning. She looked down, hiding the sudden smile that threatened. If her sister saw her grinning stupidly she would want to know why. But the agitated twitching of her lips persisted so she got up, walked around the table and pretended to search for something on the dresser, rustling through Mr. Speedwell's medical pamphlets, tidying them into piles and opening drawers.

Behind her, still slumped in a chair, Violet yawned loudly. "To think that we have fallen to this. Existing rather than living. I wonder why I even get out of bed some mornings."

Mary struggled for something merry to think about. "Christmas will soon be upon us. Surely that will bring you cheer."

"Cheer? What shall we have to celebrate? I am almost twenty, half my life is gone and I have never been to a proper ball. Here I sit, wrapping my hair every night in curling papers, but for what and for whom? Any gentleman who smiles at me in the street receives a discouraging scowl from you."

She looked over her shoulder. "You wrap your hair in curling papers, Violet, because one must keep up appearances. And since it is now solely my responsibility to protect and guide you, sister, we will not encourage attentions from the wrong sort. We may not have much, but we still have our dignity. If they were respectable gentlemen they wouldn't leer at you in the street."

"You plan to keep me here with you forever, no doubt. Just because you do not want to be alone."

Mary turned her gaze back to the dresser and bit her tongue. Did she shelter Violet too much, afraid to lose her company? Although they daily complained about each other, it would be lonely without her sister, of course. She took a breath and managed a jaunty tone, "I shan't be alone. I could always take Dr. Woodley."

Her sister was aghast at the prospect. "Surely even you couldn't be such a martyr."

"He's a very kind, good gentleman. There would be no surprises at least."

"Neither would there be any joy," Violet muttered. "You used to be so merry and carefree, Mary. Even a little daring. Once you would never have settled for a man like that. But you've changed."

To which she replied, "I was once many things."

Her days of falling for a flattering comment and a handsome face were far in the past, along with that frivolous, reckless, selfish youth. Along with the girl

103

who tossed cold water out of windows onto poor, harmless boys, and thought she had all the time in the world, plenty of opportunity to enjoy all the treasures— and cream pastries— that stretched before her.

All that had been put away in a bottle and corked, tucked away on a shelf, never to be got out again. She did not really know why she saved it there, unless it was to remind herself— a cautionary tale of pride before the fall.

Violet exhaled another listless groan. "Pass the butter, sister. I may as well eat that muffin if I can get my teeth into it, since that is the greatest pleasure I am to be allowed."

Mary thought again how fortunate it was that her sister had not witnessed Deverell's visit to the shop that morning. Out of sheer boredom she would probably have welcomed the rogue's flirting. Then where would they be? Deverell would make the most of her sister's vanity, tease her without mercy, buy her a few pretty things, seduce her without a second thought, and leave them all in a worse state than they were when he first blew through that door on a gust of icy wind.

Well, they would never see him again. That entry in the ledger would likely soon be marked with a large "PAST DUE", as several others were. Thaddeus Speedwell was not very adept at chasing down their debtors, always convinced they would pay when they could and never wanting to think ill of anybody who bought one of his books. And Mary was not allowed to collect on their behalf because it was deemed "unladylike" and he would not hear of it.

She returned to the table. "Do look on the bright side, sister. At least we are not in the workhouse. Thanks to this bookshop and Uncle Hugo's dear friend we have a home here."

Violet groaned, for in her oft-expressed opinion, living above Mr. Speedwell's shop was not much improvement on the workhouse. As for their Uncle Hugo— the black sheep of the Ashford family— Violet, who was only twelve when he died, had always been rather frightened of him. The rest of the family, except for Mary, had never approved of Uncle Hugo, seldom spoke of him, and considered his rebellious life as an artist on the outskirts of society a terrible embarrassment.

But Mary was always very fond of Uncle Hugo. She was the only one who had paid visits to him toward the end of his life, and very probably the only one who had prayed for him when he died in prison.

"I suppose that is from Raven Deverell," said Violet, nodding her head toward the letter that sat beside her sister's cup. "Nobody else ever writes to you."

"Yes. But you forget her name is no longer Deverell. She is Lady Southerton now."

"Will she come to London for the season?" A

little glimmer of hope lightened Violet's eyes at the prospect.

"I'm afraid not. Her condition will confine her at home this spring."

"Oh." Her sister's shoulders sank again. "That is unfortunate. She was our only hope for a pleasant diversion. Now we shan't even have her company to look forward to in the new year, no excuse to go out, no one to invite us anywhere, and no hope of any entertainment!"

"Yet here we sit with our health and all our limbs intact, food on our table, candles to see by, and coal for our fire, so we are better off than the vast majority of folk in this town."

"It's all very well for you, Mary!" Violet bent mournfully over the meager fire and reached for the iron poker. "Candles and coal are all *you* need now that you are old. You have no wish for excitement. You had your chance, but my good years are being wasted. My beauty blooms unseen and unadmired in this dark, dank, dismal place."

Mary looked at her sister's pouting mouth, watched her prodding the coals about with more violence than effect, and replied solemnly. "I wouldn't fret, Violet. I'm quite sure that Prince Charming— if he's worth his salt— will find you soon, even hidden away in this bookshop. All the best fairytales begin thus, do they not? One must be downtrodden and ill-used, in order to feel the benefit of good fortune when it comes."

Having made as much mess as possible on the hearth that Mary had, moments ago, swept clean, her sister set the poker back on its hook and muttered, "I wish you would remember to call me Violette. You know how I hate *Violet*."

"Unfortunately it is your name, sister."

"It shall not be any longer. Henceforth I answer only to Violette." She tipped her chin high and smoothed both hands over her skirt as she sat down again at the table. "A girl has to have something alluring about herself, and a new name costs nothing so you cannot even complain about that."

"Indeed I cannot."

Her sister looked smug and picked up her tea cup, arching her little finger.

Mary added wryly, "I can only hope that 'Violette' will be more inclined to get up early and help around the shop. I would willingly call you Cleopatra, sister, if it would make your disposition sunnier."

Chapter Seven

...And so I must rely upon you, brother, to keep our mother away from Greyledge until after the babe is born in the spring. I fear my otherwise patient husband might be driven to desperate measures should she decide to visit us again, unexpected and uninvited, for another lengthy spell. Do the best you can. I depend on you.

Your loving sister, Raven

Ransom groaned and set the letter down. Since his sister's marriage, he had been left to manage their mother mostly single-handedly. Nobody else wanted the task, of course.

Now, apparently, Lady Charlotte had been making a nuisance of herself by traveling to Oxfordshire to see her daughter far more often than she was wanted, and Raven asked her brother to intervene. Usually his sister could be very direct herself, and never lacked courage when it came to handling their mother, but he suspected she amused herself by leaving this duty to him. In the past she had mentioned, more than once, that it would do both Ransom and Lady Charlotte some good to manage with each other.

As if he had nothing else to do.

Miggs stuck his head around the office door,

looking apologetic."Your brother is below and asks to see you, sir."

He frowned. "Which brat is it this time? Not Rush again, I hope."

Only a few days ago he'd been obliged to meet with one of his younger brothers, Rush, about two habits the boy had acquired at university— gambling and brawling. Ransom had thought it best to address the issue with his brother, before their father heard about it and all hell broke loose. The quicker any matter, including a broken nose, could be resolved before True Deverell found out, the better it was for everybody.

Ransom tried his damndest to stay out of these family troubles, but somehow they kept dragging him in.

The visitor this evening was not Rush, however.

"'Tis the brother what works with them crooks, Stamp on 'em and Spit."

"Ah. Damon. I suppose I'd better see him. And I've told you before, Miggs, the name of the lawyer's office in which he works is Stempenham and Pitt."

"That were my polite version, sir. There is another word what rhymes with Pitt."

"Yes, thank you, Miggs. I had no idea of your poet's ear for a rhyme. Go and fetch my brother, if you please, and try to spare him your opinion of the legal profession."

"Very good, Mr. Deverell, sir."

Miggs lumbered off again, and Ransom lit a cigar. He stretched both arms over his head, releasing the stiffness of having sat at his desk too long.

For much of his life he'd had little fondness for his father's bastards, avoiding them as much as he could, despite True Deverell's insistence on raising all his children together. But in the last few years— against all intentions— he had formed a bond of sorts with Damon. Or rather Damon had formed it with him. Uninvited and unwelcomed at first, it had, over time, become almost comfortable.

Perhaps it had something to do with the other young man's strange habit of seeking his company so frequently and with no ulterior motive apparent. Ransom couldn't shake him off. It was almost as if the fool boy admired him somewhat. He couldn't think why.

In any case, he couldn't bring himself to turn his back on the boy, even though his mother would throw a fit if she found out that he had befriended one of her former husband's bastards. And that would be another raging female out for his blood.

Really, what did one more matter, in the larger scheme of things?

Women; nature's practical joke on man, as his father would say.

He thought suddenly of Miss Ashford again. What was she doing tonight? Did she think of the strange man who had taken refuge between her bookshelves?

Long limbs restless, he leapt out of his chair, strode to the window and looked down on the rain washed street below. The streetlamps were just being lit, their warm glow coating the cobbled road with a glittering sheen as horses and carriages passed back and forth in a constant flow. London was putting on its evening clothes now, changing with the light. In daytime it was a bustling street, but at night a new mood took hold. There was less urgency, less industry. People moved through the light and shadow like specters reluctant to show their faces.

Mary Ashford's little bookshop across town would be closed now, the window shuttered, just as his club was waking up and his night beginning. He could picture her sitting in that little parlor. Did she invite other men to sit there with her, even though she refused him entry?

He hoped not.

But why would he care, damn her?

She would not be welcomed in *his* parlor either, he thought firmly. Nor would she be allowed here at Deverell's. No women were officially allowed to enter the club — not that it stopped a few of them trying.

Deverell's gentlemen's club was contained within the four floors of three adjoining, white-painted houses. Here, members could enjoy any number of discrete entertainments, hold informal meetings, or simply find a quiet corner to read a newspaper and have their shoes polished. Many gentlemen came to escape wives, mistresses, and daughters for an hour or two. In this glorious oasis they could be just as they were, without putting on a front to please women or worry about offending their delicate sensibilities.

But the primary business of the establishment was, of course, gambling. It might seem as if the wagers and games happened incidentally in these elegant, richly decorated rooms, where gentlemen came to eat, drink, and be pampered, but that was entirely the idea.

It was more than thirty years since True Deverell first purchased one of these buildings and set up a gambling club on the premises. Nobody knew where he'd come from or how he came by his money, and he let them all wonder. He merely sprouted up one day among the blue-bloods of London, like a strong weed that could not be eradicated, and he nurtured that sense of mystery about his past by never explaining himself and never apologizing for his actions— however scandalous. True Deverell had a certain finesse, a devil-may-care confidence in his own skin that few men could copy and all envied. In very little time his club became successful, but no matter how it expanded in size behind those white-painted walls, it retained its exclusivity and an aura of discreet wealth. The club's creator had always known that gentlemen would be far more willing to part with their money in an atmosphere of luxury and comfort, than in some seedy hall in a back alley.

"But how did you know that, father?" Ransom had asked him once.

"Instinct and observation. Where would you feel you'd got most moneys-worth? In a damp alley for sixpence, or in a bed with silk sheets and a bottle of champagne beside it?"

"The bed, of course."

"Precisely. And I hadn't even told you the cost."

True Deverell still oversaw the operation of his club from a distance, but as each year passed he handed off a little more of the reins to Ransom.

"As he should," Lady Charlotte would exclaim. "You are his eldest legitimate son, and you are entitled."

But his father didn't believe in the word "entitled". True Deverell thought a man should earn his fortune and his place in life— just as he had. And he didn't care about legitimacy. He treated all his children alike, whichever side of the bed they were born.

As a result, when it came to earning their father's approval it had often been a bit of a bloody free-for-all in the Deverell litter.

"You're looking a little worse for wear, brother. Should get more sleep."

Ransom laughed, turning to greet his half-brother. "Plenty of time to sleep when I'm dead. What brings you to visit?" He shook his half-brother's

113

hand and gestured for him to sit, but Damon paced the room, glancing out of the window, unable to relax.

"I need money."

Ah. The boy did not beat around the bushes today. Ransom, not much for chit-chat himself, was grateful for it.

"Money?" He tapped his cigar against the crystal ashtray on his desk. "Does the law profession pay so badly?"

The younger man shrugged, his back to the room. "The law profession," he repeated flatly. "I hunch over my rickety little desk surrounded by rolls of parchment and the odor of dry rot. There is little chance for me to move up at present. The old fellows are going nowhere, and I get all the dull cases. Particularly all the paperwork. Before too long my spine will turn into an unsightly hump and I shall be invited nowhere because my coat always stinks of cheap tallow candles."

Ransom hid a smile. His half brother had a taste for the finer things in life and he was driven to achieve them, but nothing ever moved fast enough for the boy. "Be patient. You have not been there long. You are still young."

"I'm twenty-four!" Damon shook his head. "And I'm stuck, brother, like a horse in a box that is too small. They treat me as if I'm just another clerk. So I wondered if you might have a vacancy here. At the club." He turned to look at Ransom. "I want to earn the money, of course. And I don't want our father to know."

Returning to the chair behind his desk, Ransom leaned back and watched his brother warily. It was never a good idea to try keeping secrets from their father, and Damon ought to know that. "I cannot let you work here without father knowing," he said. "If you need financial assistance, I can give you something to tide you over, but you'd better learn to manage your budget better if you're consistently running short."

Damon was silent, frowning.

Ransom continued carefully, "Is the income of a young lawyer not enough to cover your bills in Town?" As far as he knew, his brother was not much of a gambler. When he came to the club it was usually to dine, or spend a quiet evening in the library. His university years had been full of righteous noise and havoc rendered with a merry group of drunken friends, but these days he kept to himself, his nose to the grindstone. At least, that was how it appeared.

Damon scratched his cheek and finally fell into the seat opposite, exhaling heavily. "The money is not for me. There's a certain lady friend of mine who finds herself... in an interesting condition."

Ransom groaned. "Damon!"

"Don't lecture me, brother. If I wanted a lecture, I'd go to father."

He supposed that was true and Ransom was in no position to lecture about women either, was he? But for all his enjoyment of the fairer sex he was always careful not to leave any little bastards behind. "There are things you can do to prevent the risk," he muttered.

"But not for certain. In any case," Damon shook his head, "it's too late for that now. Three months too late."

"What is the plan then? Marriage? Or do you mean to set her up in a house somewhere?

Damon cleared his throat. "I don't know yet...the circumstances are... awkward."

"Awkward?"

There was a short pause. "She's already married."

"Oh, Christ!"

A haughty expression sharpened his younger brother's features. "So you see my dilemma."

"Father would kill you if he knew."

"Hypocritical of him though, don't you think? Rather late for him to judge."

"It won't stop him ripping into you like a lion into raw meat. He's not greatly concerned with the example he set. He will tell you that he had more excuse, because he knew no better. He will say that we had every advantage he did not, and that he hoped you'd learn from his mistakes."

Damon gave a curt laugh. "Precisely why he can't know."

With a sigh, Ransom set his cigar on the ashtray and reached for the brandy decanter. He refilled his own glass and poured one for his brother. "If she's married, how do you know this child is yours?"

"Of course, it's mine." Damon grabbed his glass and drank the contents in one swig. "She and her husband have not shared a bed in years." He coughed, his eyes watering.

"That's what she tells you. I didn't think you were that gullible. You may not even be her only lover."

"When it comes to women you always expect the worst. But I believe it's my child. She would not lie or try to trick me. You don't know her as I do."

Ransom felt his insides shrivel slightly, for Damon sounded much like *him* when, ten years ago, he tried to defend the blackmailing Miss Pridemore to his father. Just after he shot True in the shoulder and watched him fall to the ground. "*She told me you seduced her. I believe her. You just couldn't keep it in your breeches, could you, father? You had to despoil the woman I love!*" But, of course, he soon discovered the fickle limits of Miss Flora Pridemore's "love" and learned of her many lies.

How long would it be before Damon had his awakening?

"Never believe a woman," he muttered, staring at the amber liquid in his glass as he lifted it to the light of the oil lamp on his desk. "Enjoy them, make the most of them, but never trust them to tell you the truth. It is best to assume that every time they open

117

their mouths a lie will come out."

"Yes, yes," Damon was not listening, of course. "But can you give me a post here? Elizabeth will need money to separate from her husband. He will seek a divorce on the grounds of her adultery. So, as you can see, I need a steady second income, not a loan."

"Divorce?" This was getting worse by the second.

"Of course. I will take responsibility for my child, and Elizabeth cannot remain under her husband's roof."

"Damon, if you're named co-respondent in a divorce, there will be no hiding it from the papers or our father. But you must have realized that. You, after all, are the lawyer in the family." He must also know how furious their father would be if the son upon whom he pinned his greatest hopes for the future, should have let himself be distracted by a woman, a mistake True always warned his sons against.

"I know, in time, it must all come out and father will be made aware," Damon groaned, fingers drumming against his glass. "But before that happens I'll be on my feet. Elizabeth and I will be living together. If I present father with a *fait accompli*, what can he say? I'll prove to him I can manage this and weather the scandal. When I was sixteen he told me that if I thought I was old enough to make decisions about my life I had better be prepared to face the consequences too. So here I am. I'm not a boy. I own up to my mistakes and don't run from them."

Ransom had been about to pour another brandy, but instead he replaced the crystal stopper in the decanter and picked up his cigar. Again he thought of Miss Mary Ashford's quiet voice.

I wouldn't run away. Usually, problems are better dealt with at once, rather than put off. It saves everybody a vast deal of trouble.

He got up, walked to the window and looked out.

"I'm sorry," Damon muttered behind him. "I didn't mean to bring that up."

"Bring what up?"

"The accident and... Sally White's death."

Ransom stared at his reflection in the window. He had not been thinking of Sally White. For the first time in years she hadn't been hovering there in the shadows. Instead his mind had been caught up on another woman, another face. It shocked him to be reminded of Sally again so suddenly.

Reflected in the glass he counted the deep lines furrowed across his brow, the weariness in his expression betraying so many nights without good, solid sleep. His shirt sleeves, rolled up to his elbows, shone white in the window, one moving like a wing as he lifted the cigar back to his mouth. "You mean that Sally's death was one of my mistakes and you suggest that I ran away from it?"

"No, I didn't mean that. I spoke about facing

consequences and not running away before I realized
how it might sound. You know what people say about
all that and about you. But I don't think the same as
them. Of course, I don't."

He knew his brother referred to the fact that he'd
left Sally on the moor after the accident and that
when she was first reported missing he had not told
anybody he was with her. His failure to be honest
immediately had, of course, increased the suspicion
against him later when her body was found. The truth
was, Ransom simply hadn't been able to find her after
he regained consciousness and so he assumed she'd
wandered off or met someone else— an absurd, all-
too convenient assumption perhaps, although at the
time he was not thinking with clarity at all. He had
been just as bloody stupid, arrogant and unthinking as
every other twenty-four-year old. As Damon was
now.

But Ransom didn't want to talk about Sally
White, so he said, "If I give you employment here in
the evenings, what will happen to your position at
Stempenham and Pitt?"

"I'll manage both, if I can. It shouldn't be
difficult. If not, I'll quit the law."

And their father would come to London at once,
looking for blood. He would blame Ransom,
undoubtedly, for "encouraging" or "supporting"
Damon's abrupt change of direction. Apparently the
boy thought money would come quicker, easier and

more abundantly working at Deverell's. With Ransom as his employer he no doubt expected a comfortable sinecure.

"But you refuse to discuss this decision with our father?"

"Not until he *must* know. Once I have everything well sorted... with Elizabeth."

Ransom strode back to his desk. "Well, if you won't seek his advice, you must let me meet this woman."

Damon exhaled a curt laugh. "To ask her intentions?"

"Yes. Why not? For your own good. For all we know she could be seeking to unload her child on you simply because you're a Deverell."

"Of course, you never trust anybody outside the family, do you?"

"With good reason." Some within the family were equally untrustworthy, but that he left unsaid.

"Very well. If you want to meet Elizabeth, I'll arrange it. I'll send her to you."

"Good. Send her to the house in a day or two, not here. Then we'll decide what we should do."

"We?"

"You're asking for my help, are you not? I can't tell you what to do— wouldn't try. But I *can* give you advice."

Reluctantly the young man agreed. He stood and reached across the desk toward the little pile of books that sat there. "What's this? Etiquette and manners?" He laughed, rocking back slightly on his heels. "*You?*"

"A woman sent them to me in error."

"How odd. What woman would be mad enough to send you books like these? Who is she?"

"Just...a woman."

Damon's eyes sparked with amusement. "I do hope, whoever she is, she does not think to change you, brother."

"Definitely not."

"Perhaps I should meet her and find out her intentions. For *your* own good."

"Most amusing. Considering your predicament, Damon, I'm astonished that you can find something to laugh at."

"Ha!" His brother's head tipped back as another guffaw exploded from his mouth. "Now you sound just like father. Are you turning into him in your old age? I confess myself disappointed, as you were always the one who said nothing should be taken seriously. I thought I would never get a lecture at least, if I came to you. Out of anybody I thought you would understand."

Naturally, Damon did not want to disappoint their father, or sully his image as the golden boy of the family. So when he found himself in difficulties he came instead to his ne'er-do-well half-brother, unloaded his troubles, and kept his own shining halo intact. For the time being.

Ransom managed a smile, clapped his brother firmly on the shoulder and sent him on his way with the reminder to send his pregnant lover for an interview. "I'll do what I can, but I still think you should stay at Stempenham and Pitt. Don't waste your education. Be patient. Father has great hopes for you."

"And that's another thing! Father never needed an education or patience. He managed brilliantly without either." Then he pointed at the books again and scoffed, "Those too. He would laugh at etiquette lessons."

Ransom opened his office door to see the boy out. "Imagine what he might have achieved if he *had* read a book once in a while."

Thus Mary Ashford was back again, wandering across his moor.

"Just imagine how much more successful you might have been, if you managed to pick up a novel once in a while," she exclaimed pertly, looking up to address the falcon that perched amid the bare branches of its tree.

Where the hell had he seen her face before? The more he thought of it, the more certain he was that he knew her from somewhere. It was as if she'd been there all along.

"Have you heard from Justify?" Damon stopped just outside the door. "When he was on leave this autumn we were supposed to meet, but he didn't arrive. It's not like him to say he'll be somewhere and then not turn up."

"I believe your brother had much on his mind at the time. I saw him only briefly this summer."

But long enough for Justify to ask for his help, turning to Ransom out of desperation. Just as they all did lately.

"Don't mention any of this to him...about Elizabeth," Damon muttered. "He'd never approve. He's always so damned upright and proper."

"Of course." But everybody had their secrets— even the most upstanding and honorable Naval Captain Justify Deverell. And for some reason, Ransom had become the brother to whom they all divulged these furtive matters. The brother to whom they looked for help, even though his own life frequently teetered out of control.

Did it make them feel better to give him custody of their problems, he wondered?

They didn't offer to help *him*, of course. But then he wouldn't ask.

He was beyond redemption, and everybody knew that.

As he looked across at the books on his desk again, it occurred to him that he'd appointed Miss Mary Ashford to an impossible, thankless task that morning. *Save me*, he'd said to her.

He couldn't remember, in the whole of his thirty years, ever asking anybody for help before. Not for anything.

Chapter Eight

To Miss Ashford;

I find these worthy tomes are not suited to me after all, and so I return them to your shelves. However, I appreciate the attempt to improve my mind, which is sadly sunk beyond rescue. So I have enclosed ten pounds for your services and inconvenience. I feel it would be remiss of me not to pay for the time you spent and the patience with which you tolerated such a troublesome customer.

Yours sincerely,

The King of Siam.

* * * *

On that Wednesday night, when sleep finally claimed him, Ransom was not chased by Sally White's ghost. Instead he dreamed of running between the shelves of a cluttered bookshop, but he was the one chasing, and had no idea who or what he chased after. Then he stumbled and managed to knock all the bookshelves over, one after the other, like dominos.

Waking as the last shelf tumbled, shaking the floor under his feet, Ransom realized he was still in his office at the club, having stayed the night on a couch as he often did if it was a busy evening. The couch was old and worn, but comfortable enough and there was no real reason to go back to the house. Nobody waited for him there. He only made more mess for the staff when he was in residence.

Briefly, with a little pang, he thought of Belle. Sweet-scented, soft-skinned, uncomplicated Belle. He wondered whether he ought to send her a gift and make it up to her for yesterday. Perhaps he'd been hasty in sending her off. She did have her good qualities...

But no, it was best to nip this thing in the bud before she became even more possessive and somebody got hurt. Miss Ashford was right about that.

Ah yes, Miss Ashford. Yesterday he'd met a different sort of woman.

Encountered might be a better word. Ran into her as painfully as he ran into that gas lamp in the street.

Sometimes a man knew when an event of significance had occurred in his life; sometimes he didn't know whether it was good or bad, just that it was noteworthy.

And that was what she was.

He took a deep breath and stretched his arms up before bending them behind his head.

Surprisingly, this morning, for the first time in many years, he woke refreshed. The possibilities for his day seemed unusually bright.

How long had he slept? As his gaze wandered

around the room, he spied his pen dropped to the blotter beside an ink stain and a list of names. Ah, yes. That was the last thing he did last night after writing his note to Miss Ashford and before dropping to the couch. Or was it very early this morning? In any case, at some point he'd decided to send those books back to the thorny bookseller and had sent a messenger boy off with the package. Better he not keep any reminder of her, he'd thought, for every time he glanced at that little pile of books he found her in his mind again, mocking him with her eyes, distracting him from his business. A puzzling, quick-witted, clever, challenging woman, the very opposite of any he ever sought out. She simply had to go.

Alas, this morning Miss Ashford was apparently still at large on his moor, despite repeated efforts to chase her off. She looked up at him with clear grey eyes, her chapped fingers tugging on his sleeve for attention.

Ransom smiled when he thought of what she would say when she saw those books returned. Ha! He liked to have the last word.

Fully awake at last, he got up and opened the sash window. It was raining out, but he enjoyed the feel of rain on his face, especially in the early morning.

Far below, the street was slowly coming to life. Flower sellers called out in sing-song voices as they wandered by with their baskets. A stout woman sold oranges from a barrel on wheels, and beside her a man puffed on a tobacco pipe while setting up his baked potato stall. It was cold and the air was smoky, as well as damp, not to mention slightly redolent of moldy cabbage leaves and horse dung. But this concoction of scents, sounds and sights was something Ransom relished. He liked the chaos of it, that feeling of standing in the midst of an ever-changing bazaar— one rich with color, drama and spice.

That was why he loved managing Deverell's, for it too was full of life, unpredictable and always evolving.

He took a deep, lusty breath of that good, honest, filthy London air, and blinked the rain from his eyelashes.

As he looked down to the awning over the steps of Deverell's, he saw a woman in a blue bonnet, with a covered basket under one arm, hastening away from the building. She glanced up at the sky, just once, squinting against the drizzle and then stopped to buy an orange.

"Ash—Mary—Miss—Miss —Ford—Ashford!" He could barely get the name out, taken by such surprise that he didn't know what to do first. Not looking up again, she paused on the pavement, waiting to cross the street.

"Miss Ashford," he shouted again, louder this time, startling a pigeon from the ledge outside his window. Alas, a large carriage drawn by four horses thundered by at that moment and then she hurried away across the street with her head bowed against the rain, putting the orange into her basket.

Ransom left the window and ran out of his office. For the second morning in a row he found himself tumbling and tripping down a set of stairs, but this time he was not the one running away. Just like his strange dream, he was the one who gave chase— he, who had never chased after anything or anyone in his life.

Miggs was just closing the front door of the club with one hand and yawning wide.

"Look out," Ransom exclaimed, pushing his way by. "Why did you let her get away?" Not stopping to hear an answer, he dashed out, down the steps and along the pavement, looking for that blue bonnet.

He was half way across the road, dodging carriages and horses, before he realized how bizarre it was that he should be chasing after a woman. Even then he didn't stop until he was forced to admit he'd lost her while turning a corner onto Jermyn Street. The crowds were thicker already now, the narrow street full of people charging this way and that. He didn't stand a chance of finding her on foot. And his shirt sleeves were now soaked as the rain came down full force.

But he knew where to find her anyway, did he not?

129

Of course.

What an idiot he was! If he really wanted to see her again, he could. Any time he wanted. Just had to find his way to that funny little bookshop hidden down an alley. If his messenger had found it, he could too.

Comforted by this thought, he turned to go back and then spied her blue bonnet as she walked into a shop across the street.

At once he hurried across, dodging between carriages, until he found himself at the window of a pawnbroker's establishment.

Holding his breath rather than steam up the glass, he peered inside and saw her there, in the shadowy depths of the shop, conferring with a plump, mustachioed fellow. She reached into her basket and brought out something in her hand, holding it so nervously for the man's appraisal that she almost dropped it.

Suddenly Ransom felt something strange. He couldn't put a name to it, but he knew he couldn't let her see him there. So he spun around and hurried back to St. James Street and the club, where Miggs held the door for him, that big, round face looking quietly amused.

"Did you enjoy that brisk morning constitutional, sir?"

"Yes," he snapped, running fingers back through his wet hair. "It was most...bracing."

"I would have recommended a hat and coat, sir. Perhaps even an umbrella, next time you go out in the rain after a bit o' petticoat."

"Thank you, Miggs." Still breathless, he added, "That was Miss Mary Ashford, was it not?"

"She didn't give her name, sir."

"Well, what did she say? Why didn't you let her in?"

Miggs stumbled to a halt and stared in surprise. An overly dramatic sort of surprise. "Women aren't allowed in the club. It's the rules."

"Well, I know women aren't allowed, of course, for Christ's sake! But the club isn't open at this moment and when she asked for me you should have let her in out of the damned rain."

Both hands behind his back, Miggs looked quizzical. "But she didn't ask for you, sir."

"She didn't...she didn't ask for me?"

"No, sir."

Now he really felt foolish. What the devil was wrong with him? Fancy racing after a bloody woman, getting drenched in a downpour, then finding her and running away again. Had he lost his mind? Were there not enough women plaguing his life already, without him chasing after that one?

Miggs sniffed loudly through his squashed, misshapen nose and abruptly held out a package that he must have been hiding behind his back the entire time. "She left this though. And, by crikey, look at that! It has your name on it, so it does."

Ransom scowled. "Then why didn't you say so, for the love of—"

"If I'd known she were an important bit o' petticoat, Mr. Deverell, as opposed to the usual soggy crumpet," Miggs cracked a slow, cheeky grin, "I would have made her come in, even though she said she were in a hurry and couldn't stay."

Snatching the package from the other man's hands, Ransom made some attempt to retrieve a little dignity. "Make sure this carpet gets well scrubbed today. It's looking grubby. And the glass chimneys on the lamps in the dining room could do with a clean."

"Yes, sir. I'll make certain."

"What about this chandelier? It's time all the crystal was washed. I want to see it shining and twinkling like new tonight."

"Yes, sir. I'll see to it. Don't you worry yourself. I can see you've other matters on your mind."

"Indeed I do. When you have a moment, come up to my office, will you, Miggs? I've got a list of people to whom I need you to pay a visit."

"A visit, sir?"

"Yes. On behalf of an acquaintance. A matter of business."

"Very good, sir."

With a satisfied nod, Ransom hurried back up to his office, carrying the parcel under his arm, not wanting to open it in front of anybody. The paper was damp with rain, the ink smudged, but yes, that was his name written there in her neat penmanship. Spelled correctly.

Had she walked all the way to St. James Street in the rain? She must have set off soon after receiving his parcel of returned books, which meant she was a very early riser and not afraid of walking a fair distance. That fussy doctor chap wouldn't like to know she'd been out chancing her health so carelessly.

But she did so for him. Well, not just for him—clearly she had other errands.

Damn it all to blazes, why was he sweating like an adolescent with his first fancy?

Impatient he tore open the wrapper and found a book with her note.

Dear Sir;

Please accept my apologies for the selection I previously sent to you in error. It was remiss of me not to provide you with reading material that you might find pleasurable. I would never want to dissuade a man from reading, and I fear my attitude yesterday has done that very thing.

Enclosed you will find a copy of 'David Copperfield' by Mr. Charles Dickens, very newly published as a complete novel. I hope you will find this story to your liking, as it concerns the struggles of a boy who overcomes much adversity in life.

Again, I must tender my deepest apology for yesterday.

I'm afraid I released in your presence some anger that <u>you</u> had not earned with me, and I should hate for that mistake to ruin any chance I might have of encouraging a new reader.

In the words of Mr. Dickens himself —

"Do not allow a trivial misunderstanding to wither the blossoms of spring, which, once put forth and blighted, cannot be renewed."

Yours sincerely,

M. A.

He stared at the letter for quite some time. Nobody, in their sober mind, had ever apologized to Ransom Deverell before. Not for anything. He didn't have the first idea how to take it. Was he even deserving of an apology? She seemed to think so.

When he turned the note over he found another line of her neat writing along the edge.

If you are agreeable, I shall deliver more books, once you have completed this one, until your ten pounds is spent to the fullest.

He had to smile at her determination to turn him into a reader.

Good of the wench to care, he supposed, even if her effort was wasted on him.

But what was in it for her? A mere ten pounds,

unless she had some sly trick up her sleeve. She must be up to something devious; she was a woman, wasn't she? Aha! Perhaps she merely wanted an excuse to visit him. Wench was obviously smitten.

Lingering over her letter, he traced the words with one finger, even smelling the paper to find her scent. As if that might tell him more.

This was bad; he was clearly in danger of letting her remain on his moor, and forgetting his rules about women. It was all the fault of her lips. Or her eyes. Or her chapped fingers. Even the way she walked away from him had a certain inexplicable allure! Since when had the back of a woman's neck, as he followed her down a crowded street, become a matter for warm contemplation? Or the slightest tilt of her head caused him to wonder what she was thinking?

Oh, Miss Mary Ashford was trouble indeed, if she did this to him without even trying.

Now to the matter of that list of names he had for Miggs...

Because he *would* have the last word, whether that stubborn woman liked it or not.

* * * *

"Where have you been, Mary?" Violet demanded. "You must be soaked to the skin!" Dashing up from her chair by the fire, she quickly helped her sister out of her bonnet and coat.

"I was in need of a brisk stroll," Mary replied, setting her basket on the table. "An early morning walk is very good for one's health, and I had a few knots to work loose in my mind. I find that the rhythm of walking helps me to do that, and as long as I go alone I have no obligation to be sociable." Reaching into her basket, she drew out the orange she'd purchased and presented it to Mr. Speedwell, with a grand curtsey.

The gentleman tore his attention from the latest pamphlet of medical advancements, and his lips flapped open in surprise.

"I know oranges are your favorite, and I had a few spare pennies today, Mr. Speedwell."

"Gracious, Mary, my dear girl! That is very kind of you indeed, but I do hope you have not gone wild and spent your windfall."

"What windfall?" Violet wanted to know at once.

"Mr. Speedwell refers to the sale of some books yesterday," Mary hung her bonnet on a hook by the door, "but that money belongs to his shop takings, not to me, and I won't hear another word about it! It is not mine to spend." She spread her wet coat over the back of a wooden chair from the table and set it by the fire to dry. "However, I do have news to cheer you, Violet— I mean Violette."

Her sister looked doubtful. "What news?"

"I decided that perhaps I have been a little harsh on you." She held her fingers before the fire to get some warmth back into the tips, for although she possessed a pair of gloves, they were very worn and the stitching had come apart in several places, making them more of a sieve against the cold, rather than a shield. "As you pointed out to me yesterday, I had my chance as a young girl and yet, because of our misfortunes and papa losing his estate before you came out, you have had very few entertainments. It isn't fair."

Violet flushed pink. "But that is not your fault, sister. I didn't mean that—"

"You are now my responsibility. We are all we have left, and I ought to make an effort for your sake." Opening her reticule she took out some bank notes and showed them to Violet. "I found some savings I had forgotten that I ever put aside. So, since it is almost Christmas, we are going to buy you some good silk and make you a pretty gown. A proper ball gown in the very latest fashion."

"Oh!" Her sister gasped in delight, hands clasped around the back of a chair, but then her smile fell. "Where shall I wear such a gown? We have nowhere to go, nothing to attend."

"I'll find somewhere, sister— even if it is merely to keep you from beating some poor soul about the head with your shoe out of frustration."

Mary had decided that she would seek assistance from Raven's mother, Lady Charlotte Rothsey Deverell, on one of her visits. That lady would surely know somewhere Violet could show-off in a new frock. Lady Charlotte might even like to discover a new, pretty young lady upon whom to practice her polishing skills and Violet would soak it all up, far more enthusiastically than Mary ever could. Violet had a head start on her sister, for she possessed the prized ivory skin and pale golden hair that gave her looks a natural advantage. Unlike Mary, whose olive complexion could only be blamed upon some distant, little-known and never mentioned branch of the Ashford family tree.

"There is nothing more troubling to me than a young woman who does not make the most of her God-given attributes, even if they are not many in number," Lady Charlotte was fond of saying, while glaring hard at Mary. "It is a vulgar sort of false modesty to pretend one does not care about one's reflection. To give up and give in to the ravages of time is a mark of laziness and the greatest error a woman can make. The less she has to work with the harder she ought to try."

Yes, she would enlist Lady Charlotte's help with her sister.

Violet was so full of glee at the prospect of a new gown and a possible outing into society that she did not stop to wonder how her sensible and organized sister could have forgotten something as important as putting money aside. Nor did she notice that Mary's favorite cameo broach and silver earrings were missing.

But what did the loss of a few material things matter, thought Mary, if it meant that her sister could finally have something to which she might look forward. The pawnbroker had given her a good price for those pieces and hadn't tried to cheat her, so she was feeling a little flush with wealth and not at all sorry.

"Let's have some sherry!" she exclaimed, rubbing her hands together as the life came back into her fingers. She raised her voice. "We do have some sherry, do we not, Mr. Speedwell?"

"Mary!" Her sister was scandalized. "It is much too early surely."

"Let's say it's medicinal then. I'm sure Dr. Woodley would approve of that." She was certainly in need of a cure, with this feverish sensation running through her veins. "It is, after all, a very cold day."

Violet stared at her.

"What now?" Mary demanded. "You recently accused me of being the most horribly sensible woman that ever lived. You ought to celebrate my wicked relapse into reckless behavior."

"I'm sure we can have a little stiffener, Mary," Mr. Speedwell exclaimed eagerly, for he was never one to let the time of day intrude on his love for a quick sip.

And so they indulged in sherry before luncheon. Whatever next, Mary mused. Clearly it was very fortunate that she didn't have a "windfall" very often, or she would go utterly mad. Probably also a very lucky thing that men like Ransom Deverell did not come into the shop every day, stirring up the dust and putting ideas into her head.

"What has prompted this change in you?" her sister wanted to know. "Surely not anything I said."

No, it was not entirely due to Violet's complaints, but she could hardly tell her sister about Deverell, how he had swept in and spun her around. Or how she had made it her project to get that man to read a novel.

It may not appear to be an achievement of much magnificence when weighed against other revolutions and rebellions in the world, but she was not a woman who expected grand things in her life anymore. Mary would be quite content with just a few good deeds fulfilled.

Chapter Nine

Two days later, that imaginary pet falcon having failed to chase Miss Mary Ashford off his moor, Ransom was at the door of his mother's suite at Mivart's Hotel. If anybody could be relied upon to remind him of the general wickedness of females, it was his mother, and he needed a dose of that dark medicine— her own particular brimstone and treacle— to put him back to normal.

"I would have come last week, mama, but I've been very busy with Deverell's. Now that father so seldom comes to London there is much for me to do."

Lady Charlotte immediately drew back from the peck he placed upon her cheek. "Your father cares nothing for you. Yet you spend all your waking hours working for him. Never can you spare a moment to visit *me*, the woman who ruined her looks to give birth to you!"

"I'm here now, aren't I?" he replied gruffly, tasting her familiar chalky powder on his lips. She wore it more thickly now than she once did. "Good afternoon to you too, mama."

"I suppose I must be grateful for the scraps of attention you throw my way. How like *him* you have become. Doling out your time to me in the tiniest of begrudging increments, the same as *him* with my allowance."

His mother was on usual form. Good. Ten minutes in her company ought to put him back on even keel and remind him of exactly why he didn't let women wander around on his moor longer than necessary.

"Why do you suppose he named you Ransom? Because you were the ransom demand he got from me, from my father, from the aristocracy he despised."

"Yes, mama," he muttered, following her across the room. Attar of Roses— her favorite scent— filled his nostrils. Anything she touched always seemed to hold a whisper of the fragrance for days after. Like Sally White's cheap perfume. He swallowed the wave of nausea that churned with sudden violence up into his throat and burned there.

"Men used to write poems about my figure," his mother added, turning with a flourish as she stood before her fireplace. "Now look at me. Your father put paid to all that with his base demands upon me." She smoothed hands over that self-maligned waist, but Ransom saw only the usual slender, corseted shape. "I had no choice, of course, but to submit. It is a wife's unhappy lot to bear children."

Ah, yes, this old rub.

For much of his youth, Ransom had been led to believe that his father forced himself on Lady Charlotte, to beget the three legitimate offspring she bore him during the miserable years of their marriage. The accusation of physical violence was never stated explicitly, but she planted the idea with partial whispers, frail and needy sighs left in her eldest son's ears. There they grew, taking root inside the impressionable mind of an unhappy, confused child. Like quick, vicious pinches they were not immediately evident, but developed later into mean little bruises under his skin.

As a grown man, when he finally found the courage to ask her directly, his mother claimed complete innocence, pretending it was all Ransom's fault that he came by such an idea about his father. But she was still doing it now— alluding to the act of sexual intercourse as if it was something beneath her, something degrading that she never wanted.

His mother had a habit of circling an issue with suggestion and conjecture, then stepping back to let someone else fire the arrow. She'd been doing it to Ransom all his life.

These days he was wiser and cut her off at the beginning. "Yes, mama, I know how you dislike intimate relations with men." He took off his hat and removed his gloves, dropping both to the table by the window. "That's why I never hear of your dalliances with various colorful, and often continental, gentlemen."

Hands resting on her waist she posed in rigid outrage, treating Ransom to her specialty— an icy stare meant to freeze his blood. Something else that no longer worked on him.

"Did you really think I could have no inkling of your affairs?" He laughed.

Perhaps she did think that. Lady Charlotte appeared to live in a fantasy of her own making. A fairytale in which she was the abused, imprisoned princess. Yet she managed to live very comfortably in this "imprisonment", which happened to be an expensive suite of rooms at Mivart's Hotel in Mayfair. Her former husband still paid many of her bills, even all these years after their divorce, and she continued to coast along on the fringes of society by using her father's name whenever possible. She was, after all, the daughter of an earl, as she would remind anybody she met.

"I have gentleman friends occasionally," she snapped. "Do you expect me to live shut away from society altogether? I suppose you are embarrassed by me too these days. Like your ingrate sister, now that she has risen to the title of a Countess and left me behind, quite forgetting the part I played in getting her a husband."

He rolled his eyes. "No, mama. Of course you don't embarrass me."

"Perhaps I should become a nun and consign myself to a convent. Is that what you want of me?"

"Mama, I may not know a vast amount about nuns, but I suspect you don't possess the qualifications to become one. And, of course, there is no reason for you, or anybody, to lead a cloistered life. I merely ask that you don't try to pull the fleece over my eyes by feigning blamelessness and piety. We are, none of us, without fault. Or sin. The world would be a far better place if everybody admitted that to be the case."

She strode across to him, adjusted his cravat and reached further upward to brush a lock of hair from his brow. He stiffened at once, always wary of her touch. "You are looking tired and worn, Ransom. You should get away from Town for a while. Why don't we both travel to Oxfordshire to see Raven?"

He moved away from her. "I'm much too busy with the club to be away this time of year, and travel in winter is an abysmal trial. I think you ought to stay here until summer. I'll take you then."

"But now that she is expecting again, Raven needs me at Greyledge."

"What for?"

"What do you mean?" Her chin went up, eyes gleaming frostily. "A daughter needs her mother's advice at such a time. I thought that was evident."

"Even though motherhood is something you would have avoided if you could? I'm not sure that qualifies you to attend Raven in her confinement and give her *any* guidance on the subject of children. She doesn't really need the additional anxiety, does she?"

"Anxiety? How could I cause her anxiety?"

His mother was, as usual, oblivious to the wreckage she left in her wake. He shook his head. "Mama, I'm not escorting you to Oxfordshire until the summer and after the brat is born, so you may as well resign yourself to waiting."

"Then I'll find someone else to take me. Or I'll go alone."

"Hale doesn't want guests at the estate until after the birth."

"I'm not a guest! I'm family!"

But he knew his sister's husband would throw a fit if Lady Charlotte turned up, uninvited yet again, especially until after the baby was born. He couldn't blame the man for wanting his mother-in-law out of the way. Raven had miscarried one child already, and her husband did not want to risk any danger to her health this time— hence her latest letter begging Ransom to keep their mother safely out of the way in Town.

It was three years since Raven married Sebastian Hale, the Earl of Southerton, but their mother had, by now, been a visitor to their estate enough times to make a nuisance of herself. Once she was there she was apparently very difficult to be rid of too. Like an infestation of ants.

"*Try to keep her occupied in Town for as long as you can. I really think my husband's head might explode if she arrives here again before she is wanted,*" his sister had written. "*But for pity's sake, do not tell her that she is not welcome here, or that I asked you to intervene! Be tactful."*

Tactful. How was he supposed to be tactful with their mother? She was much too thick-skinned for subtle ploys.

"You can play the 'doting grandmama' in July as much as you could now in December, don't you think?" he said. "In the summer there will be something for you to dote upon at least. A wet, leaking, sniveling creature that will probably upset you at once by ruining your gown and putting sticky fingers in your hair."

"But I should be with my daughter at such a time. Nothing will stop me. I shall go! I am determined."

So much for tact. He might have known that nothing less than the brutal truth would make a mark. "Mama, they don't want you there. Plain and simple."

She blinked against the lace trim of her handkerchief, feigning a tear. "How could you be so unkind!"

"Somebody has to say it. Somebody has to keep disaster from happening, and that responsibility seems to have fallen to my lot lately where this family is concerned."

Once again it was obvious to Ransom that he had become the sin-eater for his family. To him they came with their dark secrets, problems, and worries. On him they placed their burdens. When did it begin? Probably when he was a child, the vessel into which

Lady Charlotte poured her animosity and disappointment. Since then he had taken on the secrets of his brothers and sister. He knew where all the skeletons were buried and he kept the knowledge inside himself, having relieved the others of that responsibility. For some reason he had never questioned this duty. It seemed to have happened before he knew it.

Even his father had used him to dispense of an uncomfortable deed, when, six years ago, he chose Ransom to inform Lady Charlotte of his remarriage.

"Better she hear it from you, than in a letter from me," he'd said, waving a hand at his son as if it was nothing, a mere trifle. "You're her favorite."

So when Ransom delivered that news, he alone faced his mother's immediate pain and fury. Her former husband's remarriage had affected her terribly. Lady Charlotte may, or may not, have wanted True Deverell herself, but she did not want any other woman to have him. A long line of temporary mistresses she could handle, but a new wife was a bitter pill that no amount of her favorite champagne could wash down.

Ransom could have felt more pity for her, had he not, shortly before that, discovered another of her lies, one that stuck a thorn in his heart, deeper than any other. It had made him doubt everything his mother ever told him.

Because he had learned the truth about the first

time she left his father, when Ransom was a baby.

For years she'd told him how True Deverell refused to let her take her son with her when she left, how her husband cruelly separated mother and child. It was, so she had claimed, the reason why she came back and tried to bear her marriage. In effect, her years of unhappiness and degradation, were Ransom's fault.

But, six years ago, just before his father sent him to inform Lady Charlotte of his remarriage, Ransom had heard another version of that story. He discovered that his father had wanted her to take her son— that True Deverell had told her she would get no money and no help from him if she left without her baby. His mother left anyway, desperate to get away and be free, not caring about her own child. She only returned to her husband and "motherhood" when she ran out of money and found her old friends less companionable than they once were.

The story about how she had cried and begged when forced to leave Ransom behind was entirely cooked up in her own mind, to earn his sympathy, to make him her pawn, and to develop more hatred for his father.

So as he stood before her six years ago, watching her choke back angry tears at the news of his father's new marriage, Ransom had been very tempted to let it all out, to strike while she was down and weakened.

But he found that he could not do it. Enraged as

he was, he could not bring himself to wound her further when she was fragile and broken. Sometimes, when he still thought of that particular lie and that day, he wondered why he had not confronted her. She had never spared his feelings, so why did he hold back?

He did though. He let it fester inside himself and then he'd left his mother in London while he rode into the West Country to collect his new curricle in Exeter. From there he was driving to his father's castle on the coast for the wedding, but first, of course, he had encountered Sally White. And a life already begun unraveling, soon fell utterly apart.

Today the memory rushed back again, of standing in this room all those years ago, fighting the urge to tell his mother that he knew what a liar she was, what a pernicious fraud of a mother she had always been. How she had used him in her war against his father. He had left this hotel confused and angry, with a pounding headache and a dry mouth, in desperate need of libation. He could not see straight, certainly could not think prudently.

But if he blamed his mother, even partly, for what happened on the moor with Sally White, would that not make him just as bad as Lady Charlotte blaming him for her wretched marriage and "ruined" figure?

He took another breath, trying not to inhale his mother's perfume, and forced himself back to the present. "Well, that's my news delivered. You're not to go to Greyledge, so put it out of your mind. I was supposed to break it gently, but that's the best I can do since you're so bloody stubborn."

Lady Charlotte raised a hand to her pearl choker, and her eyes narrowed. "This is why you came today after staying away so long?" Her voice turned raspy as she seemed not to be able to catch her breath. "Merely to tell me that I am not welcome in my daughter's home?"

"I also came to be sure you are in good health, of course."

"You have a very strange look on your face, Ransom. Is there something more? You have more bad news for me, perhaps"

"None that I can think of."

Her face had crumpled slightly, her lips sagged at the corners. "I thought you came to tell me that your father's mousy young bride is about to give him yet another child."

"No. As far as I know, Olivia has birthed only one son. John Paul. I know of none others on the horizon."

She studied his face, as if she might catch him in a lie, then, satisfied, collected her breath, tightened her mouth and raised her chin. "Ha! Biblical names. How ironic! There will be more, no doubt, now that she has her feet under the table and *him* around her finger. I daresay she will produce a child a year and you will fall even farther in his order of consideration."

After all this time her words should not have so much power to hurt, but despite the armor of scar-tissue they still wormed their way in. His mother knew how to crawl under his skin and she, unlike the ghost of Sally White, didn't have to wait until he fell asleep to do it.

"I knew, the minute I saw that woman he married, that she had thoroughly pulled the fleece over his eyes. Never underestimate a quiet, drab woman," she added. "Those that pretend to be good and virtuous are worse than any."

"Yes, mama." Too long in her presence made him hot and sick, so he was already making his way to the door. "I'll try to call in more often now that Raven has gone back to the country and—"

"Don't put yourself out if you're too busy. I am not completely alone, you know." She flounced back to her warm fire, recovering her usual poise and carefully controlled nonchalance. "My own children may have deserted me, but I have a girl who visits several times a week."

"A girl?" He stopped and looked back at his mother. "What girl?" Ransom was suspicious of any stranger forming a connection to Lady Charlotte. He knew his mother could be indiscrete and overly-familiar with only a slight acquaintance, especially if they made themselves "useful" to her.

"A very old friend of your sister's, if you must know. A penniless spinster with no prospects, but well-bred. She is quite respectable, I assure you."

Penniless, eh? So she was sniffing after some Deverell money, whoever she was. He frowned. "I'd like to know who this person is. Raven has never mentioned this friend to me." Or had she? He tried to remember. Raven was a sociable creature certainly, but he could not recall meeting any particular female friend in her company. If she was a "very old" friend, would he not have been introduced by his sister?

"It doesn't matter who she is. When my own children are too busy to visit, I am grateful to have *any* callers." His mother now arranged herself gracefully on a Grecian chaise by the fire, her eyelids sleepily lowered, her long hands limp against the cushions. "This time of year is so dreary until the Season begins and any company is preferable to none. Well, be gone then about your wretched business. Far be it for me to keep you too long when you are needed to man the oars for your despicable father. You have done your cruel deed and cast your dagger into my heart, which you were no doubt sent to do. Now you may retreat, unless you want to watch me bleed."

Ransom bowed to his mother and made a hasty departure, before he might be tempted to say something that was even less "tactful".

* * * *

Mary tapped lightly at the door to the suite and soon heard a weary, "Enter."

She peeped in and saw Lady Charlotte draped elegantly upon the chaise with a handkerchief clutched over her eyes. "Bring me the ice-pack," she muttered. "It took you long enough, girl. I didn't realize you had to go to Antarctica to fetch the ice."

"Lady Charlotte, it's me, Mary." She came all the way in and quietly closed the door.

"Oh." The handkerchief was lowered, and two limp eyes surveyed her morosely. "I cannot think where the dratted maid has got to. My head feels likely to burst at any moment. It seems nobody cares for my health and I am left here to die alone."

Mary smiled cheerfully as she crossed the room to the window. "But I am here now so you are not alone. And you look very well, Lady Charlotte, far from the shadows of death."

The woman sighed heavily and dropped her handkerchief to her lap.

"I'm sure the maid will return shortly," Mary added, "and in the meantime, I have bought a new book to read to you—"

"Heavens, girl, I cannot hear you read today. Not one of those novels full of too many characters and too much plot! So many words! All those long names to remember! It is beyond me to concentrate. I am far too troubled."

Mary set her basket down on the table by the

window and was in the process of untying her bonnet ribbons when she noticed a gentleman's hat and gloves. "Oh. You have another caller, Lady Charlotte?" It was not rare for Raven's mother to entertain gentlemen occasionally in her suite of rooms at Mivart's Hotel, but she seldom allowed those appointments to overlap with Mary's afternoon visits.

"My wretched son," the lady exclaimed. "In such haste to leave me that he left his hat behind I see."

She felt her pulse skip. "I did not know you expected your son today." Perhaps it was another son. There were several, after all.

But the next word snatched that hope away and the man she'd tried to avoid thinking about for two days was before her again. Or rather his hat and gloves were.

"Ransom comes and goes as he pleases. I can expect him for weeks and see neither hide nor hair. Then, when I have abandoned all hope, he appears without the slightest apology for his absence, to pass on bad news and— on his father's behalf no doubt— to be sure I am behaving myself. To report my comings and goings like a spy. He cares nothing for my health and happiness. Just like his father."

"He came to give you bad news, your ladyship?" She gripped the edge of the table.

"He will not take me into Oxfordshire to visit his sister until next summer. Something he took ruthless delight in telling me."

Mary's heart beat resumed a regular pace.

But why would it matter if she encountered Ransom Deverell again? Really there was no need to make so much of it. She was in danger of giving their strange meeting more significance than it was worth, if she quaked in trepidation at the mere thought of seeing him a second time. She was turning into Violet— oops, Violette— with her unhinged imagination.

Her gaze lingered over his gloves. Grey leather, very fine, folded over and tossed down beside his upturned hat. What if he came back for them?

"Perhaps, if you have such a sore head and no need of me today—"

"But you're here now and you might as well make use of yourself, Mary. I suppose you can read to me from *Le Follet*. It is there on the windowsill ,and I should like to hear about the new Parisian fashions. That is the only thing I can bear when I am ill. It might lift my spirits."

Well, Deverell very probably had many hats and gloves at his disposal and no need to make a special trip back for those he'd left behind. If he was so eager to leave his mother's company, he would doubtless be in no rush to come back.

Quietly celebrating her narrow escape, Mary finally released the edge of the table from her fierce grip, took the magazine from the windowsill and sat in a chair across the hearth from her ladyship's chaise.

As usual there followed a short summary of all Lady Charlotte's most current aches and pains, while Mary listened patiently, giving what little support she could. Most of the time she suspected her quiet replies were not heard, and probably not needed, but she gave them anyway.

Lady Charlotte was not the most likeable of people and could be very challenging when in one of her moods, but Mary felt some sympathy for her. She did seem to be rather deserted by her children, although the lady did nothing to encourage their company. She was not the sort to apologize for past mistakes, forgive others readily for theirs, or hold out comforting arms. In fact, she was probably the most unmotherly mother Mary had ever known, and yet there was a proud, wounded sadness about her, which suggested that while she was aware of this failing she simply didn't know any other way to be.

Mary knew what it was to harden ones shell out of necessity— for one's very own survival— and then to have others misunderstand.

She had just opened the magazine and begun to read aloud when the door burst open.

"Hellfire, I left my bloody hat behind, didn't I?"

Chapter Ten

He stopped short and stared, one hand still on the door, an ice pack in the other.

"What the devil and his minions are you doing here?"

Miss Mary Ashford sat there, just as prim as you please, by his mother's fire, with a ladies' magazine open on her lap. For the life of him he couldn't make sense of her appearance there at that moment. He even thought his eyes deceived him.

But no, he was fairly sure he was not drunk or dreaming.

It was three o'clock in the afternoon, or thereabouts and she was sitting in his mother's parlor as if it was the most natural place for her to be. There on the table beside his hat and gloves was her blue bonnet— the same one he saw her in the other morning, when she left that book for him with Miggs and he followed her to a pawnbroker's.

"Ransom!" his mother exclaimed. "Bring that ice pack to me at once. I suppose you were flirting with the hotel maid again, which would explain her impertinent tardiness."

He shut the door and crossed the carpet, keeping his eyes on Miss Ashford who closed her magazine and stood. But before she could speak his mother added, "This is Raven's friend who visits me. The one

158

I told you about."

"Ah." He smirked. "The penniless spinster."

His mother, naturally, would not be at all embarrassed by the description she'd used. Neither, it seemed, was Miss Ashford, who gave a wry smile and a short curtsey. "Indeed, sir. That would be me."

So she was Raven's friend. Is that where he'd heard her name before? What a tiny world it was, after all. He was still marveling over the coincidence, when his mother yelled again,

"Ransom! The ice pack, if you please, before it all melts!" She flung out her arm as if it took all her strength to make the gesture and it might very well be her last. He finally passed the cold bag of ice to her, having crushed it quite severely in his hand.

"Miss Ashford, you did not mention being acquainted with my family when we met on that recent Wednesday." No, she had teased him instead. Called him Mr. Drivel and claimed never to have heard of him.

"It did not occur to me that you were one of the same Deverells." Her eyes were wide, clear grey pools. All innocence.

"Really? What other Deverell might I be?"

"Do fetch my son's hat, Mary. Let him be gone again so we can have peace, or my head will never recover."

Miss Ashford quickly obeyed, collecting his hat and gloves from the table, but Ransom was no longer in great hurry to leave. He simply dropped his seat into the nearest chair and when she handed the forgotten items to him, he set the hat over his knee and exclaimed, "As you said, mama, I have not spent as much time with you as I should. Perhaps leaving my hat behind was an unconscious admission of guilt, ensuring I must return."

"But I don't need you now. I have Mary. Sit, Mary! You know I don't like it when you hover. It makes the room untidy."

Once again Miss Ashford calmly did as she was ordered without comment. Ransom was amused. "Yes, I can see she must be a vast improvement on my uncouth, disobedient company. Miss Ashford appears to be well trained." He knew there must be a reason behind this quiet compliance from a woman he knew to be quick witted, much too intelligent and opinionated to tolerate his mother's nonsense, and not in the least subservient.

"Since when have you felt guilt?" his mother demanded sharply, rings and bracelets sparkling, as her clawed fingers clasped the ice bag to her brow. "You have no conscience, so don't pretend you're sitting there now because you feel sorry."

"You've caught me, mama. Of course I have no conscience. I learned from the best." He smiled broadly. "As a matter of fact it's raining like billy-ho out there and I'd rather wait out the worst of it, so this delay is entirely for my own selfish convenience.

But I suppose, in return for putting up with me, I can escort Miss Ashford home, when she is ready to leave."

Those grey eyes turned to him with surprise. She looked younger and less sinister today, out of her usual grim habitat. Perhaps it was the light in his mother's suite. This afternoon she was neither shrouded in cobwebs nor drenched in rain.

"It shouldn't put me out too much," he added with a sigh. "It's not *too* far out of my way. She needn't think I'll make a habit of it. Gallant gestures are hardly my province."

After a slight pause to find her place again, his mother's obliging visitor resumed reading from the ladies' magazine. It was not long, however, before she was interrupted in the midst of a sentence, proving that she was not being listened to by Lady Charlotte, any more than she was by him.

"Where did you meet my son, Mary? You did not mention it to me."

She looked up from the magazine, but Ransom replied before she could. "I met Miss Ashford in the bookshop where she works."

"A bookshop?" Lady Charlotte lowered her ice pack. "*Works?* I did not know this, Mary."

"Indeed, madam. And I live there too."

"You live. *In.* The shop?" Each word fell like a heavy weight.

"Above the shop, your ladyship."

"How ghastly!"

"Not at all. We are quite cozy there, my sister and I. A dear friend of my uncle's offered us the rooms when our father died, and since my uncle had passed on to me his shares in the bookshop it made a sound solution to the problem of our living arrangements."

"But that is very odd for two genteel, well-bred young women. I knew your family had fallen on hard times, but I cannot imagine why I did not know the very depths to which you are sunk."

"I doubt you ever asked her," Ransom muttered.

"It is not at all a bad place to live," the young woman said firmly, "and I prefer not to think of it as *sunken depths*, madam. We are still, currently, afloat." A very little smile tugged at her lips. "I do not believe anything is ever sunk beyond rescue."

Ransom knew she referred to his mind, of course, because that is how he had described it in his note when he returned the books.

That mercury gaze returned once again to the magazine, she read on.

Cunning wench.

He relaxed deeper into the chair with one leg stretched out, fingers steepled under his chin. He watched her thoughtfully, still trying to make sense of why she was there. Why she was *really* there. Surely nobody would voluntarily seek out Lady Charlotte's company and with Raven no longer in London, Miss Ashford had no other connection to the family. There must be an ulterior motive to her presence.

His mother hadn't lost her appalled expression, her thoughts obviously stuck on the subject of Mary Ashford's living arrangements. Lady Charlotte was never comfortable around great poverty, perhaps because it reminded her of where she might be if not for her former husband's financial generosity. She liked to complain of being "poor" and hard done by, but of course she was not. Indeed she was fortunate that True Deverell had never cut her off, despite all the terrible things she said of him. So when faced with the evidence of real hardship she froze, became almost incapacitated.

Miss Ashford pretended not to notice and read on in a low, pleasing voice, describing the latest hideous fashions of Paris, as if this was the most important news ever put to print.

It might be quite pleasing to have her read to him too, he decided, for she could make the dullest of articles sound interesting. But he would enjoy it more if they were alone together. Although he'd be in danger of falling asleep, if he could take her calm, melodious voice with him into his dreams, it might not be so bad. Would she protect him from Sally White too, as she saved him from Belle?

No. She thought he should stand up for himself instead of running away from the demons that pursued him. Not that she'd used those particular words; it was what she meant. He could pretend to her that he didn't understand, but he could not pretend to himself.

The fact that she had known who he was when they met, cast a thoroughly new light on their encounter and that conversation.

Before too long his mother interrupted again. "I thought Lord Ashford left some provision for your living arrangements when he died, Mary. I cannot think he would approve of his daughters in a *bookshop*." She spoke the words as if they might be a euphemism for a brothel.

"Whether he would approve or not, we had nowhere else to go. And I'm afraid he would have approved even less of the alternatives."

"But you are a Baron's daughter and educated. A governess post with a good family would be far more respectable for you. Far better than to be in trade."

"I would not like to be separated from my sister, madam. She has been left in my charge, and I promised to take care of her."

"Surely you could find some distant relative or childless couple to take her in. Little girls are always wanted as they are less trouble than boys."

"My sister is almost twenty, Lady Charlotte, not a child."

"Goodness gracious! Then she can fend for herself. Can you not get her married off? I suppose you have nothing much in the way of a dowry to offer, but perhaps a dreary little clerk of some sort will take her for a small sum."

"He very well might." Miss Ashford's lips drew another swift smile. "But she would never take *him* for anything less than love. I'm afraid my sister has romantic ideas."

"Then she'd better come to her senses," his mother scoffed. "You're both too poor to have that luxury, and in another few years she will be in danger of losing her bloom too. Like you."

Now he could see that Miss Ashford's unruffled demeanor was endangered, as if she was a hedgehog and his mother's questions and comments poked at her like a sharp stick. Her expression became very proud. Her spikes were up.

His mother, of course, had no capacity for reading another person's posture or their expression. "I cannot think why Raven never told me of this dire situation."

"Because I asked her not to, madam. I prefer to keep such matters private. I'm sure you understand."

But, of course, Ransom knew his mother would not understand that either. Very little about her own life was private. Discretion had never been hers in great commodity and when she married True Deverell she lost any chance she might have had for a quiet life. Not, Ransom suspected, that she had ever wanted one. Lady Charlotte thrived on drama and if nobody was interested in her comings and goings anymore she would very probably shrivel away and die. In the meantime, however, she complained at every opportunity about the society matrons who gave her the cut, and the vile gossips who, she was certain, were merely jealous of her continued good looks.

He watched as Miss Ashford bent over the magazine and continued reading aloud. There had been just the hint of a blush— suggestive of a mounting temper— but it was gone now already.

A few days ago in that dusty little shop he had asked her, "*What keeps you so busy then?*"

To which she'd replied, "*The sheer effort it takes for a small, unimportant woman to survive. Not everybody has the liberty of running away from their problems.*"

So apparently Miss Mary Ashford had nobody to go to with her troubles. That balding, bespectacled fellow with his nose in a book and buttery finger marks on the skewed knot of his cravat, was not likely to provide much guidance. In fact, he did not seem to be aware of much at all going on around him. Clearly she was left alone to manage her sister.

Ransom's thoughts turned to his own siblings— full and half-blood— and their many trials and tribulations, which had all, lately, been laid at his door.

He and Miss Ashford had something in common after all. Would she not be surprised to know it?

Studying her profile, he tried to understand what it was about her that drew his attention and held it. Her hair was smooth, straight and dark brown, tied back in a knot of some sort. There was no hint of a curl, no ringlets like those favored by some young women. Her nose was slender with a gentle, aquiline slope; her skin had a slightly olive tone and that, in addition to her solemn face and graceful composure gave her the look of a Renaissance Madonna in an oil painting.

And that was it! Now he knew what it was that had fascinated him.

La Contessa.

But how could that be?

He didn't realize he'd been tapping his fingers on his hat, until she shot him a cross scowl. At once he stopped and curled his fingers into a fist.

"Ransom, stop fidgeting and distracting Miss Ashford," his mother exclaimed. "You take after your father with that tiresome, vulgar inability to sit still. You disrupt the serenity of a room simply by being in it."

Abruptly he got up.

Both women looked at him expectantly.

"I'm sorry," he muttered stiffly. "I just remembered some business I must take care of today. Excuse me." With that he left the room hurriedly, this time taking his hat and gloves with him.

* * * *

Well, she thought, with a strange mixture of relief and disappointment, that was over with.

"Now you see what I mean, Mary. He comes and goes quite without warning, whenever the mood betakes him."

"Yes. I see."

"So very rude and shamefully ill-bred. His father's influence. I was never allowed to interfere in the raising of my own children. I was shut out of their lives. Just another of *his* cruel strikes against me."

Mary had managed not to look at Ransom too much, to keep her mind on the article she read for Lady Charlotte, but his presence had a fairly calamitous affect on her senses. It made his every slightest move echo in her ears, so that she found herself talking louder to drown it out. Even now that he'd left she remained distracted.

On this occasion he was dressed properly and decently. Very elegantly, in fact. Richly. But he wore those fine clothes with a casual, understated carelessness. He was a tall, dark, broad-shouldered shape in her peripheral vision. A menacing shape she could not ignore.

After he left, his mother could not return her attention to the fashions of Paris. She seemed unduly perturbed by the idea of Mary living above a shop, although it was unclear which part of this discovery she found most dreadful. Perhaps she saw it as affecting her own circumstances in some way. But if her son hadn't raised the subject she would never have known about those living arrangements, for

Mary did not like to talk about herself and Lady
Charlotte seldom liked to talk about anything but her
own problems. Mary had hoped to maintain some last
little vestige of dignity for the remains of her family
for as long as possible. Now, thanks to Ransom
Deverell's imprudent mouth, the sad facts were
exposed to the least discreet person she knew.

For the past few years, since her father's death,
Mary had kept up appearances as best she could.
Whenever she went out she made sure to dress neatly,
so that if she met anyone she knew they would be
none the wiser. Most people were aware that the
Ashfords had lost their estate, many knew about
Uncle Hugo, but they did not need to know all the
details of how Mary and her sister lived now. When
she encountered old acquaintances in the street, Mary
was quick to inquire into their health, carefully
remembering the names of their children and
spouses, even their dogs, rapidly leading the
conversation so that they had slim chance of quizzing
her in return. It was always her hope that they would
walk on thinking how well she looked and how happy
she seemed. Even if that thought was promptly
followed by the modifier, "all things considered".

But these visits to Lady Charlotte gave Mary the
opportunity to converse with someone who had no
idea about that cramped, lumpy bed she shared with
her sister, or of the holes in her stockings and the
hunger pains in her stomach— a lady who was

blissfully ignorant of most things Mary had to face every day. For that short time in Lady Charlotte's presence, where a hangnail was often the most pressing problem, she could forget it all herself and be immersed in the respite of silly nothingness.

Now all that was spoiled. In one sentence, Ransom Deverell had pulled down the curtain behind which she hid her true circumstances and exposed her pitiful plight.

Lady Charlotte "concerned", Mary now learned, was much worse than Lady Charlotte unaware or detached from reality. Raven had often told her that, but then her friend said a lot of things about her mother— particularly when in a temper— and Mary had not understood exactly what she meant. After all, Mary had been without a mother for many years and secretly thought Raven complained more than she should about her own.

But she was about to find herself the target of what Raven termed Lady Charlotte's "clucking".

"To think of you abandoned to the life of a shopkeeper, Mary! I wonder at my daughter leaving you behind when she went off to Oxfordshire. Some friend she has been."

"Madam, your daughter has remained a true friend to me through some very challenging times, and when many others were less than kind. For that I will always be grateful."

"Now she has deserted you, just as she deserted

170

me. We are abandoned as she goes on with her life away from us."

Mary smiled. "We have her letters to entertain us, Lady Charlotte."

"Hmph. My daughter is a sadly infrequent correspondent, and she has a lazy penmanship that causes me to squint. And I have more than enough lines about my eyes already." The lady sighed deeply, sinking against the rolled arm of the chaise. "Raven has always said she prefers living her life, rather than wasting time writing about it. Now, of course, she has so much life to live while you and I have none."

"Then, until she is able to return to London for a visit, we must take consolation in the company of each other, Lady Charlotte."

This did not seem to be much compensation. "Now my son refuses to take me to Greyledge this winter. It is ridiculous that I am trapped here and cannot be there for my daughter in her time of need."

"But travel is most unreliable this time of year. I suppose he thinks of your comfort, Lady Charlotte."

"My comfort, indeed! Ransom thinks only of himself. Just like his father, he has no time for me. None of my children care what becomes of me as I sit here all alone with nothing and nobody of any consequence to help fill my days."

Mary might have been insulted, if she was not so relieved that her ladyship had, for the time being, forgotten about the bookshop. Now, thankfully, Mary was back in her small role at the side of somebody else's stage, and Lady Charlotte embarked upon one of her favorite complaints about uncaring offspring, her hateful former husband, her deceased father, and anybody else that had ever slighted her.

Then, suddenly, she said, "You shall travel with me to Greyledge, Mary. We'll go together and surprise Raven. I shall not mind the journey if I have a companion."

"Oh, Lady Charlotte, I do not think that is a good idea. Your son does not think you should—"

"Pah! What does he know? Men know nothing of childbirth."

But Mary had no intention of going where she was not invited. She could well imagine Raven's expression if they turned up at Greyledge unexpected, and the last letter from her friend had hinted at great hopes for a very quiet, calm, peaceful Yuletide season at the estate.

Besides, Mary had travelled into Oxfordshire with Lady Charlotte once three years ago and still had not fully recovered from the embarrassment caused by listening to the lady berate servants, coachmen, toll-keepers, grooms and innkeepers' wives— whom she found "slovenly, bacon-faced and ill-kempt"— along their route.

Mary looked down at the magazine in her lap, searching desperately for a distraction. "Goodness what a lovely pattern for a ball gown. Princess-line with the bodice and skirt in one piece. I have never seen such a dress. I wonder if it might suit my sister, but I suppose it would require a great many yards of material."

Lady Charlotte demanded to see the picture so that she could give her own opinion— even though she had never met Violet.

This was Mary's chance to divert her ladyship's attention and her "clucking". Violet, at least, could benefit from it, while Mary would only chafe under the attention. She would much rather be left to the quiet enjoyment of a good novel.

So she told Lady Charlotte all about her idea to give Violet an outing into society and her hopes of finding her sister a good match. Nobody enjoyed the prospect of meddling, matchmaking and a fashionable foray, quite so much as Lady Charlotte, and she was soon in a much better humor, quite forgetting her sore head.

When Mary left Mivart's Hotel a little over half an hour later, she found a Hansom cab waiting in the street. The driver leapt forward to greet her just as she took the last step down to the wet pavement.

"Are you Miss Ashford?"

She halted, gripping her basket before her. "I am."

"Ah, good!" He tipped his hat to her. "A gentleman sent me here to wait for you, Miss. He said you would be the young lady in the blue bonnet, and he paid the fee for your journey in advance."

She was so startled she didn't know what to say for a moment. "This gentleman..." she managed finally, "did he give his name?"

"He said he was the King of Siam, miss. I don't reckon that was entirely honest, but since he paid me double the fee, I didn't think it right to argue."

Mary looked up at the grim sky and blinked against the rain which had just begun again. "It is so very damp out, I shall accept his generosity." She knew when to be practical, put her emotions aside— and ignore her pride a little. After all, it wasn't as if anybody would see her accepting the favor. The sky was already getting dark and she did not relish the thought of walking all the way home.

"Very good, miss. I'm glad you are agreeable, for he said he would chase me down if I didn't succeed in my mission of transporting you safely."

"Did he indeed?" Stepping up into the seat, she just happened to glance out through the side window and, in the soft glow of a street lamp, observed a man on horseback turning away down a side street. She didn't have to see his face to know it was Ransom Deverell. He must have been waiting around all this time in the rain, instead of dashing off to that important business he supposedly remembered.

How very odd. Even stranger that he didn't wait a moment longer to let her thank him. If she had not accepted the offer of a Hansom cab, would he have ridden after her?

But she soon had something else to worry about, when she realized that wherever the driver was taking her, it was not to Trinity Place and *Beloved Books*. She leaned out, looking back to shout. Alas, the driver, sitting high up behind the cab, was whistling too loudly to hear, and had his collar up against the rain. Mary got the sense that he *would* not have heard her even if he could.

* * * *

Ransom galloped home, handed his horse off to the groom, dashed into his house and looked about anxiously to be sure the place had been tidied since he left it a few days ago. It had popped into his thoughts— at the last minute— that some female might still be there waiting for him, so he was glad to find the place quiet and mostly put back together after the last party.

The butler must have heard him clattering about in the hall and swearing at the wet mud he'd brought in on his own boots, for he appeared a few moments later to see whether the master of the house required anything.

Ransom spun around. "Ah, Smith. You did give that money to the young Indian woman as I requested? I left instructions with Mrs. Clay on Wednesday."

"Oh yes, sir. She seemed very grateful. Unlike the

French lady, who caused rather more ruckus while she was here."

He cringed. "Yes, I'm sorry about that. I was not expecting Mademoiselle Saint Clair so early. Nothing broken, I hope."

"A Royal Doulton figurine, I believe, sir, came to a sad end when the fight broke out."

"I'm sorry."

The butler looked him up and down with weary eyes. "At least you survived unscathed, sir?"

"Mostly. And the other three ladies?"

"Enjoyed a hearty breakfast before departing the house in recuperated spirits."

"Excellent." Ransom took the candelabra from the hall table and carried it into the drawing room to see that the fire was lit, and the furniture back where it should be. "Any moment now, Smith, a young lady by the name of Miss Ashford will be at the door." He set the candelabra down and rubbed his hands together. "Look out for her, will you?"

"Is this a lady to be sent away or permitted entry, sir?"

"Permitted entry, Smith! Indeed, you are not to let her get away." He hadn't gone to all this trouble for nothing.

"Very good, sir. And I'll send a maid in to light the gas lamps in here?"

"No, no. Candles will do." He'd heard somewhere— couldn't think where— that candlelight

176

was more likely to make a woman spill her secrets. Apparently it was more "romantic" than gaslight. Perhaps because it made them think of taking off their clothes. He gave a little snort of amusement at the thought of women and their foibles.

The butler retreated with his smooth, silent glide and Ransom went to the window, watching to see her mood when she approached his house. He had a feeling it would not be a merry one. She was not the sort to appreciate being abducted and interrogated, but he would damn well get to the bottom of this woman one way or another. Sending him books and apologies, pretending not to know him when she was, all the time, an old friend of his sister's and apparently known to his mother. Looking at him from his bedchamber wall with those cool grey eyes as if he was a boy in need of a spanking.

Trying to make him feel as if he ought to impress her by reading a blasted book.

As if he ought to kiss those sly lips. That might be the only way to be free of them.

Uh oh, here she came now.

Pulse uneven, he dropped to a seat by the fire, loosened his cravat slightly, ran a hand back through his hair and then tried to find an appropriate pose. Casual would be best, so that she didn't know he'd been waiting and watching for her. He grabbed a newspaper from the floor beside his chair, but when he realized it was several weeks out of date and that he had penned rabbit ears and a pirate eye-patch onto a sketch of the Prime Minister on the front page, he tossed it quickly aside again.

Eventually he propped one muddy heel up on the velvet covered fender, sank deeper into the old chair, lowered his eyelids to half mast and feigned sleep.

He couldn't think why he, a grown man, was in such a state again. This was absurd. She was hardly the first woman he'd had brought to his lair.

But as he heard her quick step crossing his hall tiles, he could have sworn the flames in his fire leapt taller, like long tongues lapping, curling and spitting through the fringe of his dark eyelashes.

Did she have any idea of the heat into which she was walking?

He rather felt as if there ought to be a grand organ playing to accompany her arrival, for he'd begun to think of her as his Nemesis, punisher of hubris, a winged goddess out for divine retribution and wielding a whip— her tongue, of course. She would be, he had suspected almost from the first glance over his shoulder, the agent of his downfall.

Here she came, his Nemesis in a Blue Bonnet.

Chapter Eleven

"Mr. Deverell, what can be the meaning of this? I am expected home shortly, and the alarm will be raised if I am not."

He jumped a little, as if she woke him. With one heel still up on the fender, he turned only his head to peer around the wing of his chair. "Miss Ashford. How good of you to allow me a moment of your time."

"Did I have a choice?" She stood just inside the door of the drawing room, holding the handle of her basket with both hands. "I must ask again, Mr. Deverell, why you had the Hansom cab bring me here? It is late and I—"

"Come around into the light, woman, so I can see you properly. I'm getting a crick in my neck while you skulk there by the door."

With an exasperated sigh, she moved forward and then stopped a few feet from his chair and the fire.

"You must be cold," he said, gesturing to a chair on the opposite side of the hearth. "Won't you sit?"

"No. Thank you." Her gaze slid quickly around the room, as if she was almost afraid to look too closely. "I will not stay long, but you may as well explain yourself before I go. It must be something very important that caused you to have me brought here."

Ransom was still, watching her intently. Finally he spoke. "I want to know what you're up to with my mother." He still had not changed his lazy pose in the chair, but inside he was anything other than relaxed. How strange that she did this to him when many very beautiful women had failed to catch his attention for more than an hour or two. She'd had his for two full days, all while pretending it was accidental and she didn't want it at all.

A faint frown marked her brow. "Lady Charlotte seems in need of a companion once in a while. Since her daughter is now married and moved away—"

"You stepped in to take her place. And get what? Money and trinkets, I suppose. Take care, Miss Ashford, for whenever my mother gives anything there is always a string attached."

He saw her fingers tighten around the basket handle. Instincts warned he should prepare to duck. "Lady Charlotte does not pay me to visit her. I wouldn't accept payment if she tried." Her voice was tight and hoarse with anger.

"Then what do you get out of it?"

Her lips parted and then snapped shut.

"Well?" he demanded. "Don't try to tell me you have no motive for your own advantage. Women always have a cunning scheme in play, and nobody would spend time with my mother unless there was something in it for them. I'm waiting, Miss Ashford.

180

You told me you never fib."

Head on one side now, she seemed puzzled, her anger fading. Already he had seen how her temper mounted quickly and dissipated in the same way. Almost as if she didn't think it was worth the trouble to be angry. "Mr. Deverell, is there anything about our brief acquaintance that makes you think me a woman capable of cunning schemes?"

"Yes," he snapped, pushing himself more upright and setting both booted feet on the carpet. "You tricked me into buying books, didn't you? Only the devil knows what you'll talk my mother into. My mother is...susceptible to influences."

He saw the tip of her tongue travel swiftly across her lower lip and she looked down at his feet. The corner of her mouth moved. Was she laughing at him? Inside, where he couldn't damn well see what was going on? She probably had many intricate, sly-moving parts.

"Did I say something amusing, Miss Ashford?"

"Mr. Deverell," she said softly, "your mother is not in any danger from me. I read to her, and sometimes we play cards. Very occasionally, in fair weather, we go out to a museum or an art gallery." He watched her fingers open and then close again around the woven basket handle. "We discuss fashion and other frivolous matters that please her and take her mind off her troubles for a while."

"What else?" He knew there had to be more.

181

"I tell her when a new bonnet makes her look youthful," she admitted.

"Ha! So you flatter her to get into her confidence. I knew it! Somebody sent you to spy on her and acquire gossip about our family." He glowered hard, but she met his gaze without flinching.

"Is it difficult to acquire gossip about your family? I thought everybody knew everything about the Deverells already. And what they don't know, they make up." She paused, looking down for a moment. "I am touched by your concern for Lady Charlotte, but you may rest assured that I know what it is to have a family wounded by scandal, and I would never contribute to vile gossip."

He hesitated to believe her and yet there was honest warmth in her voice. It curled around him like a blanket of light, soft down, not smothering by holding too tightly, but seeking to comfort. Careful and polite.

"And to answer your question— no, I do not flatter your mother," she added. "I only tell her the truth. If I have nothing good to say I remain silent."

Ransom fell back in his chair, knees spread and hands on his thighs. He laughed gruffly. "Yes, you *are* a cunning creature."

"It's called civility and diplomacy, Mr. Deverell. These characteristics, so Lady Charlotte tells me, are not much known in your family. I think she feels the value greatly now."

182

"I'm sure she finds much of worth in your company." It came out of his mouth before he could stop the words forming. "You're quite exceptional."

She looked surprised. As was he.

Again her fingers flexed around the basket handle. "I am neither difficult nor argumentative. But I do not prostrate myself timidly at her feet either."

"Good." He recovered the stern gruffness with which he'd meant to interrogate her. "Because if you're not careful, Miss Ashford, she will take over your life and have you at her beck and call. She tried to do that with my sister."

Her gaze had once more drifted away from him and gone off on a tour of the drawing room. Apparently he was less interesting to look at than the furnishings and the paintings on the wall.

He hitched to the edge of his seat. "She'll probably try to make you travel into Oxfordshire with her, since I refused."

"Yes, I know."

"And you also know better I hope."

She sighed. "I do."

"You'll let her down with that civility and diplomacy, will you?" He smirked. "Better than I did."

"Yes."

She said nothing more, but left the word there, as if it was all he needed, as if he should have no doubt that she knew exactly how to manage his mother. Her eyes now watched him with a calm confidence, an

183

ease in her own skin. Unusual in a woman. Discomforting for a man who thought he knew all the ins and outs, all the ways around, over and under an obstacle.

"So you're a Baron's daughter. I should address you as The Honorable Miss Mary Ashford, should I?"

"Only when formally addressing a letter," she replied crisply. "It only means something on paper, and I wouldn't be in the least offended if you forgot it altogether."

"And how did you come to be living in a bookshop?"

"My father's estate could only be inherited along the male line. The Ashfords have always been a very proud family, and above all else it was important that the name never die out. Ironically, that same feudal sense of pride and duty caused us to lose everything when we simply ran out of men. An event inconceivable to my ancestors, no doubt."

He frowned. "Ah. But what about all those brothers you mentioned?"

"My brothers both died in the Afghan war. They defied my father to go off together. I had an uncle, but he never married. My father sold the estate to the railway to cover his debts, and so the Ashfords are no more. Women don't count in our family. You see now the futility of the Honorable."

Ransom nodded slowly. "How long have you known Raven?"

"Since I was fifteen."

All those years when they might have been better acquainted.

Her eyes narrowed as they returned to his boots and then, slowly, traveled upward. "This is why you had me delivered here like a basket of cabbages? To quiz me about my past and my connection to your family?"

"Why else? My mother and sister are notoriously careless about associations they form. Someone has to keep an eye on things."

"Who keeps an eye on you and the associations you form?"

He gave a slow grin. "Nobody. I'm quite unmanageable."

A quick huff escaped her pretty lips. "So I see."

"Well, when we met you did complain to me that nobody ever goes to great lengths to seek out your company. I thought you might be impressed if I did."

"Why on earth would you want to impress me?"

He was thoughtful, studying the elegant line of her neck and shoulders. She was very poised, very upright. A credit to her nanny, assuming she had one as a child. Today she wore a gown with a high, lace neck that was visible under the collar of her coat, and his eyes were constantly drawn there to the sensual curve were her slender neck met her shoulders. Whenever she swallowed a tiny flutter of lace was visible to his observant eye. "I really couldn't say why

I felt the need to impress you," he growled. "It's not like me at all."

She almost smiled, or perhaps it was merely that her lips had a habit of pressing together tightly with impatience. "May I go now then? If you are done with me, of course."

"What makes you think I am done with you, my little basket of cabbages?"

"If my only sin was making you buy a book, Mr. Deverell, I cannot comprehend that you truly think I have any bad intentions in visiting Lady Charlotte. Are you afraid of what I might make her read too?"

"Undoubtedly. We can't have a bold wench like you putting thoughts into her head. Her mind is better left fallow with nothing more than the appearance of a grey hair to worry about."

"Why did you not question me like this in her presence? Why go to these lengths?"

"I couldn't very well ask you all this in my mother's parlor, could I?"

"Why ever not? What difference does it make where you question me?"

Because he didn't want his mother to see he had any interest in Mary Ashford. That would only cause trouble for both of them.

Interest? Was that what it was? He didn't know. Certainly he was curious to know how she came to be entombed among the cobwebs of that bookshop. And why she had pretended not to know who he was.

Why she had teased him.

Leaning forward with his feet apart, forearms resting on his thighs, hands clasped together, he eyed her thoughtfully in the dancing reflection of candles and fire. The two sources of light seemed to fence with each other, thrusting and parrying with fluid, graceful skill. But Mary was the trophy for which they fought, a slender figure with dignified bearing and the stillness of self-possession.

"I wonder why my sister never introduced us."

"I daresay she thought I'd be a very wicked influence on you," she quipped.

He laughed. "Yes. Something like that."

A coal tumbled from the fire, making her start and look across at the hearth.

"Or she wanted to keep you to herself," he added. "She was always very selfish with her toys and possessions. Although it didn't stop her from wanting to play with mine too."

"I should be going, Mr. Deverell. As I said, I am expected home and —"

"Dine with me."

He had not planned that, but there it was. Just like the last time he asked, it sputtered out of him with no warning, no preamble. No possible good motive.

The woman gripped her basket as if someone might try and wrench it from her. "I told you the last time we met that it wouldn't be possible."

"Yet it's not out of fear for your reputation?"

"No. A reputation is as meaningless to me as the Honorable."

"Why is that?" He was genuinely curious, wanting to understand this woman. It had never been important to see beneath the surface before, but this was different. She was different. She talked to him naturally, easily and he felt a warmth in her company. As if nothing bad could ever happen if she was near.

He did not want to stop looking at her, or hearing her voice.

This was a startling discovery and somewhat worrisome.

"My family has fallen on hard times, Mr. Deverell," she said. "Unfortunately that is what happens when men are in charge. But now it is just me and my sister, and our misfortunes have helped me see life through clearer eyes. My Uncle Hugo used to say it is easier to see the larger picture when one stands outside the frame and is not part of the bright, rich, busy canvas. Now I know what he meant, for I am on the outside, no longer caught up in the rules and expectations of society. I see now what is important."

"Which is?"

"People. I have lost many people I loved and I wish...I wish I had helped them more while they were here, done more for them, that I had not been so selfishly caught up in myself and that world of the

bright canvas. It is people that are important. Family."
She looked away, her gaze wandering over a
landscape painting above the fire. "We should look
after each other."

Ransom put out his hands, palm up, and
exclaimed impatiently, "What about you and I then?"
He was a little annoyed, he realized, that she
befriended his sister and his mother, but wanted
nothing to do with him.

"Are you suggesting you could look after me?"
She sounded amused.

"No. Good God," he teased. "I'm no use for
anybody. But why can't you look after me? Clearly I
need it. Look at me!"

"There is nothing I could do for you," she replied
drily. "I'm quite sure you have everything exactly the
way you want it."

He shrugged. "Not all the time."

"Oh, poor you. The degradations of not having
everything *all the time*." She began making those little
movements that meant she was ready to leave—
checking her gloves, adjusting her bonnet.

"It is only dinner I offer, Miss Ashford. Not an
unbridled orgy."

Her lashes lowered, and he saw her chewing on
her lip, struggling for an answer. Ransom stood.

"I'll send a message to that sister of yours and let
her know you're in safe hands. Then we can dine
together without causing anybody undue concern."

"No," she said firmly. "Thank you, but I cannot."

He stood. "What if I was to tell you that your sister will eat very well this evening and manage perfectly without you?"

"I must still tell her where I was and with whom."

"For pity's sake, woman, you're here now—"

"So you thought that if you had me kidnapped and brought here I'd dine with you?" Her eyes twinkled up at him. "I suspected before that you'd seldom heard the word 'no', but your sister failed to warn me of the steps you would take to get your own way."

"I don't know why you make such a fuss," he muttered, digging his hands into the pockets of his riding breeches. "It is only pork chops with apple sauce on a Friday. If we're lucky there might be a pudding. By nine o'clock I'll be back at the club, so I won't bother you for long and you'll be safely home, tucked up in bed in a chaste, maidenly nightgown by the hour of ten."

"Surely *you* haven't run out of other ladies to entertain you?"

"Surely *you* have nothing better to do in your predictable world. Or has the gallant but dithering doctor staked his claim finally?"

Her lips wobbled and parted. Beneath her lashes there was a flare of something— anger? Frustration? Amusement? He couldn't tell. Never had concerned himself overmuch with the thoughts and feelings of women in his company. But he wanted to learn all about this one.

"As you heard me tell your mother, I have the charge of my younger sister. It is my dearest hope to find her a steady, marriageable gentleman and then to see her comfortably settled. Since I have sole responsibility for her now, I must set the example. I cannot have my sister knowing that I dined alone with a man who has no intention to marry. A man who infamously prides himself on having no principles. She will then think there is no harm in it for herself, and that would be a dangerous path to set her on. But please understand, I am concerned for her heart, her health and her future happiness, not how others would perceive the idea of my dining with you."

He squinted. "So you sacrifice your own pleasure just to teach your sister a lesson. Very noble of you."

"I prefer to think of it as practical, sir. A peck of caution saves a pound of misery, as they say." She made for the door, edging around him with her basket between them.

"And I must wait until your sister is safely married, before you would spare a moment for me? Or for yourself."

"She is my first responsibility."

"But why shouldn't you and I be acquainted?" he exclaimed. "It could be perfectly innocent. Friends.

Like you and my sister Raven."

She looked askance.

"Perhaps not entirely the same," he added with a rueful smile. "I shall admit I find you intriguing, Miss Ashford, and I have thoughts that are not entirely innocent when I look at you. Damn! See, you already force me to be honest. Whatever next? Scruples?" He shuddered dramatically. "Ugh!"

There was a soft pink tint to her cheeks as she backed away toward the brighter light of the hall.

He followed. "You worry about my possible influence on you and your sister, but what if it works both ways? You might do me some good, Mary Ashford."

"I know very well that you prefer ladies like your French companion," she exclaimed in a voice not much above a whisper. "They are better suited to your way of life."

"What way would that be?"

"Late hours, expensive tastes, high wagers, the pursuit of your pleasure at the expense of all else."

Ransom lengthened his stride to pass and cut her off, standing in the open doorway and blocking her exit. "What choice do I have since a well-behaved lady like yourself won't give me the time of day?"

She stopped, a look of confusion passing over her face beneath the brim of her bonnet. The temptation to catch hold of her around her waist and steal a kiss was almost overwhelming. For so many years he had looked up at the portrait on the wall of his bedchamber and wondered about his "Contessa", making up stories about her life, all the while thinking her long since dead and gone. He imagined he'd known her in a previous time, a previous incarnation. Yet she was here, all the time, almost under his damned nose.

His voice scraped over his tongue, the words forming jagged tears all the way up his throat as he felt that powerful desire take hold. "If I had a good woman, Mary Ashford, to put me to rights, I might become a worthier man. In time." He took a breath and suddenly his fingers were tugging on the grosgrain ribbon under her chin. "Don't you think?"

As the bow came apart under his determined fingers, she apparently puzzled over his question, too distracted to know what he did, or how to stop him.

"Do you believe that my wickedness is stronger than your good?" he added. "That I might change you for the worse, before you could help me?"

She shook her head slowly and raised one hand to his, halting its progress. "I am not *that* good, Mr. Deverell. I am no better than anybody else and not without my share of sins. I am just an ordinary woman, trying to live the best way I can, without causing anybody any harm."

"I doubt you'd know a real sin if it bit you on the nose," he grumbled. "You need a little of my wicked misbehavior in your life for balance."

Having inspected his face for a moment, she laughed. "You are proud of that reputation, aren't you? I suspected it from the first."

He scowled. Nobody had ever laughed at him the way she did. Men were generally too afraid and women too eager to please.

"Ransom Deverell, you don't really want saving. You don't want a *good* woman. You wouldn't know what to do with her, except see to her utter corruption and heartbreak."

"Then what do I want, Miss Ashford of the all-knowing mind?"

"A spanking quite probably." Her eyes held a sultry glimmer as she looked up at him. "But it's much too late for that."

Although her hand had stopped his, the bow was undone and her ribbon hung loose. Now, with his other hand he grabbed the bonnet off her head and put it behind his back. "I thought nobody was sunk too far for rescue?"

She blinked and when that clear, shining grey appeared again he felt drawn down to it, like a bee to nectar. "But a person has to want to be rescued. It takes effort and toil on their own behalf too, sir. It takes a person not giving up on themselves. And you seem content to be the villain."

He couldn't think what to reply, too consumed with the need to kiss her. If she only knew what he'd dealt with in his life, how he'd raised himself not to care about anyone or anything. Or tried.

"We all have troubles in our life," she added, as if she read his mind. "Just when I think life cannot get any harder, someone or something else I love is taken from me, or another obstacle is thrown up in my way. But I look to the next day and the next, because sooner or later it must get better. It must. I'm a fighter, sir, for myself and my sister. We've been through enough tragedy, and I won't succumb to the lure of transient pleasure just for a temporary respite. I will give my sister a good future. A lasting one."

Without her bonnet and the broad shadow it had cast over her face, she seemed more vulnerable, younger. Exposed. And yet her gaze met his bravely, unwavering, and she made no attempt to get her bonnet back.

Suddenly he wanted to put his hands around her face, very gently, and reassure her that she was safe with him. That he would never hurt her or let her be hurt. He would do anything for her.

It was an intense sensation such as he'd never before felt.

"So please forgive me, for declining your offer of pork chops and misbehavior, Mr. Deverell, but I have enough troubles already. I am trying to save *myself*, as well as my sister, and that, at present, takes up much of my time."

He huffed. "You need a man's help, of course."

"Despite the fact that, as my family history can

prove, when they are in charge of matters all is rapidly laid to waste?"

"Yes. You need the right sort of man. And I don't mean a man just to reach the top bookshelf."

A half laugh, half gasp shot out of her. "One like you, I suppose?"

"Why not?"

"Mr. Deverell, rest assured that if I suddenly find myself suffering tedium and desirous of another calamity, I will certainly let you know." She leaned closer, feigning solemnity with a whisper. "You'll be the first man I come to. When I am desperate enough to need one."

She prepared to walk around him, looking very determined. Still holding her bonnet ribbons in one hand, he stretched out both arms in the frame of the door to prevent her passing. "Perhaps I shan't let you go. I'm a powerful man, you know. Could keep you here and who would know? Who would object?"

"I would." She set her lips in a firm line and eyed the doorway again, probably trying to measure the possibility of getting around him without actually touching his wretched, wicked person. "Be warned, Mr. Deverell, I may be a *meek little bookseller*, but I am not a woman who balks at the application of violence when it is required."

"Oh. What are you going to do to me? It cannot be any worse than the usual."

"The usual?"

196

"What women usually want to do to me. I seem to bring out the worst in them. Or is it the best?"

While she was still thinking up a response, he suddenly put his free hand under her chin.

"Pardon me, Miss Ashford, but I've wanted to do this since Wednesday and I cannot seem think about anything else until it is done." He lifted her face, paused a brief moment, just to watch the color in her eyes turn incandescent as the moon, and then he bent and kissed her.

It was a tame kiss by his standards, a soft brush of flesh on flesh. Yet it felt like much more. Her lips were warm and tasted sweet. He had a memory suddenly of stealing cherries from a fruit cart in the market when he was very young. Until that moment he had never thought of it, but the picture was clear as if it happened yesterday. He and his sister had escaped their nanny to run wild in the crowded market. They filled their pockets with stolen cherries, but the crime was discovered when Raven ate so many that she had a stomach ache and became sick. Ransom, being the eldest, was the one punished for it. But he didn't care because the cherries were so very sweet and succulent. He never cared about the punishment as long as he enjoyed himself to the fullest before he was apprehended in his mischief.

As he drew back, he waited for Mary Ashford's retaliation, an angry accusation. Perhaps a slapped face.

Instead, all she said was, "I hope that helps clear your mind."

"So do I," he managed, slightly hoarse.

"Anything to be of service."

"Anything?"

"Within reason."

He stroked the pad of his thumb along her jaw. How soft she was, yet not in the least delicate. "The dreadfully sensible and level-headed Mary Ashford. Have you ever done anything that was not reasonable, I wonder? Ever done anything reckless?"

"Of course. When I was a girl. But one grows up. Circumstances change. One must adapt to one's lot."

He drew his thumb back again to stroke her lips, tracing the gentle bow which had, from the beginning, captured his attention. "Circumstances could change again, if you were not so damnably stubborn and wretchedly sensible."

"My good sense is most inconvenient for you, I'm sure."

"Damn it all, woman. I thought you'd appreciate the candles."

She frowned. "Candlelight strains the eyes when one wants to read."

With a low growl of frustration, he lowered his mouth to hers again and this time the kiss was firmer, more demanding. His hand swept around to the nape of her neck, feeling that lace under his fingertips, the warmth of her hair and wanting to be lost in it. He wanted to rip apart the tight knot of hair and then her clothes. He wanted to devour her, claim her for his alone.

Never had he felt possessive, so full of desire. And yet so helpless to know how to capture his prey.

There was a sudden sharp pinch and he realized the damn woman had bitten his lip. Her eyes were wide open, regarding him again in that partly alarmed, partly bemused way.

"I warned you," she said.

Breathing hard, he wiped the back of his hand across his lip and saw the little speck of blood she'd drawn. He raised an eyebrow. "That was quite unnecessary, Miss Ashford. I'm appalled."

"Excellent. You ought to be." She calmly reached into the potted palm beside the door. "Do return this to the lady who misplaced it here, amongst other items she lost in this house no doubt." She held out a lady's slipper that must have been overlooked during the house cleaning after the party. "I don't believe it's one of yours. It looks a little too dainty for your feet."

Frowning, he snatched it from her hand, and since he had removed both arms now from the doorway, she was able to escape through the gap, into the hall.

"If you ever get around to reading that book I sent you, Mr. Deverell, then we might have something to talk about. But don't think you can summon me, or have me brought here to amuse you

199

on a whim. I've encountered handsome and arrogant before, and my shelves are thoroughly full up with men who think I need their advice. If you truly want to impress me, you'll have to employ a little more than *the usual* effort and one sorry candelabra." She laughed again. "Do not look so crestfallen. You'll soon decide it's not worth the struggle, I'm sure. Good evening. Oh, and there is a matching shoe to that one under the red sofa. The practical side of my nature shudders to think how the lady got home, unshod, in this weather." Her little speech delivered smugly, she curtseyed and turned to leave.

A footman was opening the front door already.

"Have it your way, Miss Stubborn," he grumbled as he strode after her, "but I already have you in my bedchamber in any case so it matters not to me."

Lips parted, she looked at him in astonishment, cheeks blushing pink.

"I can show you if you don't believe me," he said, glowering.

The footman holding the door open did his best attempt to pretend he hadn't heard. But a new arrival, standing on the top step with her hand on the bell pull, wearing a hooded, fur-lined cloak and waiting to come in, definitely had heard.

Both his departing guest and the new one froze and stared at each other.

"I know you, don't I?" said the second woman.

Mary Ashford shook her head and hurried away

down the steps to the waiting horse and cab. Ransom signaled to let the driver know that he would pay for this trip too, and then he watched her leave. She did not look back.

Meanwhile the other woman was waiting, her frown deepening with irritation, which suggested she didn't wait very often for anybody. "I am Lady Elizabeth Stanbury. Your brother said you were expecting me."

Oh, lord. He'd completely forgotten about Damon's problem. He scratched his head with the slipper and winced. "Ah, yes. I suppose you'd better come in and get it over with. Smith, please take Lady Stanbury through to my father's study." His lips were feeling a little odd. As if they were stung. But surprisingly they still worked, despite being savaged by that "meek little bookseller".

"There is no fire in the study, sir," the butler intoned gravely. "Should I have one lit?"

"No. No. Lady Stanbury won't be here long, and my father's study is more suitable." He always referred to it as his "father's study", because he still thought of the house as belonging to True Deverell. Ransom was merely a cuckoo who probably didn't deserve such a grand house. That was the way he had felt since he first moved in and the sensation had not decreased over time. Touches of his father were everywhere— in the art and treasure that he'd purchased to decorate the place. Even the staff were chosen and hired by

True. Ransom had no inclination to change anything. Why bother? Everything in life was temporary and one should never get attached. People inevitably let one down.

"Sir, is that blood on your lip?"

"Ah." He wiped his lip again and managed a sheepish smile. "A slight mishap, Smith. Nothing to worry about."

The butler swept Lady Stanbury away, while also relieving Ransom of the discarded lady's shoe.

So Miss Ashford— his reluctant savior from irate Frenchwomen— was gone, carried away into the darkening night by a stout horse and a creaking chariot. Well, he might have known he couldn't persuade her to stay. It had been a rather clumsy attempt, not up to his usual seductive standards. Truth was, he did not know how to win this one over. As she'd said, it required more effort than he was accustomed to making when it came to women.

What did he think he was doing with her anyway? Where could such an interest possibly lead? He really did not want a Daisy Do-good under his feet, casting her disapproving eyes all over him, as if he didn't already know how very wicked he was.

"Shut the door, Thomas," he growled to the footman. "We failed to keep that one, I'm afraid. We must release her into the wild."

"She seemed rather different to the usual ladies, sir."

"Different? In what way, Thomas?" Had she bitten his footman too? She'd only been in the man's presence with her damnable lips for a moment.

"Careworn, sir. But kindly. Was she collecting for charity, sir?"

He smirked. "No. Unfortunately. She might have been a bit more obliging then, if she wanted money out of me."

Hmmm. That was a point. Why hadn't she taken advantage of the fact that he had money and she had none? Most women would get what they could from him if they managed to catch his eye— drunk or sober. As his father would say, nothing made its way faster to a woman's heart than money. But apparently she didn't want any of his.

All she wanted was for him to read a book.

Chapter Twelve

As the horse took her away from Deverell's house, hooves sloshing wearily through puddles, Mary's insides tumbled through a gamut of emotions. None of which she wanted to identify. She let her body bounce and sway carelessly with every bump, her basket in her lap, her gaze fixed to the cobbled road ahead.

Elizabeth Grosvenor.

Now Lady Elizabeth Stanbury, of course. Wife of George Stanbury— the man once engaged to marry Mary.

In that other lifetime.

It was several years since Mary had seen Elizabeth, but there was a time when they moved in the same social circles, attended the same balls and parties. She would have recognized her anywhere, although Elizabeth had not known who *she* was, only that there was something familiar. Well, she supposed time had changed her appearance and not for the better. Worries and responsibilities did that to a person, Mary thought grimly, fingers tightening around her basket.

In comparison Elizabeth had looked very well standing on Ransom Deverell's steps. She was older than Mary, but very well preserved, positively glowing with health and contentment. A woman who glided smoothly through life. A woman for whom nothing ever went wrong. A woman who would trample her own grandmother to get a foot up the social ladder.

"I know you, don't I?" spoken in that clipped, cut-glass, aristocratic voice.

Mary was surprised the woman dared admit they had ever known each other.

Blowing out a hefty sigh, she turned her head to watch the light of the street lamps slipping by. There were fewer lights here, of course, for the horses were taking her farther away from the affluent part of town. The stripes of darkness became broader and longer, briefly lit faces sucked away into shadow, until she might as well be the only one out on the road.

Did George know his wife paid visits to Ransom Deverell under cover of darkness?

She imagined Violet's voice then, "*Serve him right, the blackguard!*"

But it was years since Mary had felt any real anger against George. As she'd said to her sister, she could hardly fault the man for wanting to secure his father's estate and keep his home. Besides, he had forgotten her so easily, set her aside with so little apparent qualm, did that not suggest he could have done the same even if they married?

During their courtship, Mary had never pried too far beneath George Stanbury's fine surface. He was charming and lively, but they had never been alone together, of course. There were always other people there, chaperones and friends to keep them from the "temptation of improper intimacies". The knowledge they had of each other, however many times they were in company, could have been noted on a card no larger than four inches square.

But when her father and brothers encouraged the match, Mary had found herself swept up in the merriment. She agreed to marry him, aware that their engagement must be of some lengthy duration. His father was very ill and George did not think it right to plan a wedding until his health had improved. Mary understood. The delay, she'd thought, would give them time to know each other better, hopefully in less formal settings.

Alas, his father never rallied and then there was a period of mourning to be observed. Once again Mary waited with patience, for George's time was greatly taken up with responsibilities when he inherited his father's title.

It was not long before she had her own grief to manage when her brothers— who had always done everything together, including defy their father to join the 3rd Light Dragoons— were killed at the Battle of Kabul. Silence and an awful stillness descended upon their world. A dark rain cloud covered them as if it would never be summer again. Uncle Hugo was then the last male heir for the Ashford estate, but at the age of fifty-five he had no wife and no children, nor did he possess the slightest inclination to get any. He preferred to travel and paint, to live an unconventional life, unfettered by the responsibility of a great estate and not beholden to society's rules. Mary couldn't blame him, for what had the estate and his family ever done for him except turn their backs on his way of life and try to pretend he did not exist?

But her father never forgave Hugo for that refusal to conform. He believed that his brother had failed to do his duty for the estate by not marrying and producing sons. It was that simple, and he did not care whether marriage might have been against Hugo's nature. He did not care whether his brother would have been miserable leading a false life. "Your Uncle Hugo is an embarrassment to the Ashford name," he said once to Mary. It was one of the few times she ever heard him speak of his brother, and one of the last that actually referred to him by name.

So Mary's father, buried in debt and without male heirs, was obliged to sell everything.

"We shall need that wedding now, Mary, my girl, to lift our spirits," her father had said, his eyes heavy with sorrow. "The sooner the better. What can be keeping that young man of yours from our door?"

But of course, it would not be proper to rush the proceedings, no matter how urgent one party felt in the matter. "Father, we cannot have a wedding while we're in mourning." Nor would she lower *her* Ashford Pride to push George into action.

So the delay stretched on.

When her father moved his daughters permanently to London, Mary still had hopes of a marriage occurring in the not too distant future, despite the growing infrequency of George's letters and visits. The Ashfords— what remained of them— kept up appearances as long as possible.

Always she found excuses for her absent fiancé: he must be busy; must still be in the country at a shooting party; or his family obligations kept him dashing about Town— the fashionable part, of course, not the area where they now lived. He would visit when he could. She must be patient and understanding.

Then, finally, she read the announcement of his wedding one morning in the newspaper.

Mary vividly remembered the life draining out of her as she sat at the breakfast table and stared at the printed words, reading them five times before they fully sunk in.

She never saw or heard from him again. Not even a letter attempting to explain.

Her father, trying to remain optimistic, had promised there would be other chances and other gentlemen, but unlike George she could not simply adjust her plans to new circumstances and replace one face with another. Men had turned out to be much less trustworthy than expected. Her naiveté, innocence, and a certain amount of self-confidence, was lost along with hope.

As she had remarked to Ransom Deverell, people had a habit of leaving her life, one by one, whether intentionally or by death.

Not long after George's surprise marriage, Uncle Hugo was arrested and so the storm over their heads grew even darker, until there seemed no chance of a break in it.

Poor, dear Hugo, who had only ever wanted to be happy on his own terms.

Some of it was kept out of the papers. What was put in alluded to his "crime" in the vague terms used so as not to offend anybody's moral sensibilities. It was still enough to make her father go white as a lily when he read about it. He'd known about his brother's love life for a long time, of course. How could he not? But seeing it in print, put out for public consumption, was another matter.

"I suppose Lord Stanbury congratulates himself now at narrowly escaping such an association," was the only comment he made to Mary on the matter. And that came out as if he momentarily forgot where he was and who she was.

She was not supposed to understand the details, of course. Being a well-raised, maidenly creature, she should not be aware of such things. Sex and anything related to it was never talked of in frank terms and if she was ever to know anything about it, she would be told on her wedding night, by her husband. But Mary was far from stupid, and she was not blind or deaf.

209

She knew of her uncle's preferences and how they were forbidden, considered a criminal offense. She also understood that his long relationship with Thaddeus Speedwell was something more than two confirmed bachelors living under the same roof, even though it was never talked of.

At first she had found it difficult to understand. She adored her uncle, but Mary would have loved the companionship of an aunt, especially after the death of her mother. For a long time, she wished he could simply follow the established path and not be stubborn. But she came to see what a selfish thought that was. She also understood that when one was lucky enough to find true love— like a glorious, chocolate-covered, French cream pastry— one must never let it out of one's sight.

Love was a precious rarity and not everybody would be fortunate enough to find it, so why should Uncle Hugo be forced to give up his treasure and his happiness?

And so Young Mary had come to a tentative acceptance that secretly grew stronger over time. Her love for her uncle was too deep at the root to be disturbed. As her father had said— and as Violet had recently reminded her— when Mary loved she did so with her whole being.

Thaddeus Speedwell was a very gentle, reserved gentleman who never raised his voice, but Hugo had an effervescent character that could not be tamed or quieted. He was outspoken in his rebellion, his own sense of pride and determination just as strong as that of any Ashford. And he possessed three other things that were sure to get him into trouble— a quickly roused temper, an acutely felt abhorrence for injustice, and an extreme aversion to letting anybody else tell him how to live. Or die.

But this unapologetic flouting of convention made him few friends in high society and one day he crossed the wrong person for the last time. Hugo's enemies had him arrested for "acts of indecency", and he was sent to prison where he contracted pneumonia and died.

In typical Uncle Hugo form, as he lay dying, he dictated a long confession to several crimes that he could not possibly have committed, including the murder of an art critic— a gory, unsolved crime that had plagued authorities on both sides of the English Channel for months.

"Weep not for me, Mary my kitten," he'd written to her. "They would have preferred to put a noose around my neck, because I am not like them and refuse to be so. They are angry that I shall die now, before they can have that opportunity. But I shall go out with style and take responsibility for something I would dearly love to have done. Better that than to have the last report of me be that I died of so insipid and pedestrian a sickness."

Thus he told a very lurid tale of stabbing an art

critic— who had given his latest exhibition a very bad review— through the forehead with an oyster fork, outside a Paris restaurant. It was all very garish, overwrought and macabre.

"Much like my work on canvas, according to the blackguard's review," he'd said.

When her father read an account of this deathbed "confession" in the newspaper, he was silently furious, veins bulging from his neck.

Some thought Hugo Ashford was mad, unhinged. Kinder folk called it eccentric. Mary suspected it was much simpler than that. She came to believe that her Uncle Hugo confessed to murder because he thought, in some odd way, that a killer in the family might be less shameful to his brother than the truth of why he was really imprisoned in the first place.

In actual fact, to her deep sadness, he was right. The Ashford pride was so deeply ingrained in her father that his brother's "unnatural love" for another man was far worse than murder.

Her father died not long after Hugo and so, in the space of a few years, she went from being a young debutante with everything in her future— quite content to pass up a French cream pastry, certain there would be many others— to a perennially hungry spinster, struggling to manage her sister.

One by one all the people she loved had left her. Now all she had was Violet. And even Violet wanted to vanish and become 'Violette'.

Perhaps, one of these days, Mary thought morosely, staring at the streaks of muddy puddle water that stained the hem of her skirt, she would be the one who got to escape reality. She could call herself Marietta and take up fortune-telling.

She pressed a hand to her heart and closed her eyes. If only she hadn't laid eyes on Elizabeth Grosvenor Stanbury tonight she would not have been forced to feel all of this misery again. All the loss and the frustration at not being able to stop any of it from happening. Wasted feelings that did nobody any good. Revisiting the past was only for people who liked to dwell on painful memories and wallow in self-pity. How many times had she said that to her sister? She should heed her own damned advice. But the sudden sight of Elizabeth had acted like a door opening on that past, taking her back there.

The last time she saw Elizabeth— before tonight— was the morning of her uncle's confession in the newspaper. Mary, trying to keep up appearances that day, was in Mayfair on her way to visit Raven, when she passed Elizabeth in the street.

No acknowledgement was made on Elizabeth's side, although Mary stopped, prepared to greet her politely. Instead Lady Elizabeth Stanbury passed her without stopping, commenting loudly to her companion, "I'm surprised she can show her face in public. I should have died of shame."

It hadn't helped that the painting above Ransom Deverell's mantle tonight happened to be one of Uncle Hugo's early works, jolting memories of him too. Of happier times, when he laughed a great deal, and used to let her daub paint on an old canvas beside his while he worked. Those were the days when he was funny and light-hearted, before he became louder, angrier and more obstreperous in old age. Before he started telling fanciful tales and believing them.

Struggling against the potent sadness that seemed to have found a violent grip on her heart that night, she brought her mind back to the present. To Ransom Deverell— an effective, colorful, and noisy distraction for which she was grateful. She whispered his name to herself a few times and found that, after a while, it began to sound like "Handsome Devil." Very fitting.

Oh, pork chops with apple sauce and possibly a pudding! Almost as tempting as the man who offered them. Alas, the sacrifices one must make for the good of one's impressionable younger sister.

Chapter Thirteen

"But I do not want to marry your brother." Lady Stanbury's blue eyes gleamed briefly with cool amusement. "Why would I leave my wealthy husband and settled life for scandal, exile, and uncertainty with a twenty-four-year-old, restless, unpredictable boy?"

Ransom felt something sinking in his chest, leaving a hollow. Ah, he should have realized, but Damon had seemed so certain. "He has not mentioned marriage to you?"

"Certainly not. We never spoke of such a thing."

"But my brother is under the impression that you want a divorce from your husband, madam. He's making plans for a new life with you and the child."

She laughed curtly. "Then he should have consulted me instead of you. I certainly never encouraged such an idea. What can he be thinking?"

Elizabeth Stanbury was a handsome woman with sharp features, ivory skin and a long, swan-like neck. Everything about her was slender— willowy he supposed was the right word—and perfectly arranged. Even the ringlets on each side of her face were identically balanced. He could see what had attracted his brother Damon, who always sought the prettiest, fastest, most expensive and newest— whatever he thought others would say he shouldn't, or couldn't have. Especially if somebody told him he was not entitled to it, being only a bastard Deverell.

But Ransom could also see that this well-maintained lady was not likely to throw herself whole-heartedly into a love affair that meant abandoning her status in life. She was far too composed and orderly, a woman with everything she wanted.

Almost everything, apparently.

"I am thirty-four," she said, "and my child-bearing years are not infinite. After eight years of marriage my husband had begun to despair of producing an heir, but now at last he will have one."

"You've told your husband about the child then?"

"Of course. He is overjoyed. We both are. It is a miracle."

He stared. "Madam, if you imagine Damon will give up his child, and sit quietly by to see it raised by another, you must not know him very well at all."

"What would your brother want with a child?" she scoffed. "He is not much more than one himself."

Ransom studied her through narrowed eyes, his anger and disgust quickly mounting. The longer she talked the less attractive her face became. Miss Ashford's calm, quiet poise, even in much less fashionable attire and lacking a few of those willowy inches, was more pleasing to the eye. "Yet Damon was old enough to share your bed."

She did not blink or blush, merely kept her glassy gaze fixed to his, unashamed. There was a hint of weariness in her tone now when she replied, "Every

216

marriage encounters a difficult patch occasionally. Boredom sets in. Wives, as well as husbands, have been known to seek recreation outside the marital bed. In some cases an affair can rejuvenate a tired marriage."

"So my brother relieved your ennui. I don't believe he realized that was his sole purpose. From the way he spoke to me, he thought a great deal more of the affair and of you. He thinks he's in love, madam."

"Love? Surely *you* do not believe in that any more than I do?" she sneered. "Your reputation precedes you, Ransom Deverell."

"Yes. I am irredeemable. My younger brother, on the other hand, is an optimist and something of a romantic. Life has not yet crushed that out of him. Not quite."

"Then perhaps this will stand as a lesson for which he will thank me later."

Suddenly the room felt very cold. He had instructed Smith not to bother lighting a fire in the study because he didn't intend to make Lady Elizabeth feel too welcome, and he seldom used this room anyway — most of his business matters were taken care of at the club. But now the chill crept into his bones and he wished they did have a fire. It was almost as if this woman emitted her own frost.

Ransom's mind flashed to an image of Miss Flora Pridemore, smug and spiteful— his own uncomfortable lesson in the cruelties of mercenary female cunning. He wished he could have spared his brother that pain. Now he understood the frustration his father must have felt as he watched his sons making these mistakes. A litter of young men all insistent on finding out for themselves. All thinking they knew better than the man who came before them.

"I cannot be held responsible for any expectation or misunderstanding on your brother's behalf," the woman added. "I never led him to think there could be anything more between us."

Now she reminded him of how he had ended his affair with Belle Saint Clair. Christ, he had been an ass. Perhaps he had wanted her to find those other women in his bed. He thought he had forgotten the date of her return from France, but it was possible that somewhere, in the depths of his mind, he had known that she was becoming too possessive, outstaying her welcome. He took the easy path out, like a coward.

"So you have no feelings for my brother at all," he muttered. "He was merely a plaything to break the monotony of your life."

"Yes, he made a change from my husband's inattention, and I was thankful for the diversion. Damon was a very good lover...although rather too demanding of my time and too often in a jealous temper. But I'm afraid he overestimated his place in

218

my life if he thought this was *love*."

He turned away, one hand on the back of his neck. Suddenly he caught his reflection in the mirror above the dark fire place. Was that him? He did look tired. There were more creases across his brow than he remembered the last time he looked.

Maybe his mother was right and he did need to get away from town, but how could he when he had so much to do? Besides, he much preferred London, the noise, the activity and the crowds. The country was too quiet. Like a silenced scream.

His head began to feel tight and heavy when he thought of what he must say to Damon. The boy was not going to take this well at all.

He rubbed a hand along his jaw where it ached from grinding his teeth. "Why did you tell him about the baby? Now he knows, it's going to be much harder on him. You should not have told him."

"Yes, I rather regret that, but I was indisposed one morning in his company and he guessed the cause before I did." There was not a quiver of guilt or pity on her face. If he stuck her with a pin he suspected she wouldn't move. "Soon I leave for Kent. I will spend my confinement there. I do not want your brother to follow, or try to see me. That's why I agreed to come here and meet with you."

Meanwhile, Damon was making plans to take a second job and become a doting family man. If Ransom didn't care so much for his half-brother, it might have been amusing. But there was nothing humorous about the way this would all end. He always knew it was a mistake to care, of course, but he couldn't prevent it. The devil knew he'd tried.

"What if your husband finds out that the child you carry is not his?"

She drew herself even taller, as if to face a firing squad, and said firmly, "I have never said it is not my husband's child." Again her eyes were coolly superior, daring him to argue.

There was a pause. He thought he could see the breath in front of his mouth. "I see." So that was the way she meant to play her game. "Damon will be very angry when he learns that you have used him."

She opened the small, beaded reticule that dangled on a string from her thin wrist. "You can persuade him against any nonsense. I have seen him talk of you, and I know how he looks up to you. Give him this if it will help." Holding out a folded bank cheque, she added, "This should be a satisfactory fee for any inconvenience he might suffer."

Rather than take the note, he put his hands into the pockets of his riding breeches. That was better, get some warmth back in his fingers. "Inconvenience, madam?"

"Of giving up any foolish claim he might try to make."

"Damon is certain he sired your child, and he won't be persuaded otherwise."

"That's a pity," she snapped, "because if I say the child is not his he has no evidence to the contrary."

Ransom nodded his head at the bank note in her hand. "That looks like a stud fee to me, madam. Proof enough, surely."

She stuffed the note back into her reticule, drawing the string tightly closed. "Very well then. Perhaps you're right and to go away will be enough. But I want you to make it clear to your brother that this is over with. It is done. I do not want to hear from him again."

"Would that not be better coming directly from you, madam?"

"I have tried." Her shoulders softened, rounding almost imperceptibly. For the first and only time, he saw a glimmer of sadness in her pale eyes, although whether she felt it for Damon or herself was debatable. "But I found it challenging to be firm. He can be...persuasive."

Ransom shook his head.

"I am told all Deverells are the same," she added. "It was a mistake to become involved with one."

"But now you bring another one of us into the world."

The woman looked down at herself only briefly, her pale lashes sweeping quickly back up again. "This child is a Stanbury, heir to a title and an estate, not the offspring of a bastard Deverell."

She was lying; he was sure of it. Lying to the tips

of her ice-blonde hair.

Now, however, the visit was ended. Like a grand empress who had benevolently granted *him* an audience, she slipped back into her cloak and fastened the frog clasps at her throat. With a cold, distant smile, she said suddenly, "Was that not Mary Ashford I saw leaving as I arrived? Mary Ashford once of Allacott Manor in Somersetshire?"

He pulled his hands from his pockets. "No. It was a basket of cabbages."

She squinted. "It was Mary Ashford. I am certain. What on earth was she doing here with you?"

"I daresay she wondered the same of you, madam."

"Gracious, I did not expect to see Mary in this part of town," she sneered, pulling up her hood. "The years have not been kind to her. I can see why she did not want to admit I knew her."

Ransom thought of the way Mary had bowed her head and hurried into the Hansom cab. "Perhaps she did not want to admit she knew *you*, madam. She may have thought to spare you the embarrassment of being seen and recognized at my door. Miss Ashford strikes me as the rare sort who worries more about the comfort and well-being of other people than she does about herself." He knew that about her already. Indeed, he felt as if he'd known her forever. "Very different to dark, jaded, selfish souls like you and I."

Lady Stanbury's features, briefly amused by Mary

Ashford's plight, snapped back into rigid hauteur. "I came to see you at Damon's insistence, but I desire no further connection with your family. Keep your brother away from me. For his own good."

Ah, one more unsavory task dropped into his hands. Why not?

Eager to see the back of her as soon as possible, he rang for Smith to show her out and then poured himself a large glass of brandy. Something to warm him up.

If only Miss Ashford had stayed. Her wry honesty would have been a very welcome respite, something to make him smile— better even than brandy. But no, she wouldn't stay. Now he was alone with his demons until he got to the club later tonight.

Just how was he going to break this news to Damon?

It seemed to have been a year of trouble for the Deverell men when it came to women and he, for one, would be glad to see it draw to an end. Perhaps, in the new year, he could make a resolution to fast, giving up his favorite pastime.

Hmph. He swigged his glass of brandy. Sudden chastity? Good luck with that.

Besides, any such effort on his behalf —unlikely as it was to meet success—would not keep his brothers out of similar turmoil.

This past summer, Damon's elder brother, Naval Captain Justify Deverell, who was usually the epitome of good sense and propriety— at least by the standards of their family— had, for some god-forsaken reason, purchased an Indian woman at an illegal "Wife Sale". Although Justify would never admit it, Ransom suspected his half-brother had been as drunk as any self-respecting sailor on shore leave should be. But since Justify was required to sail off again soon after the sale, this pretty purchase had been left in Ransom's hands to manage too.

Of course, their father had yet to be informed of the curious acquisition, for if there was one thing he wanted it was for his sons to choose a bride wisely. It was highly unlikely that, even with his dark sense of humor, True Deverell would consider a woman purchased from her previous husband for six pounds, and who could neither speak nor understand English, to be a wise choice.

Ransom had been called upon to help find lodgings and respectable employment for the newest Mrs. Deverell, while Justify returned to his command at sea. Meanwhile, he was expected to keep all this a secret from the rest of the family, until Justify found— as he called it— "a perfect opportunity to break the news gently to our father".

"Best of fortune in that endeavor," Ransom had said to his brother when they parted company.

Best of fortune in that endeavor. It might as well be the Deverell motto when it came to women.

Distracted by these troubles that had been put

into his hands, he found he had no appetite for dinner after all. No desire to eat all alone at that long table. Instead he decided to leave early for the club. Perhaps he'd send for Damon tonight and break the news. The sooner he got it over with, the better, as a certain lady would advise.

He rode at his usual clip, his thoughts finally settling on the pleasing image of Miss Ashford without her bonnet. How could he explain his desire to have her remain in his company? She would roll her eyes and say he needed a dose of gripe water. But her portrait on his bedchamber wall had looked down on him for eight years, solemnly waiting for something, and on Wednesday it had tried to tell him that the "something" was about to happen.

Since then he'd looked at his world through new eyes. He couldn't be sure it was all due to her, but it seemed more than likely. Why else would he find himself smiling whenever he thought of her? He raised a hand to his lip. She'd drawn first blood. That ought to be warning enough.

Ought to be. But Ransom Deverell, in common with most of his family, had always taken issue with the word "ought".

* * * *

When Mary arrived back at the bookshop that evening, she found Thaddeus Speedwell in a very jolly mood. Even her sister was laughing giddily as she stuck mistletoe in her hair. There was a large fire in the hearth tonight, extra candles lit and bunches of holly decorating the mantle.

"Your sister thinks she must have a secret admirer, Mary," said Thaddeus, gripping her arm in his excitement, "for somebody sent us a large hamper this evening, full of Yuletide cheer. Look!"

It had come from Fortnum and Mason— a big, heavy wicker hamper filled with an abundance of Christmas delights, including savory pies, bottles of wine, fruit, nuts, smoked salmon, cheeses, marzipan and plum cake.

She knew at once who had done this. Who else? It was perhaps what he had been up to while he waited for her to leave his mother's suite.

What if I was to tell you that your sister will eat very well this evening and manage perfectly without you?

"You look very pale, Mary," her sister exclaimed. "I hope you're not going to be peevish and say we should send it back to the shop."

She took a deep breath. "No. Of course not. It is a wonderful gift. It would be ungracious to refuse it. And impractical."

Violet wrinkled her nose. "You're not going to weep, are you? You look odd."

"Really, Violet! When was the last time you saw me shed a tear?"

"When you climbed that tree on a dare and got stung by a wasps' nest."

Yes, fifteen years ago or thereabouts. "I'm surprised you remember," she muttered. "You couldn't have been more than five or six at the time."

"Naturally I remember," her sister replied pertly, the little clump of mistletoe nodding above her ear. "I remember because it *is* such a rare occurrence and hasn't happened since."

It had happened since, of course, but only when she was alone and nobody would know. Tears, like regrets, were ineffectual. Unless one was lucky enough to look endearing when sobbing copious tears, and Mary was not. She merely looked moist and droopy, as if she had a very bad cold, which had the effect of making people back away from her in alarm, rather than offer a hug of reassurance and comfort.

"Where's your bonnet?" her sister demanded.

Oh no. She had abandoned it to Deverell's clutches! What wickedness would befall her bonnet in his house?

Although she had tried to pretend his kisses did nothing to her, they had left her in a state of intoxication so that she could barely put one foot before the other. Hopefully he had not noticed. But now she was no better than those women who left dancing slippers— and probably a great many other things— behind in his house.

She licked her lips. They felt somewhat bruised, but warm too, despite the weather.

"I must have left it somewhere," she managed

eventually, one hand checking that her hair was not in too great a disorder. "Never mind. It was a rather old and sad bonnet. If some beggar in the street has found it, they are welcome to keep it."

"Soon you shall be able to buy another, Mary my dear," Thaddeus exclaimed, "for I have more good news." He had fetched the ledger from under the counter. "A great many of our debtors have paid their bills today, quite suddenly. I wonder if it is the Christmas spirit we have to thank for all this."

Mary studied the ledger and saw that a handful of "PAST DUE"s were scratched out and "PAID IN FULL" written in, along with the amount.

"We shall have a very merry Christmas indeed," he added, eyes gleaming up at her through his spectacles.

She thought of Ransom Deverell reading that ledger upside down. the calculating light apparent under his lowered lashes. His gaze had scanned the lines in a matter of seconds, far less than a minute, as far as she knew. Yet he must have memorized the names and addresses of all those debtors.

Again there was no doubt in her mind that he was behind this change of fortune, however it was achieved. She was not certain she wanted to know how.

Why had he done all this? Of all the things she'd ever overheard or read about that man, she would never guess him to be generous.

228

On the other hand, Mary already knew how gossip favored bad news and scandal. Good deeds were far less likely to be mentioned.

As her Uncle Hugo would remark airily, "The loudest critics are always those who have nothing good to say." Of course, being a man who liked to raise questions, tempers and eyebrows, Hugo always turned it to his advantage. "One must remember, a bad review often provides an artiste with their best exposure. A *very* bad review will make others curious to see for themselves. To be liked all the time would be a dreadful bore."

What she *did* know about Ransom Deverell for certain was that he always got what he wanted. Even Raven had told her that. He was outspoken and straightforward. And seldom still for long. She had seen for herself that he did not hide his attraction for a woman. On Wednesday she thought it was simply a habit of his, to flirt. But was this his method of seduction— to overcome her protests with gifts and favors?

Whatever he was up to, it would last only until another woman caught his eager eye.

Perhaps he merely felt pity for her. That idea rattled her Ashford Pride.

"Mary! You're pulling all the berries off that sprig of holly!"

She hastily dropped the partially massacred clump of seasonal cheer and left her sister to finish decorating the mantle.

Again she thought of Elizabeth Stanbury in his doorway that evening. And of the French whirlwind who had chased him down the street only a few days before. Of the other woman whose scent had clung to him when he came to her shop.

If I had a good woman, Mary Ashford, to put me to rights, I might become a worthier man. In time. Don't you think?

Such a man was impossible to trust or take seriously. But he was not— so she had discovered— difficult to smile at, or even to forgive for his blunders.

And it was certainly not at all challenging to become enchanted by that man. It was all too easy. Even to fall a little bit in love. Just a little. Not with her "whole being" this time.

Just a little in love. Nonsensical as it was for her to feel that way about Ransom Deverell.

He'd probably forgotten all about her already.

But when she glanced down, Mary realized she'd made a little arrangement of scarlet berries on the table, forming a dramatic letter R.

She allowed herself to look at it for just a moment, feeling rather naughty, and then, before anyone else might see, she quickly swept the berries into her palm and tossed them into the fire.

Whatever might happen to her bonnet in his custody, she almost envied the damnable thing.

Chapter Fourteen

Lady Charlotte had expressed an interest in meeting Violet, so Mary took her sister to Mivart's Hotel on her next visit. As she could have predicted— knowing her ladyship's penchant for pretty things— the introduction was a success.

"Violette is a charming, sweet little thing, and it is time I took on a new project," she told Mary. "I will chaperone her in society this winter, for I know how desperately frugal you are, Mary! No expense should be spared, and I shall see to it that it is not."

Many of Lady Charlotte's old connections in society no longer existed, since her scandalous marriage to True Deverell and then her even more scandalous divorce. However, she still clung bitterly to the few remaining "friends" and, since Raven married the Earl of Southerton, her circle had begun to enlarge again. Not liked by many, they considered her a necessary evil to remain on her influential son-in-law's good side, and she knew this. But she was not a woman to let dignity get in her way. She made the most of her daughter's advancement.

"Do not look at me with that fearful expression, Mary. I have funds of my own and since my one and only daughter declines my assistance at present, why should I not find another protégée? Lord knows, I have tried with you, Mary, and you simply have no care for fashion. It is most frustrating for a woman of my tastes and sensitivities to be faced with you in that burgundy day gown that has been out of fashion for five years and has a visible darn at the elbow."

Violet beamed happily. "My sister prefers to be dowdy so that she is not smiled at in the street by gentlemen who are not respectable."

They both laughed and shook their heads at Mary, as if she was a little girl standing there with cake crumbs on her face and in her hair.

But she did not mind it. Putting up with Lady Charlotte's less than flattering remarks would be worthwhile if it gave Violet something to be happy about at last. It was also true, of course, that supervising this "debut" would give her ladyship something to occupy her mind, and keep her from thinking about Oxfordshire and her daughter. In addition, Mary's knowledge and interest in fashion could, in no way, satisfy her sister's thirst for that subject. All things considered it seemed an advantageous connection from both sides.

A few days later, a trip to the haberdashers was organized and soon Lady Charlotte and "Violette" were lost among the rolls of fabric, while Mary — with no book in her possession at that moment— was obliged to occupy her mind by reading an advertisement for Beecham's Pills and another beside it for French corsets and petticoat frames. She was just wondering whose idea it was to put women into cages, be they French or of any other origin, when she was aware of a warm movement of air behind her and then a deep male voice muttered,

"I do hope you're not thinking of purchasing one of those contraptions, Miss Ashford. Disguising the natural female shape in such an unwieldy manner, so that a man cannot admire it, is deplorable and vastly unfair. Disguising yours would be an abomination."

She turned quickly and found Deverell very close. It was almost a week since he had her brought to his house. By now she had expected him to forget about her entirely. But his eyes were just as heated and demanding today as they had been then. As if no time at all had elapsed since he kissed her, and as if their conversation had never been interrupted.

"You have no idea what my legs look like." Alas, that was the best she could do, too startled by his sudden appearance to prepare any better, more ladylike retort.

A devilish grin meandered across his mouth, as if it had all the time in the world. and she, equally lazy, watched it. "As I told you, there is nothing amiss with my imagination."

"What are you doing here?" Another remark blurted out. She felt sixteen again, light in the head and feet, capricious and scatter-brained.

"I like to keep an eye on the enemy."

"I beg your pardon?"

"If one wants to know what women are up to, a

haberdashery is the ideal place. Here one learns all manner of secrets and tricks of the trade." He tapped the handle of his walking cane at the corset advertisement. "And be prepared for whatever devilry one might encounter. Under a lady's clothes."

The man was exceedingly improper. He was also despicably handsome— and unavoidable in such close quarters. If he had the limbs of an octopus Mary could not have felt more surrounded. Anxiously glancing over his shoulder, to be sure no other customer in the shop was looking their way, she said, "Your mother is here. I'm certain she'll be pleased to see you."

"Is she, by Jove?" But he didn't turn to look. His dark gaze remained fixed upon Mary.

"Thank you, sir," she managed finally, "for the hamper of Yuletide cheer. I wish you had not gone to such trouble and expense. I cannot think why you did."

"Don't be unduly modest, Miss Ashford. It's very tiresome. You know why I did it. I am, if nothing else, straightforward in my purpose when I take pursuit."

Yes, but had she not made her position clear? She took a deep breath, which only succeeded in letting his scent invade her lungs, his presence filling her senses completely yet again. No floral undertones today, thank goodness.

Had he swayed toward her another half inch? She could have sworn she felt a sigh of breath against her temple, and the sly stroke of his finger moved the pleats of her skirt.

"You left your bonnet behind," he said, not even bothering to lower his voice.

"It does not matter. It is old and frayed. Burn it for all I care." That came out with more insolence than she'd meant, but his proximity and the powerful feelings he evoked, triumphed mercilessly over Mary's ability to remain unruffled and civil.

"As you desire. I prefer you without it in any case."

She looked up and found his gaze questing over her hair with the sort of blatant, lusty admiration a proper gentleman ought to hide. Her fingers itched to pull the hood of her cloak up again, just to keep him from looking. But her brain issued no approving command and so her hands remained at her sides, flapping about uselessly, as if they had turned into two ham slices.

Suddenly, much to her abject horror, he slid his hand through the opening in her cloak and settled his hand on her waist. It was heavy, warm, the fingers spread, the thumb stroking the material of her bodice.

"Mary," he whispered. "I could get you out of that corset as easily as I once got you free of that knotted string. Then I would show you exactly how imaginative I can be. I would tell you a story you won't find in one of your books, and I would do it all without a word spoken."

She urged her feet to move, but they were as helpless as her hands. He drew her closer still and his mouth...oh, his mouth touched her hair.

"You deserve much more than this. Never limit yourself."

In the next aching breath, he was gone again, striding out of the shop without another word. The door slammed loudly shut, and several folk looked over, curious.

Lady Charlotte was one whose attention had been caught, and she immediately gestured Mary over to the counter. "Was that my son? I thought it was him. The surly boy would not bother to greet me, would he?"

Mary gave no answer and pretended to peruse the fabric samples with her sister, although she could not touch them because her hands were trembling. What did he mean by saying she deserved more? More than what?

"I told him we were coming here today. One would think he'd take the time to stop and speak to his own mama. But I suppose I expect too much. He was here, no doubt, to buy some common slattern a trinket. Probably that actress hussy he's been running about with. What did he say to you, Mary?"

She swallowed hard, trying to dislodge the lump that stuck there. "Nothing very much. I hardly heard. He seemed in a great hurry."

"Hmph. As always. Never a moment for polite

conversation. I quite despair of him."

I am, if nothing else, straightforward in my purpose when I take pursuit.

It was ten years since anybody had seriously pursued Mary. Eight since her heart and pride were unceremoniously trampled. She had, as she was always telling Violet, resigned herself to her lot and her only hope now was to see her sister well and happily married. In the meantime she had her novels, the bookshop, and all those little things in which she took pleasure.

But was it enough for her?

You deserve much more than this.

Even when her father and brothers were alive, nobody had ever suggested she deserved anything special. Daughters were never as important as sons. Women took whatever chance they were given and made what they could of it. They did not carve out their own opportunities, or else they were accused of being forward. It was not dignified to grasp. Certainly Mary had never dared suggest she wanted more than she was likely to be offered.

Why would she, when she did not know what else she could have?

Suddenly the possibilities before her had expanded.

As she glanced through the window of the haberdasher's, pretending to examine the weather, Mary saw that Ransom lingered outside the shop, apparently caught in conversation with another man. He ran fingers back through his hair and laughed. People passing on the street turned to look at him, because he was too beautiful to be ignored. Men and women alike stumbled into each other, too busy wondering who he was to pay heed to their steps on the crowded pavement.

But suddenly the hammering beat of Mary's heart ceased again when she saw a face from her past. There, across the street, also watching Ransom, was a tall, distinguished gentleman in a fine grey coat. His hair was a little whiter than it had been the last time she saw him, and the skin had a few more folds, but there was no mistaking the hard, proud features of George Stanbury.

She moved away from the window, fearing he might see her.

Then, chiding herself for being so foolish as to think he could see her in the window from across a busy street, she peered out again. This time he had crossed the road and was walking toward the shop. But his steps slowed. He stopped, half turned, consulted his fob-watch. People did not look at George as they passed, for there was nothing especially interesting that drew their notice, but she saw how they instinctively gave him a wide berth. His forbidding air of grandeur kept them from any attempt at contact, even that of the eye.

Had he seen her?

No. He walked on, passing the shop, moving with the flow of people, just a few feet behind Ransom Deverell.

She could breathe again. George Stanbury had no idea how close he came to being beaten by Violet's shoe.

* * * *

He had called in at the law offices of Stempenham and Pitt, but Damon was not there. A visit to the boy's lodgings also yielded nothing.

Deciding he did not have the time to trudge up and down town looking for his brother, just to give him bad news, Ransom gave up. Damon would find him when he was ready. In all likelihood the boy was sulking over a bottle of brandy somewhere, licking his wounds.

And Ransom had other, more pleasant, subjects upon which to dwell. Sitting in his office at the club, thinking about the sensuous arc of Mary's waist under his palm and the perfume of her hair, he grew restless again and got up to pace around his desk.

Finally his gaze fell to the book, still sitting where he had left it after unwrapping the parcel and reading her note of apology.

If you ever get around to reading that book I sent you, Mr. Deverell, then we might have something to talk about.

He had expected to be over this fascination by now, but it was worse, spreading throughout his body. And seizing his mind like some sort of tropical fever.

With a heavy sigh, he tapped one finger to the cover and then walked around his desk in the other direction to pour a brandy and light a cigar.

Below, in the club, business was brisk. The sound of male voices and laughter echoed up from the main floor. Later he would go down and walk around, greet some of the regulars, ensure that all ran smoothly. But for now he had a moment to himself.

He sat and reached for the book. Miss Ashford, for all her clever insights, did not know that Ransom had an extraordinary ability to read a vast number of pages in a short time. Not only that, but his mind absorbed the words and kept them there, exactly as he read them on the page. This was yet another peculiarity of his that irritated tutors and fellow students, and from the first moment he discovered this talent he used it to annoy them even more.

But one had to make one's entertainment somehow.

Wouldn't do any harm to peruse a few pages of this book Miss Ashford thought he might enjoy. Slowly he opened it and began to read.

I am born. Whether I shall turn out to be the hero of my own life, or whether that station will be held by anybody else, these pages must show. To begin my life with the beginning of my life, I record that I was born (as I have been informed and

believe) on a Friday, at twelve o'clock at night. It was
remarked that the clock began to strike, and I began to cry,
simultaneously...

* * * *

Ransom did not leave the club until much later.
It was full night by then, but the rain had paused and
a handful of stars speckled the cold, inky black sky.
The air tasted like snow. By morning the ground
would have its first crust of white, no doubt.

After a few words with Miggs, who would close
up that night, he set off for the house and his bed.
For once he was actually looking forward to sleep.
His thoughts had lately been so full of Mary Ashford
that there was no room for the ghost of Sally White.

Ahead of him, in a pool of gas light, a figure
stepped off the pavement and raised a hand in
greeting.

"Deverell! I knew it was you."

He slowed the horse, wondering who it was, not
recognizing the voice.

That crisp glitter of starry night sky was reflected
too in a puddle that stretched across the road.

Those stars— first the pattern on the ground and
then, once again, those in the sky— were the last
thing he would remember seeing that night, just after
he dismounted and the first blow struck the side of
his head.

241

* * * *

Hell was considerably colder than he'd expected. Once again somebody must have let the fire go out.

And once again Ransom Deverell felt certain the end was upon him.

Some would say, "Not before time considering the way he lived his life."

If only he had found a good woman to keep him out of trouble, but he was a man beyond redemption and everybody knew it to be so.

Distantly he heard a church bell ringing. It was midnight.

It was midnight on a Friday— the same day and hour that Dickens' Davy Copperfield was born.

If only *he* could begin all over again.

He knew what he would do, if given that chance.

Part Two
A Moderately Sensible Woman

Chapter Fifteen

Excerpt from the memoirs of True Deverell.

From the very beginning he knew he had already lost his son. The boy he named "Ransom" belonged to his wife, her creature, a weapon to be used against him in the war of their marriage. But even so, after thirty years of bloody battle, when the sudden end came and his son lay dying, the father was not prepared to say goodbye. In that dark moment, True Deverell's thoughts returned to birth.

To the moment it all went wrong.

This child was made where there was no love—much the same as True's own beginning. But he could have tried harder, he could have been a better father. Instead, his son had suffered as the consequence of an unhappy, unholy union that left him, by turns, neglected and abused.

Lacking maternal instinct, his mother, Lady Charlotte, was never happier than when she could complain about her life, and her eyes lit up with glee when she told her eldest son of the "degradations" to which his common, uncouth father supposedly exposed her. She spared no details in her eagerness to win the boy over to her side.

But Ransom, unlike his mother, endured pain in silence. He was a withdrawn child, and a nervous, restless adolescent, all too cognizant of the seething hatred between his parents. He grew into adulthood learning to duck and run as thrown glasses flew speedily over his head. All the while knowing that his father looked at him and saw only the woman who had trapped him in marriage.

"You have your mother's eyes," he heard more than once and it was not meant in a kindly way.

By the time True realized the error he'd made in not fighting for his son, it was too late. The die was cast.

As soon as Ransom was old enough to talk, Charlotte had taught him that he was her only ally, the only one who could protect her from his father. And because Ransom wanted to believe he was needed by his mother—by anybody—he absorbed everything she told him, which meant that when her betrayal came it was worse than a dagger to the boy's heart. After that he trusted nobody.

The damage seemed irreparable, but as an adult Ransom did not want to be repaired in any case. He was, as he liked to say proudly to his father, irredeemable.

True understood, for that which was not made whole could never be broken again.

Now death came too soon and his son would never be mended.

But while True Deverell stood by the ailing man's couch and asked, "What do you need, son? What can I fetch for you?" a sign of spring's slender hope showed its face. A snowdrop sprouted.

For his son gestured him close, finally letting him near, and then he whispered in his father's ear...

Chapter Sixteen

She woke, for once, without the usual pinching pains of hunger, and as she lay there, staring up at the starlit cracks in the ceiling, Mary had the distinct impression that she had not come to the end of her natural dream, but that something had woken her. Quickly she sat up, her senses on alert, her breath forming a grey mist before her mouth. But all was still and silent.

Beside her in the bed, her sister snored on, limbs spread out to take up as much room as possible. It was very early, still dark out, a thin trickle of silver starlight falling through the threadbare curtains to trace her sister's form as she turned over, muttering in her sleep. Mary exhaled a heavy sigh that lingered before her lips again, taking ghostly shape not long after the last breath had faded. She did not relish the idea of facing the cold at this hour, but once awake like this she found it impossible to go back to sleep.

A half hour later, she was dressed and, with a gas lamp lit, had made her way down the narrow stairs to the parlor. The room still smelled of pine and cinnamon— good, comforting scents of the Yuletide. It cheered her spirits at once and made her smile.

Her gaze moved over the table, where the material for Violet's new gown, waited wrapped in paper. It was to be made up in a pattern selected by

Lady Charlotte from one of her magazines and the material— a lush, deep raspberry silk— was chosen by Violet. They were all in agreement that it would suit her perfectly. Lady Charlotte had suggested a seamstress, which is where Mary and Violet would take the material today.

"This will be a wonderful Christmas," Violet had exclaimed last night, her cheeks flushed and eyes shining.

Mary, having over-indulged herself with an extra glass of wine, had briefly felt a similar state of elation. But in the back of her mind, when she went to bed, there was something worrying her, a nagging thought that would not be silenced.

As if she had overlooked something.

A sudden draft caught her ankles and made her shiver.

"Wake up, Mary, and get to work," she chided herself crossly.

First order of business was lighting the fire and then she could put the water kettle on to boil. She was still busy with that task when she heard a loud, frantic banging at the shop door.

"Miss Ashford. Miss Mary Ashford? It's a matter of urgency, miss!"

Good lord! What on earth...?

Taking her lamp in one hand, she went to see what was happening. A big, moon-like face peered in at her through the window, anxious and white. "Miss

Ashford, come quick! It's Mr. Deverell, Miss. He sent me to fetch you."

Deverell. What was he up to now?

She set down her lamp and cautiously unlocked the door. A giant figure emerged through the whirling snow and stepped over the threshold. Cap in hand, his wide shoulders heaving under an inch-deep layer of snowflakes, crisp and glittering, he pleaded urgently, "Miss Mary Ashford, is it? Will you come?"

She backed up a step, reaching for her lamp, raising it to bathe his rugged features in the amber glow. "Sir, it is not yet daylight. What can you—"

"I should introduce myself, shouldn't I? My name's Miggs, Miss." He rubbed his flat nose with one red thumb that stuck through a hole in his leather glove. "You might remember, I opened the door to you last week at the club, when you delivered that parcel for Mr. Deverell the younger."

"Of course. I remember." His was not a face one could forget and if she had not known him she would never have unlocked the door.

"He's been hurt, Miss. 'Tis very bad." His words came out in a series of quick gasps, like hiccups. "He may not have long left, I reckon, but he opened his eyes at last and the only thing he could whisper to his father were your name and that you must come. So I were sent here to fetch you."

"Hurt? What do you mean hurt?" Her heart thumped unevenly as she closed the door behind him.

"He were set upon by thugs last Friday night on his way home from the club, Miss. Well, very early Saturday morning, I reckon it might have been. I heard a ruckus in the alley, but the cowards scattered when I came, and I found him there on the cobbles, cold as a corpse, beaten and bloody. Didn't even have time to get his knife out, so they must have jumped him. Three or four men it must have been. Now will you come, Miss? There's no time to waste."

"But what can I—?" Her mind spun. Friday. This happened Friday night and it was now Monday morning. And she had felt something amiss. "Why would he ask for *me*?"

"I know not, Miss. But he won't have nobody else. Only you. His father will be right mad at me, if I return without you."

Miggs looked hopeful and yet helpless at the same time, crushing his cap in both humongous hands, his eyes wide and watery. If Deverell was badly injured...

"I do not know what I can do for him," she muttered, as he followed her back to the parlor to get her coat. "But I suppose, if he has asked for me—"

"He said you're the only one he wants, Miss."

"What about a doctor?"

"Yes, Miss," he nodded slowly. "One o' them fellows came to the house, but, as Mr. Deverell the elder says, he were as much use as a sieve to keep out rain. He chased the fellow out again with a boot up

250

the backside. Neither him, nor the master, hold much liking for sawbones."

By then Thaddeus Speedwell had come down in his slippers and nightcap, so she quickly explained where she was going and asked him to get a message to Dr. Woodley. If the Deverells would let another man of medicine in the house, he was the only doctor she knew and this was the one thing she could do to help. Dr. Woodley was surely trustworthy and always keen to give his learned opinion. On this occasion he could put it to good use.

"Are you sure you should go alone with this fellow, my dear?" Thaddeus glanced doubtfully at her giant chaperone. "Perhaps it is not proper."

"I daresay it is not, but I am a moderately sensible woman, of an age to bear the consequences, and I shall do so with as much equanimity as I can muster. Now, I shall entrust Violet to your care until I return. Do not be deceived into letting *her* out of your sight. Please tell her I have gone to tend a sick neighbor." It was more or less true.

Miggs had not come with a carriage, but rode on a dray horse the size of a barn. It had to be that large, she supposed, to carry a man of his size.

"You'll have to ride up with me, Miss. Try not to mind the stench of me too much, but I haven't had chance to bathe of late."

She looked around for a box, or something to help her mount, and when nothing could be found,

the big man took matters into his own hands.
Literally. Mary found herself boosted upward at some
sudden speed with those hands on her derriere. There
was no saddle, so she was obliged to hold on to the
horse's mane and hope for the best. A moment later
Miggs was seated behind her and reaching round to
gather the reins.

Again she thought how unreal it all seemed.
Little more than a half hour ago she'd been in bed
and now here she was on her way to who-knew-what.

She certainly could not say her life was
predictable this morning.

It had begun to snow harder, fat, heavier flakes
drifting in the wind, speckling the horse's mane.
Probably doing the same to her own, for Mary
realized she had left her hair in a braid over her
shoulder, not sparing the time to pin it up before she
left the shop. She had not even thought to wrap a
scarf around her head, or find her hooded cloak.

Oh well, she supposed it wouldn't matter that
much since this was an emergency. Although what on
earth he wanted with her she could not imagine.

It was only just turning light out, but there were
folk on the streets already going about their daily
business, and some turned to watch the strange sight
of that giant horse and its burden.

She imagined what anybody who knew her
would say when they saw her like this: *There goes Miss
Mary Ashford, formerly of Allacott Manor, fallen on hard*

times and off to join the travelling circus.

* * * *

When Mary first set eyes on True Deverell she was ready to turn on her heel and storm out again, certain that this had all been a cruel jest and that Ransom was actually in perfect health. But after that first flare of surprise, she realized that the silver sprigs around this man's temples proved him to be the father, not the son. The gas lamps in the hall were turned down low so that too had aided in the illusion, making the similarity in looks quite remarkable, but once she was close enough, Mary saw that True Deverell's eyes were not so dark as his sons. They were cool pewter and cloudy with worry.

"Miss Ashford." He took her hand in his firm grip. "I regret we meet under these circumstances. My son told me nothing about you before this, but then, of course he has never been one to share his confidences with me. Or with anybody. We never know what he might do from one day to the next." He smiled crookedly and briefly down at her. His gaze quickly, thoroughly assessed her appearance, followed by the puzzled quirk of an eyebrow. "That boy never ceases to surprise me. This time, at least, the surprise is pleasant, even if it comes late."

The manner in which he held her hand within both of his and shook it so warmly, suggested that he thought her a close and dear acquaintance of his son's. Still unsure what she was doing there, Mary politely asked when he had arrived in London.

"I came down yesterday, meaning to persuade my son to ride back with me to Cornwall and spend Christmas with us at Roscarrock Castle." He sighed. "The boy insists upon staying alone in Town every year, but my wife thought he might agree to come if I asked in person and if it only kept him away from the club for a few days. When I arrived, I found him in this state."

"How dreadful. I'm sorry that I did not—"

"I hope you are not upset that you have only just been sent for. I'm afraid my son faded in and out of consciousness after he was attacked. His first sane words to me, when he finally spoke, were about you. Had I known, of course, I would have sent for you sooner. But nobody knew, it seems."

Before she could respond to that strange comment, he was escorting her into the drawing room, one hand under her elbow.

"My son has refused to be taken to a hospital or even to his bed above stairs. At present he lays on the couch. He says he doesn't want to get blood on his bed sheets and cause more work for the maids. While he is in this mood, he is an insufferable wretch. I can barely hold my temper, I don't mind telling you. He can be stubborn as a bull. And a martyr, like his mother."

Ransom Deverell was stretched out on the red

couch before the fire, swaddled in blankets and with a bloodied cloth tied around his forehead. A bare foot stuck out at the end of the blanket, the heel resting on the arm of the couch. It was the sight of that naked foot which suddenly and unexpectedly caused a tear to spring up in her eye.

Must be the shock, she supposed, and the suddenness of all this. It was early and she had not eaten breakfast. Yes, she could find many excuses for a little tear. But there had better not be any others to embarrass her.

She must remember that bruises sustained in a fight often looked much worse than they truly were. So she prepared herself for what she might see.

"Ransom," said his father in a louder voice, "Miss Ashford is here, as you asked." He turned to the butler, who hovered by the door looking ashen. "Please bring some tea, will you— or," he looked at Mary again, "perhaps you prefer coffee? Or chocolate?"

"Coffee, thank you. That would be most welcome." Tea seemed too tame and ladylike for the occasion and chocolate too much of a treat.

The man on the couch moved finally to show he was still living and reached out his hand from the blankets. "Don't lurk where I can't see you, Mary," he wheezed.

His father took her coat and pulled up a chair for her beside the couch, angling it so she could face the sick man. "I'm sure your visit will do him some good, Miss Ashford." He lowered his voice again. "Perhaps you can persuade him that he will be far more comfortable upstairs in a proper bed."

"Don't fuss, sir," Ransom groaned. "The reason I wanted her here is because she *won't* fuss. There is nobody more level-headed than Miss Mary Ashford." And she caught just a very little glint of amusement from under his black lashes. "She won't take my nonsense, or be overcome with pity." Then his eyes opened wider. Or one did, for the other was too badly swollen. He tried to sit up, staring at her as if she might be a ghost.

She touched her braid, feeling self-conscious. "I'm afraid Mr. Miggs startled me this morning, and I completely forgot to put it up. I must look a sight." It all added to the dream-like strangeness of this situation. In fact, looking down at herself, she was only surprised not to see her nightgown.

"Yes. A very pleasant sight, all disheveled and not long out of your sleep." The corner of his mouth twitched in a pained smile, before he fell back to the pillows again. Someone had made the couch up, as best they could, with extra pillows and blankets to create a makeshift bed.

"I'm very sorry to see you like this, Mr. Deverell. What happened?"

"They sprung upon me in the dark. I got in a few punches of my own, but there were too many."

"You do not know who is responsible? It should be reported, surely."

"Better we handle the matter ourselves," his father growled. "Keep the peelers and the law out of it. I'll deliver the punishment."

"Could have been anybody," Ransom muttered, sullen. "I've been told I make enemies. Too many enemies."

His face was very bruised and puffy, his lip cut. She could tell from the way he moved and spoke that his chest and ribs must hurt too. "I have asked Dr. Woodley to call upon you. Will you see him?"

Pressing his head back into the pillow, he exhaled a low moan and a curse.

"You ought to be examined," she urged gently. "He could give you something for pain and help you to sleep."

"I don't want to sleep." Horror darkened his gaze. "I never want to sleep."

"But you must. It will help you heal."

"I'll sleep when I'm dead, which will be soon enough now, Mary."

She heard his father pacing back and forth behind her. Or prowling, rather, anxious as a caged leopard.

"I'm quite sure you're much more durable than that," she said with all the confidence she could muster, for his father's benefit as well as his. But she was rather alarmed at his appearance. Usually so tall

257

and vital, so restless, he looked very different today—broken and bloody. Mary knew that the most dangerous wounds were often those on the inside, things that could not be seen. Sometimes they caused a slow descent into death; sometimes the end came suddenly, with no real warning. But when the worst peril was hidden from the human eye there was little to be done about it.

"I was assured recently that I would only see the error of my ways once I was on my deathbed," he said. "It turns out this was correct. I see things much clearer now, so that must be what it means."

Mary studied him cautiously, trying to ascertain whether he really believed he was dying or not. Ransom's expression would usually give him away, but with his features distorted and discolored he may as well be wearing a mask. His father was clearly concerned, although he appeared to be trying to hide it under a brusque temper. She had seen how upset Mr. Miggs was, and when Mary first arrived at the house she observed a stout lady by the door to the kitchens, sobbing into her apron. The mood in the house was definitely somber as the grave.

Much of the furniture in the drawing room had been rearranged around the couch, newspapers, handkerchiefs, pillows, dishes and brandy glass, all placed and piled within his reach, but in messy disarray that suggested it was all done in haste. The curtains were kept closed, the gas lamps low.

Everybody, except his father, walked about as if on tiptoe, and she was surprised they had not yet put straw out in the street to quiet passing horses' hooves.

At that moment the butler brought in the coffee pot and cups, steering them carefully on a wheeled trolley. "Mrs. Clay hoped she might tempt you to eat something today, sir. To that end she's made a dozen delights— all your favorite. There is cinnamon toast *and* plain, Madeira cake with apple jam, pork pie, kippers, boiled eggs and porridge, to name but a few things, waiting in the dining room for the guests and I can bring you a tray in here, sir, if—"

"Good God, no. I couldn't eat. But Mrs. Clay's efforts must not go to waste. I daresay Mary might be hungry."

Why did he keep calling her by her Christian name? His father did not raise an eyebrow at the familiarity, but then they *were* Deverells and did things differently.

While the butler poured coffee, she looked at Ransom and said cautiously, "Why did you send for me? What can I do?" Perhaps he wanted her to take a message to his mother, she thought. He had enough people here attending to his every need.

His eyes narrowed. "Where else should you be but at my side at such a time, Mary? If you have something more important to do than bring comfort to a dying man, then don't let me keep you."

"You are not dying," she said firmly.

"You say that as if you have power over life and death. I ought to know whether I'm dying or not. If you start being argumentative, I'll send you home again."

"Feeling sorry for yourself is no excuse to be rude," his father interrupted, terse. "Although I daresay Miss Ashford ought to know what she's getting herself into. She must be able to manage you or she wouldn't be here."

She tried a sip of coffee, but it too hot and burned her tongue.

Getting herself into? What on earth—

"I sent for you, Mary, because I knew you would not fuss, nor flinch at the sight of blood, nor be indiscreet and gossip. You are, in fact, the only decent and rational woman I could think of. Sensible," the wounded man gave another pained grimace, "to a fault."

His father, who apparently had as much ability to be still as the son, had walked out into the hall with the butler, discussing some matter of the house.

"And to think—I never believed I'd have much use for a woman like that," the injured man continued wryly. "But now I do."

"Ransom Deverell, I cannot be the only woman of good sense that you have ever known."

"None other came to mind, I assure you."

Mary understood why he wouldn't want his mother there— Lady Charlotte did not like to speak of blood and sickness, let alone see it, and did not know how to be sympathetic, invariably turning the matter to being something about herself. But surely..."Of all the other women you know—"

"I do not know them. Not the way I know you."

"In slightly less than a fortnight?"

"But I have *known* you longer." He poked a finger at the ceiling.

Having no idea what he meant, Mary could only assume that his mental state was disturbed. "I suppose some of the women you know are married and therefore could not be summoned," she muttered.

He looked at her, his eyes blank, as if he was thinking about something else and not listening to her at all.

Mary cleared her throat. "Lady Elizabeth Stanbury, for instance," she added.

"The icicle? She wasn't here for me. Well, not exactly."

She waited, eyebrows raised.

"That woman is one of my brother's problems. Not mine."

"I see."

"And I gave up Belle Saint Clair the same day I met you. Finding you was like walking into that lamp post, Mary Ashford. You both put a stop to me."

But there were others, probably. Or there would be, once he was back on his feet. Could a man like

Ransom Deverell ever keep his gaze from wandering? He needed blinkers, like a plow horse, she mused.

As if he read her mind again, he huffed, head falling back to the pillow. "You won't believe me, so why bother? Besides, there have been other women, of course, and you know that. I'm no angel. But that's all in the past now. I'm starting again, for the time I have left."

"The time you have left? A good forty years at least."

"I fear not even forty hours, Mary. I can feel nothing from the waist down and breathing itself is a deuced struggle." He exhaled a frail sigh to demonstrate. "Will you fluff up my pillow, Mary?"

She put her coffee cup on the trolley and then, while he held his head up, she rearranged his pillow.

But he took advantage of the moment to grab her hand and press it to his lips, apparently less sleepy than he appeared. "It was a lucky day when we finally met in person, Contessa."

His father's footsteps were returning to the room and Mary tried to regain custody of her own hand, but Ransom held it tighter still.

"You're remarkably strong for a dying man," she noted drily.

"It is a strength born of desperation. I am determined to make the most of my last days."

True Deverell re-entered the room, strode around the couch and stood behind Mary, one foot tapping. "Will you stay to breakfast, Miss Ashford?"

"Oh, I —"

"Please do. I should like to get to know more about the woman who has captured my son's heart. I promise I am not as fearsome as you might have been told."

Mary's first instinct was to believe her ears were playing tricks upon her. She did not turn to look at the man behind her, but kept her gaze fixed to Ransom's face. He had closed his eyes again, as if in great pain, but was he merely hiding from her? His hand still held Mary's in an unwavering grip. "Sir," her throat was dry, making her tongue feel awkward, thick and clumsy, "I think there must be some sort of misunderstanding—"

But his father had resumed that long stride back and forth across the carpet, not listening. "I began to think it would never be. Some men are simply not made for marriage. Nor are some women. It is always a business of chance and risk."

Her pulse was racing and Ransom Deverell's sly thumb was pressed hard to it, measuring the reckless pace.

He opened his eyes and said, "I think we should be married directly now, Mary. Under the circumstances. Since I do not know how long I have."

Surely she was dreaming. None of this had happened. She must still be in bed beside the snoring "Violette". It could be the only explanation for any of it. And by some trick of the mind, in this somnolent state of being, she was unable to move her tongue to argue, just as it was sometimes in a dream when she could not make her feet move forward.

Ransom's dark gaze held hers. She could not blink or look away. Slowly his thumb stroked her wrist.

"Mary is the only woman who can save me. I knew it the moment we met. She knew it too."

Save me, he'd entreated her, with his strong hands clasped around her arms, *and I'll be in your debt.*

Behind her, his father had picked up a newspaper and rustled it, while murmuring a distracted, "Hmm."

Mary mouthed anxiously at the man on the couch, "What is this mischief?"

But he ignored her. "To rephrase Mr. Dickens and Master David Copperfield—*Whatever she has tried to do in life, she has tried with all her heart to do well; that whatever she has devoted herself to, she has devoted herself to completely...in great aims and in small, she has always been thoroughly in earnest.*" He paused, his gaze searching her face. "I believe she will serve her husband with the same devotion as she takes on other tasks."

The quote she recognized from *David Copperfield*. So he must have begun to read it after all. Mary was shocked into silence. When she thought she was a woman who had seen and heard everything, he still surprised her.

What other tricks might he have up his sleeve?

He had memorized that passage for her, to show her that he understood, that he could make an effort.

Mary felt another terrible tear threaten her composure, but she fought it back. Oh no! He would not make her fall in love with him more than the little bit she had allowed in already. He was unpredictable and everything bad for her. She ought to consider, for instance, her combustible petticoats.

If only she had not such a weakness for a good novel.

He squeezed her hand. "My future wife does not suffer fools gladly, or indeed, in any other way, sir. She let me know that from the start. If I can have her at my side for my last hours, I shall be content."

"Well, I see she has improved your bloody mood already," his father gruffly, tossing the newspaper aside. She felt a hand on her shoulder then and looked up. "You can give my son something to live for, Miss Ashford. Perhaps he will finally slow his horses, although it seems almost too remarkable to be believed."

Ransom looked away, wincing. "I knew it would be a trial for you to believe I could win the hand of a good woman, sir. I am the son least likely to make anything of my life, is that not the case?"

"That's up to you, boy. Man holds his own fate in his hands."

Now Mary was in a most awkward position. How could she speak? True Deverell had shown a tentative measure of relief at the idea of his son soon to be married, and with Ransom in the sorry state of an invalid, supposedly convinced he lingered at the threshold of death, Mary was reluctant to spoil the moment of fragile peace between father and son.

If Ransom currently amused himself with a wicked game at her expense, he was likely to grow bored eventually and give it up. And if his brain truly suffered from some momentary confusion which caused him to believe things had happened which had not, then he could soon recover, be back to his normal self, and remember that he was not the marrying kind. He did not like "leashes".

Finally she freed her hand from his, reaching for her coffee cup again. "We will talk *properly* of this matter later, when you have rested and recovered your strength." When they had all cooled down, like the coffee, and when she knew exactly what was going on inside his mind. As well as her own.

What if Ransom really was dying? How could she turn her back and walk away from someone in need? She'd lost too many people already. Life and its opportunities were so fleeting.

The truth was she *did* feel as if they'd known each another longer. Perhaps because of her long friendship with his sister? And she did...she did care about him. Very much. Far more than she should in light of their short acquaintance and his reputation.

"I had to find some way to keep her company,

266

sir," he muttered drowsily, as his eyes began to close again, "and she is too respectable to dine alone with a man like me, so I had to ask her to marry me. It was the only thing to be done."

"Hmm." His father, while wearing a hole in the carpet with his booted feet, and turning the air blue with the curses he threw out under his breath, succeeded in producing only dust and bumping into the misplaced furniture, adding to the sense of chaos. He did not draw close to the couch, but on this circling, pacing guard, kept a distance from his son as if a line were marked on the carpet to show a boundary.

"What do you think of her, sir? Is she not a Renaissance Madonna?"

"Hmm. If you say so."

Mary decided that she had better take charge, since Ransom Deverell had put her in this unenviable position and everybody else appeared to be letting him get his own way, yielding to his every whim as if he were a spoiled prince. Girding her Ashford loins, she stood. "Why don't you let your father and Mr. Miggs help you up to bed? It will be much more comfortable there."

Behind her his father tripped to a halt.

"But this couch is red," the patient complained. "The blood won't show." His lips turned down at the corners. "I do not want to be a bother. Heaven forbid."

"Don't be foolish. Did you not send for me so that I could talk sense into you? Then you had better listen, otherwise I have had a wasted journey across town in the snow."

His eyes narrowed as he looked up at her, peevish.

She continued briskly, "You need a bath, or, if that cannot be managed, at least a once over with a wash rag. Then a warm bed." Walking to the end of the couch to adjust the blanket over his bare foot, she slyly pinched his big toe.

The patient jumped a few inches.

"It seems your numbness is wearing off," she commented wryly.

After a few more grumbles he agreed to being moved, "But only to please you, Mary dearest."

She watched as his father, Mr. Miggs, the butler, and a footman ferried the patient out into the hall and up the stairs, utilizing an old dressing-screen panel as a stretcher. It required shouting, grunting, and maneuvering that had probably not been witnessed since the construction of St. Paul's Cathedral.

When the front door bell rang, Mary was the only one with a free hand to answer it and so she did, to find a very perplexed Dr. Woodley waiting on the step, come in answer to her summons.

Chapter Seventeen

"He exaggerates his condition, no doubt— loves the drama, like his mother. But I was damned concerned when I arrived yesterday and found him barely conscious, unmoving..." True Deverell helped himself to kippers from the sideboard and sat across the table from Mary, tossing his plate down with a clatter. "Of all my sons he's always been the most trouble, of course. Blasted boy!"

He seemed angry with everything— even the salt-cellar raised his ire. But it was clear the man had endured a tiring few days. He was unshaven, his clothes disheveled, boots still spattered with dried mud from his journey. The way he speedily and ruthlessly dispatched that smoked kipper also suggested he had not eaten since his arrival.

"It must have been a dreadful shock, sir."

A slice of toast went to its fate immediately after the kipper. "Hmmm." He growled through a mouthful and shook his knife before pointing it at her, "And when I find out who is responsible I'll give them a shock too. One they shan't recover from."

Mary slowly spread butter on her own toast. "There is no idea who did this? Or why?"

"I'll find out, don't you worry. Luckily I came when I did, for he would never have sent word to me." He scowled hard across the room at some invisible foe and then drained his coffee cup. Finally he pulled himself back from dark thoughts, wiped his lips on a napkin, cleared his throat, and said, "But tell me— what is Miss Mary Ashford's story? You appear sane enough, but looks can be deceptive."

"I am a friend of your daughter's, sir. We have known each other for a decade."

"And Ransom?" He dropped his knife to the floor and swore lavishly, looking at his fingers as if he could not understand why they had failed him.

"We met but recently."

"What about your family?" he demanded brusquely. "They surely don't approve of my son."

She hesitated.

"Don't be afraid to tell me," he added with a smirk and a wink. "I am well aware of society's general opinion when it comes to me and my litter. You won't tell me anything I haven't heard before, but it will be useful to know where we stand in your case."

It occurred to Mary that he was wondering whether *she* might be the cause of this attack against his son. "I only have one sister left, sir," she assured him hastily. "A younger sister left in my care. In fact, she will be waiting for me, as we have an important errand today at the dressmaker."

"Just the two of you, eh? What happened to your parents?"

"My family once resided at Allacott Manor in

Somersetshire, but—"

Getting up abruptly, he returned to the sideboard to fill a second plate.

"My father had to sell the estate." Mary left it there. The name had registered nothing on his face and he did not seem to be listening now anyway. No need to mention the gambling habits of her brothers, or their reckless decision to go off together to battle. Or of her father's unwise investments, the succession of poor harvests, his stubborn refusal to try new methods of farming, and the loss of many land laborers to war and to the factories. All the frustration of watching her father make bad decisions for the estate and having no power to intervene, because she was only a daughter. Only a woman who should be decorative and obedient, and preferably silent.

No reason to dig all that up again and let the bitterness seep through her veins like poison. She was a "meek little bookseller" now and adjusted to her lot. Or she had been until a certain Wednesday morning when a draft blew through her new life and brought a mischievous genie with it.

"Damned shame," he muttered, "but those old houses are a drain on any man's pockets. The world is changing. Mark my words, Miss Ashford, more of those old estates will crumble unless the old aristocracy learn to adapt, use their imagination, work hard. Stop sitting by and expecting other people to do it for them." Then he stopped and looked at her over his shoulder. "I don't suppose that's much comfort to you now though, eh?"

She couldn't answer that and fortunately he didn't wait long before he continued spooning a mound of scrambled egg from a chafing dish onto his new plate. The way he addressed her was very familiar— like his son. He did not stand on ceremony and expressed himself, with a generous measure of curse words, as if he felt quite at ease in her presence. But it was a welcome change that he did not speak to her as if she was inferior, stupid or in any need of his pity.

"Any relation to the artist Hugo Ashford?"

Mary almost choked on her bite of toast. Nobody ever raised his name in front of her these days. "Yes," she managed tentatively. "He was my uncle."

Deverell nodded and moved along to cut a large slice of pork pie, then stabbed some plump sausages with the same knife, adding them to his overcrowded plate. "A great artist. Underappreciated I always thought."

Warm gratitude swept through Mary's heart at this unexpected praise for her uncle. In the blade of her butter knife, she saw a deep flush color her face. "Yes. He was a very special man and a fine artist." To be able to talk of dear Uncle Hugo openly with anybody felt like a wondrous treat, but at the same time rather naughty since it was a subject strongly discouraged by her father when he was alive.

"There are many folk who say I have no eye for art. How can I have any? An uneducated bastard like me?" He laughed curtly. "Those *cultured* experts think a foundling like me has no right to own any of it. I bought all the art in the house. My son would never buy art himself, for then he'd need a permanent abode of his own in which to put it all."

"This house is yours then, sir?"

He nodded. "Bought it thirty years ago or thereabout. My first real home. I never had a permanent roof over my head until then. This was my chance to show off the wealth I'd acquired. My first attempt at breaking the 'Upper Crust' and a most successful one."

"It is a very beautiful building."

"But it was never a happy home. All for show." Returning to the table, he shuddered and his eyes darkened. "There are too many memories of my first marriage. Sometimes it seems as if they cling to the curtains. Like smoke."

She knew what it was to suffer too many memories, whether unhappy or not. If she ever went back to Allacott Manor she was sure the ghosts that lingered would tear her apart and all these years of carefully built composure would shatter, revealing the silly, irresponsible, vulnerable girl who still dwelt inside her and occasionally came up with fanciful ideas.

"My son did not want the place, but when he took over at Deverell's I decided he ought to live here— have a separate house to escape to once in a while. Sometimes I think he would be more content living in a hayloft over a barn." He gave a little snort. "Ironic, considering how hard I worked to escape such humble dwellings."

Somehow she could not see Ransom, in his fine garments, living in a hayloft. But she stayed quiet and let his father speak, learning more about this man who had, like a cuckoo, invaded her life and tried to make himself a part of it. And True Deverell held nothing back. He did not speak in polite words, selected not to upset a lady; he spoke bluntly, as if to another man at his table.

"My son disdains permanency. He prefers to be the free, wayfaring, limitless bachelor running from commitment and his own shadow. Instead of investing in property that will appreciate in value, he spends his money on ephemeral moments— races, parties, champagne, and fancy curricles that will lose their worth the moment they've been ridden."

Was he telling her all this to warn her, or put her off? She looked at the crumbs on her plate. "But he...he is generous."

"Is he?"

"He has been to me, sir."

Deverell hunched over his second plate of food, both elbows on the table. "It *must* be love then," he muttered wryly. "He's always been more selfish than altruistic. Damn cub enjoys his devious pranks." Looking up at her, he added, "Indeed, I thought this sudden plan to marry was just another hoax. His idea of a jest. When he sent for you, I expected a strumpet with a backside fit to rest a tankard on, rouge troweled onto her cheeks, and bubbies hoisted up to her chin. The sort you can find, three for sixpence and a bottle of sherry-sack, down by the docks."

It didn't seem right to laugh while Ransom was in such a bad way upstairs, but Mary felt a smile threaten as his father painted that lurid image in her mind. No man had ever spoken so straightforwardly to her.

"Frankly, Miss Ashford, you were something of a mule kick to the whirlygigs," he added dourly.

Did that mean she'd been a disappointment, she wondered. Perhaps he didn't like to be proven wrong by his son.

While Mary struggled to hide her amusement, she watched him devour the second helping of food.

"So what can you possibly find alluring about that boy? The money, eh?"

She stared. "I can assure you, sir, I don't care about the money."

"Of course you do. You're not an imbecile, are you? Everybody needs money. The game of life requires money. If you haven't any you can't play the game."

Mary gathered her thoughts, rearranged the
275

crumbs on her plate, and said, "When I first met your son I dismissed him as the typical rake about town, but I have since found that he has many more layers. I believe...I believe he wants to be different. Perhaps..."

She had surprised herself. Her voice trailed away.

If I had a good woman, Mary Ashford, to put me to rights, I might become a worthier man.

Why did she even believe he meant that? The man was an accomplished, infamous seducer. He knew how to appeal to her weaknesses, just as he knew how to find any woman's soft spots.

But his words echoed inside her. It was as if, even before he ever laid a finger on her person, he had already touched her soul.

The fire in the grate crackled softly, and snow still tumbled against the tall windows.

Across the table, True Deverell spoke again through his food. "I have no right to advise you. You're not my cub, of course. But I hope you have your eyes open, Miss Ashford."

"I always do, sir."

"And I hope that this isn't just some momentary fancy on my son's part. Some prank. Forgive me if I seem harsh, but no woman has ever kept his interest beyond a month. Once he's had her she's usually swiftly forgotten."

What could one say to that?

"I shall be glad, of course, if this marriage comes

276

to pass and I was cheerful to keep up my son's spirits, but one must look at the odds. You're a sensible woman, so you must know the risk."

Mary was amused to hear that True Deverell had considered his demeanor "cheerful".

This time she was saved the trouble of answering, when the butler entered to announce that Dr. Woodley had completed his examination.

Deverell scowled, exhaling a low curse. His gaze fixed Mary in a stern beam of silvery light. "You had better see to the sawbones. I might just bite his bloody head off."

"I hope you are not offended that I asked him to come, sir."

He shrugged. "That was up to you, Miss Ashford. My son could very soon be your responsibility completely so you may as well start now. I hold little faith in doctors and their leech-craft, but I shall defer to you on this occasion." He gave her a very brisk, crooked smile that left her wondering what he really thought of her, and immediately looked back at his sausages. "Tell the fool to send me his bill."

Mary curtseyed, although it did not appear to be expected, and followed the butler out.

* * * *

Dr. Woodley stood in the hall, putting on his gloves, hat tucked under his arm. "Miss Ashford!

How astonished I was to receive your message this morning. I had no idea you were acquainted with the Deverell family."

Mary was in no mood for pointless chatter. "How is he, Doctor?"

He looked very dour and even greyer than usual as he shook his head. "Many of his wounds are cuts and bruises, the like of which need only time and patience to mend."

She clasped her hands together and felt hope lift her mood. For just a moment.

"However, he complains of severe pain in the chest. These things are not easy to diagnose, but I fear it likely the gentleman has a wounded lung," he added. "It could be a puncture to the tissue. I was unable to examine him fully, as Deverell was... most difficult." His countenance became very white and stiff, nostrils flared. "He refused to be handled."

"I see."

"Such injuries can, sometimes, heal themselves, but with such an injury there is a great risk of septic infection spreading throughout the body."

Hope fell like a bird pierced by an arrow. The flint blade of fear ripped through the flesh of her heart, and left a hollow that filled with sadness. Ransom Deverell had his faults— as did they all— but he did not deserve this. Such a vicious attack could never be justified.

"I cannot say it is certain, but from the location

278

and intensity of the pain I would say a putrid effluvium of the lung is likely."

"And what...what can be done?"

He shook his head, eyes closed and lips pursed. "Very little unless the lung rebuilds naturally, which is doubtful, especially if there is a broken rib. His breathing is constricted now, and it will only continue its decline."

Mary thought quickly, searching her mind as if it were a shelf of books, each binding engraved with a memory of something she'd heard or learned. She suddenly remembered reading one of Mr. Speedwell's pamphlets extolling the virtues of pure air therapy administered through an inhalation apparatus. As a voracious reader, Mary devoured any written material at hand, however dry the subject matter, especially if it took her mind off hunger at breakfast. "If he struggles to breathe, doctor, could pure air not be applied to assist? I read that—"

"Oh, I doubt it could do any good in this case."

"But I read of it in one of Mr. Speedwell's medical journals."

He granted her a condescending smile and stopped just short of patting her on the head. "Leeches applied to the area will surely do more good. Tried and true remedies are seldom improved upon, Miss Ashford. It is best to leave these matters to learned men. Do not fill your brain with ideas beyond your understanding. The collection of those booklets is an amusing hobby for Thaddeus Speedwell, but for a young lady like yourself to study them...I fear, it can only be dangerous."

She tried to keep her temper, to steady her thoughts and be practical. To remember that he meant well.

Dr. Woodley advanced a step closer and lowered his voice to a deep, gloomy rumble. "I understand congratulations are in order, Miss Ashford. The gentleman tells me that you and he are to be married."

Mary's heart was beating far too quickly, the tiles under her feet spinning. Her head felt light, empty. Slyly, with both hands, she reached for the ankle of a statue behind her and held it tightly. The coolness against her damp palms was a welcome, soothing relief.

"I cannot imagine how this came to pass, but I wish you every happiness, of course," he went on in the same tone. "I have only myself to blame for being such a foolish old procrastinator."

Forcing herself to pay attention, she blinked and then frowned. "I do not understand what you mean, Dr. Woodley."

"For these past few years I...I had planned to ask you myself, Miss Ashford. Surely you were aware of my interest. Of my growing attachment."

"Oh." Her face felt very hot. She was embarrassed on his behalf and considerably shocked. Violet had often joked about the doctor's interest, but

Mary never took it seriously as a possibility.

"Your blushes concede it to be so. You *were* aware." His lips bent in a tepid smile, but his eyes retained their usual limp, dolorous aspect. "Do not distress yourself, my poor, dear lady, for I will not press upon the matter. It would have been a comfortable match for you, even if I say so myself. A *respectable* match. However, I left it too late to ply my suit, while you waited patiently. The fault is entirely mine. I am a dithering old fool, and I let the chance slip through my fingers. I kept you waiting too long and now, out of desperation, you have resorted to this match. I fear I have wounded us both. Can you forgive me?"

She awoke slowly to the realization that, despite the severity of his patient's health, Dr. Woodley was still talking about himself. Now she could not deny the engagement to Ransom Deverell, or else the doctor might mistake it as a hint that he should make his offer after all.

Let him go now with some pride intact, she decided. Let him imagine that she might have said 'yes', if only he had asked in time.

So Mary released her grip on the marble statue, gave a sad smile and said, "Dr. Woodley, you have been a very good friend and I hope that will not change in the future."

"My dear Miss Ashford!" He clasped her hand and kissed it with more fervor than she had ever seen from him. "I will not turn my back upon you in the dark days to come, although others undoubtedly shall when they learn of this strange choice."

Apparently an engagement to Ransom Deverell was the first step in her descent to hell. After a pause to arrange her thoughts and calm her temper, she replied, "I must ask you to keep this matter a secret for now, Dr. Woodley. You are, in fact, the only person outside this house who knows."

As she walked him to the door, he promised not to speak a word of her engagement to anybody.

"What about the patient's head, doctor?" she asked. "Could he be suffering confusion?"

"He may have had a slight concussion, but he seems to have his wits about him now. Certainly knows where he is and who he is." He sniffed. "Had enough arrogance to give me short shrift."

Taking his bag from the footman, he was about to leave when Mary stopped him.

"But what can be done for his comfort while he heals?" She refused to think that Ransom Deverell might die.

Dr. Woodley paused as he waited for the footman to open the door. "Keep him rested, the head of the bed elevated. I shall send over some laudanum to help with the pain. But in all likelihood rot will set in and the lung will thoroughly flatten, unable to take in air. The tissue will continue the decay once it is begun." He exhaled a gusty sigh.

"Unless, of course, he recovers."

"So in your *learned* opinion," she said with just one stubborn, wiry vine of anger creeping through her voice, "he might die. Or he might live."

He tipped his hat. "Precisely, my dear Miss Ashford. You see the lot you have taken on. I will send the bill to Mr. Deverell, shall I? The sooner the better, I expect." And he walked out into the snow.

She stood for a moment in the silent hall, watching the footman close the front door.

There was one final glimpse of Dr. Woodley pulling up the collar of his coat before he stepped into his carriage and then the outside world was shut out.

It felt significant to her in that moment— the deep thud of that door, keeping her here, in this strange world, while everything else she once knew went on as it always did on the other side.

Here, she had turned onto a new path, to walk in the unpredictable world of the Deverells, where men cursed freely in front of women and spoke to them as if they were equals. Where passionate tempers flared without any attempt to hold them in. Where orgies had been held— according to gossip. Where men declared they were going to marry women they hadn't even asked. And where "Peelers" and the law were not welcome. They dispensed their own justice, it seemed.

Well, she could not turn her back on Ransom

now, could she? Whatever happened, fate had brought him to her and he had asked her to save him. Dr. Woodley called it the "lot" that she had taken on.

He might die, or he might live. But could that not be said of anybody, every single day?

Chapter Eighteen

Smith had bathed him with water from the washbasin, dressed him in a nightgown he didn't even know he possessed and then put him to bed. There he sat, propped up with pillows and bolsters, extra blankets spread over him, curtains drawn to keep out daylight, and the fire lit to chase off any chill. He was meant to be sleeping, but for Ransom it was too quiet.

He hated the quiet.

Where had they all gone?

Earlier, that somber doctor had come and poked him about for five minutes, but all examination had ceased when Ransom told him that he was going to marry Mary. The fellow couldn't get out quickly enough then.

Now they left him alone with only the gentle tap of snow at his window for company.

The pain burned like fire, and sometimes it felt as if the flames touched every part of his body. Other times the blaze decreased to a smolder, glowing ashes dropping from one bone to the next. Breathing was less of a Herculean struggle than it had been when he first regained consciousness, but it was still a challenge.

Feeling very sorry for himself, he was about to throw an ornament at the wall just to make a noise that would bring somebody to his room, when he heard the soft click of a door opening and turned his head to see Mary Ashford's face peeping in.

"About time you came to see me," he exclaimed. "Were you hoping I'd be dead by now?"

Still she hovered by the door. "I merely wanted to be sure you were in bed and resting, before I go home."

"Then come here, woman. I'm not going to eat you. Not today anyway." He managed a little grin, although it hurt. "I haven't the appetite at present."

"I really shouldn't come in."

"Why not? Who's going to tell? Besides, we'll be man and wife soon enough."

From what he could make out of her face in the flickering firelight, her lips had gathered in tight disapproval. It frustrated him that he couldn't see her clearer.

"Oh for pity's sake, Mary, come in and open my curtains. Let in some light from outside before I suffocate. For some reason Smith decided to make the room as dark and stifling as the grave. I need to see some life, even if it's only pigeons."

So she finally came in, leaving the door ajar, to cross his chamber and open the curtains. Snow piled on the ledge outside although it had mostly stopped falling now. He felt instant relief now that he could see daylight. Air. And Mary.

"I hear you were rather difficult with Dr.

Woodley," she said.

"He wanted to poke me about. I wasn't having it."

"He's a doctor. How do you expect him to examine you?"

"That's his conundrum to solve, not mine. Besides, the fellow is my rival for your hand. He might have tried to finish me off."

"Rival! What nonsense you speak."

Framed in that cool, angelic white light as she tied back his curtains, Mary was a tidy, graceful figure, her noble profile the sort that could be very accurately captured in a silhouette. Some women had features that were less well-formed, little smudged noses and chins without character. They were badly formed watercolors compared to his "Contessa", and their profiles would be indistinguishable from any other. But not Mary.

He did not know why she had this hold over him. From the start he'd tried to keep her in his company for as long as he could, in order to uncover all her secrets and get to the root of this fascination. Was it simply because she had resisted him, while other women could not? No, it was something more than that. Something indefinable.

"Why are you going home already?" he muttered, belatedly realizing what she'd said. "You're supposed to be lifting my spirits and sitting here with me. I'll pay you twenty guineas for the service."

"I have an appointment with a dressmaker for my sister, but I will return to visit you later. If I am still needed."

"You are."

"And there is no fee required."

Her movements were quick and efficient, her fingers deftly adjusting the pleats of damask silk where they tumbled to the carpet. She stood a moment, looking out into the street.

"I hope you are pleased with this infernal mischief," she said, her back still turned to him. "How long do you expect to get away with it?"

"I beg your pardon, Mary, to which infernal mischief of mine do you refer?"

She turned, hands clasped before her. "This marriage lark."

He said nothing. In truth, he was surprised she'd gone along with it so far. He'd expected her to deny it vehemently to his father the moment she heard about it. The fact that she hadn't protested, gave him a slender ray of hope. But then, she was always very polite and soft-spoken, even when telling him off.

Head tilted to one side she looked at him. "I thought at first you did not have your wits about you— that you were merely confused. But now I wonder if you meant to sport with your father. He tells me you are fond of tricks and pranks. He is not, however, so easily taken in as you think."

"Is that what you imagine you are to me? A joke?

288

You told me that you know yourself, Mary, and I thought you knew me too. It certainly felt as if you could read me like one of your *beloved books*."

Watching him steadily, she did not reply.

"The truth is, Mary, when I lay in the street, kicked and beaten, I could think only of you and of how I should have known you sooner. I've been given another chance, however long it lasts— one night or two— and I intend to make the most of it."

Her lips parted slightly. Had she been holding her breath? Here he was, struggling for his, while she withheld hers deliberately, rationing herself. Ransom knew that once he recovered he would never take his breath for granted again and every gasp of air he inhaled would be put to good use.

"I should have asked you properly, I suppose. But you weren't there at the time to ask."

For a moment it looked as if she might laugh. Her brows lifted, her eyes glittered, the corners of her beautiful mouth wavered.

"Would you marry me, Mary Ashford? I shan't trouble you long, but I ought to have somebody visit my grave and I'd rather have it be you than anybody else."

* * * *

How long did he have? How long did anybody have? Life was not permanent and circumstances could change in the blink of an eye. She should know.

"Your father is very anxious and concerned about you," she said, changing the subject, moving closer to the bed.

He gave a little snort. "He hides it well."

"That doesn't make it any less genuine."

"My father and I have a difficult association, of a sort that was foisted upon us both against our will," he wheezed. "You would do better to stay out of it."

But if she married him, would she not become a part of his family? A Deverell?

If she married him...*if she married him*...

A half hour ago it stunned her that she was even considering it, but when all was said and done he was just a man in need. And she was a woman with needs.

He was attracted to her and she to him. But to more than the outer surface.

Engagements were often arranged between people who knew less about each other than they did. Look at her and George Stanbury, for instance. She had already spent more time alone in the company of Ransom Deverell than she ever had with George. Probably more time alone with him than most engaged couples spent.

Yes, she could find plenty of reasons to make it seem quite reasonable.

If I had a good woman, Mary Ashford, to put me to rights, I might become a worthier man.

She looked around his room until her gaze stumbled to a sudden halt. On the far wall was one of

290

Uncle Hugo's paintings she had not seen in years—
so many years that she'd forgotten its existence. He
had painted it one summer, dressing her up to look
like a young woman of the Renaissance. "There is an
innocence and purity to you, Mary, and it will not be
there much longer. I should capture it while I can,"
he'd said. "These moments are so fleeting and when
you are older you will forget."

"See." Ransom Deverell winced at her from his
bed. "I told you, didn't I?"

It seemed rather indecent that her portrait had
been hanging on his bedchamber wall all this time.
His father must have purchased it, of course.

"You've been witness to my antics since I moved
in," the patient teased. "Finally you decided to step
out of the frame and put a stop to my wickedness
once and for all."

"That sounds rather brave of me."

"You are brave, Mary. Look how you stood up to
me!"

"I was hungry. I'm very curt when I'm hungry."

He eyed her with gentle bemusement.

Uneasy, she touched her braid again, wishing her
hair was pinned up and tidy.

"Oh, before I forget," he pointed to the
mahogany dresser. "I have something of yours in the
top drawer."

"Mine?"

"Go on. Look." His arm dropped wearily, his

eyes drifting shut.

Mary crossed to the dresser and opened the drawer. There was a small package inside with her name penned upon the paper, the handwriting surprisingly careful and neat.

"I meant to give it to you that evening I had you brought here, but you left in a confounded huff before I could. You may as well have it now."

Cautious, she removed the parcel and unwrapped it. "My mother's brooch! And the silver earrings. But how did you...?"

She couldn't finish, too overcome.

"I saw you on Jermyn Street, the morning you brought me *David Copperfield*. Don't be embarrassed and don't mention another thing about it. From now on if you need money, you come to me and I won't want any of your precious treasures in return. Well..." he chuckled and then flinched, one hand to his side, "not that sort of treasure."

He must have followed her that morning then and seen what she did. At the thought of him chasing her down St James Street and around the corner in the rain, she was astonished and yet very grateful. "You really should not have done all these things for me... the hamper...and the collection of overdue bills...that was all you too, was it not?"

Squirming against the pillows he was reluctant to accept her thanks, brushing it all aside as if it was nothing. "So what is your answer, Mary? Will you save me?"

"Are you going to offer me twenty guineas again?"

"Mary, I would give you anything you want to be the companion of my last hours. I thought I'd made that clear."

"Companion?"

"To sit here with me, read to me, tell me what's going on in the world. Wait with me while I sleep, so that you can wake me if you see me having a nightmare..." He paused then, out of breath for a moment, apparently. She saw genuine fear in his eyes before he could blink it away and continue in a more teasing tone. "The sort of thing you do for my mother. Although I don't need to be told when a bonnet makes me look younger." Impatiently, he gestured her closer. "I know you could never sit at my bedside unless we have a formal arrangement between us. We must think of your impressionable younger sister, of course."

Mary regarded him skeptically. "That is all you want from me?"

"For now it's all I can have, is it not? Once we're properly married and if I improve, naturally, your duties will expand." His eyes had recovered their customary naughty gleam as he followed her progress toward his bed. "But we can address those matters when we come to them. Your sawbones suitor said that in my state I shouldn't get too...agitated. So don't tease me, temptress."

She shook her head as she leaned over to straighten his quilt. "Why would I agree to an engagement with a man like you?"

He thought for a moment and then said somberly, "It is a risk, of course. But on both sides. You'll have to place a bet on me behaving myself, and I'll have to place a bet on whether or not we are compatible in bed, since I'll be marrying a woman of whom I have no..." he wheezed, "previous intimate experience."

Her fingers knitted together, she looked down at him. "Perhaps we should swap wagers. After all, I'd be marrying a man of whom *I* have no intimate knowledge. And you shouldn't be so sure I'd behave myself."

His frown eased, his eyes slowly growing lighter. "Very well, my truculent, persistent wench. What do you want from me?"

"I can agree to an engagement, sir, and we will see what happens. After all, we have known each other for only a short time and your health is more important than thoughts of marriage."

"I'll have to be satisfied with that then. For now. I suppose you hesitate because I may *not* recover the strength to service you physically and you want your chance to wriggle out of it, should I fall short in the breeches."

"Nothing could be further from my mind," she

exclaimed. "I meant only that your recovery is a priority and, after that, we can talk of the future. Whatever it holds for both of us." Aware of the fact that he did not make promises, she did not want him to feel cornered.

"Well, I can't imagine what else there is to think about. It's on *my* mind most of the time."

"What is?"

"Taking you to bed." Catching his breath, he managed a pained grin that was oddly endearing. "You might as well know that, if you mean to marry me."

"I appreciate the warning, but I'm sure I shall endure. If you will." Without thinking she reached over and swept a dark lock of hair back from his bandaged brow. He closed his eyes and opened them again, staring heatedly.

Oh, what had she done? Had she just said 'yes'?

Suddenly she thought of her sister. How would she tell Violet? How did one broach such a subject? Would it show all over her face immediately?

She had resisted dinner with the rogue, and now she had agreed to an engagement. Perhaps *she* was the one with concussion.

Warm fingers tangled with hers, drawing her hand to his chest. "I think you'd better kiss me," he said. "And make our agreement binding. Just don't bite me this time."

She looked at his bruised, scraped and swollen

face, all his good looks gone. Never had he been more handsome in her eyes.

Carefully she bent over and delivered a shy kiss to the corner of his mouth, not wanting to hurt.

There was no sound in the room suddenly but the beat of her own heart.

* * * *

The last time he thought he was at the gates of hell, he had been angry, full of spit and fire, but this time was different. He was not that same foolish young man anymore, of course. Six years had passed since then and he had, against all expectations, matured.

Now he was engaged. Ransom Deverell, the Determined Malefactor, the man who said he'd never marry, had allowed this woman to take up residency on his moor. In a matter of weeks, she had caused him to act like a love-sick fool, yet she claimed not to know how it was done.

Suddenly the door flew wide open and Damon strode in, already shouting, "What the devil did you say to Elizabeth? You sent her away, didn't you? You put her off and told her to leave me! How dare you interfere?"

Smith followed close behind, looking apologetic. "Sir, your brother would not—"

"Why are you hiding up here?" Damon halted, stared. "Good God!"

Ransom felt his wounds burning again as he saw his brother's appalled expression. Yes, he must be a sight. He'd resisted looking in any mirrors. Didn't need to.

"What the hell happened to you?"

"Somebody seems to have taken a severe dislike to me," he replied. "But that's no reason for you to race up my stairs and into my room as if the place is on fire."

Damon looked at Mary, who still stood by his bed. Ransom reached for her hand again and held it.

"This is my fiancée, Miss Mary Ashford." A strange whisper of something new swept through him when he said it. He wrapped his fingers tighter around hers.

"Who? What?" his brother scoffed. "Since when?"

"Since now."

Damon's eyes flared with anger. "Well, how nice for you. I'm glad that your affairs are all in order. What about mine? I should never have entrusted them to you, should I?"

"You refer to Elizabeth?" Flames shot through his lung and he strained to get the words out.

"She's gone. Left London. I've been searching for days. Finally I received her short letter telling me that if I wanted to know why she left, I should ask you. So what the deuce did you tell her? I suppose you paid her off, is that it?"

Behind Damon their father had just entered the room, but he moved so stealthily that the younger brother didn't know it. Ransom did his best to cut the conversation short. "Let's talk of this matter another time. I think we—"

"No! I want to know what you said or did to send her away on that Friday evening when she came to see you. Elizabeth is carrying my child, and I intend to make a life for us together, whatever you think and whatever father has to say about it!"

Chapter Nineteen

"Good morning, Damon. I thought I heard your voice in the hall."

The young man froze, wide eyed.

For a moment nobody spoke. Ransom sagged against his pillows, still holding Mary's hand. The wind picked up, blowing snow at the window and dancing with the flames in the fireplace. Mary, he noted, seemed to be holding her breath again. He stole a quick glance at her face and saw she was paler than usual, very somber.

Finally Damon turned to greet their father, his face red. "I...did not know you were here in London."

"No. Clearly."

Another silence.

Their father walked up to the fire and stood with his back to it, warming his seat. "I believe Miss Ashford said she has another appointment today, so perhaps it is time we let her go. We shouldn't keep her longer than necessary." He gave Mary a stiff smile. She quickly released Ransom's hand, muttered a promise to return later, and hurried out.

As soon as the door was closed and they heard her quick step descending the stairs, their father sighed deeply and said, "So who wants to tell me about this woman who is carrying Damon's child and why I have not been consulted in the matter?"

* * * *

Her heart was thumping like a rabbit's foot when alerted to danger. Elizabeth— she had no doubt they talked of Lady Elizabeth Stanbury— was pregnant with Damon Deverell's child? That must be the Elizabeth about whom Damon accused his brother of interfering. Unless Ransom made a habit of meeting women called Elizabeth on Friday evenings. Besides, he had told her that the woman she saw at his house was one of "his brother's problems" and not one of his own. He spoke truthfully then, she thought with relief.

Oh, but she should not know about this. It was a wretched business and a very private matter.

Did George know?

Proud, haughty, conceited Elizabeth! It seemed unbelievable. The Stanburys were such a rigid, conventional family. Bloodline was everything to them. Pedigree *and* money, of course. And Damon was ten years her junior at least.

Surely it couldn't be true.

The butler met her in the hall with her coat and the bonnet she'd left behind on Friday.

"Mr. Deverell the elder insists that you take his carriage, Miss."

"Oh, I couldn't!" Her sister would certainly have questions if she returned in that luxurious splendor.

"He *insists*, Miss. And he says you are to keep it

all day for your errands. He has no need to go out in it anymore today and will stay inside to watch over his son." He paused, looked at her gravely and repeated, "He *insists*, Miss."

She could hear raised voices coming from the room above now, although the words were muffled.

The butler leaned toward her and added, "It is not wise to get Mr. Deverell the elder in a temper, Miss."

"No. I suppose not."

A comfortable carriage ride did sound very nice, especially with the streets in such a mess, and she was tired, wilting, her nerves stretched to their limit by the events of the morning.

"If you don't mind me saying, Miss, you may as well get used to it. If you plan to become a Deverell."

Yes, he was right. People would know sooner or later. Mary would have to get accustomed to questions and curious looks again, to people making assumptions about her. They would all think she'd married for the money, of course. The servants in his house must already be discussing it.

She would no longer be a peripheral player on the stage; she was about to take on a more prominent role.

Was she prepared for it?

Oops. Something hard had just hit the wall upstairs. Sounded like a body. She hoped her portrait would survive.

Time, perhaps, to be as brave as Ransom thought she was.

* * * *

When Damon was gone again— in just as high dudgeon as he first arrived— their father stayed in the bedchamber, sweating and furious.

"A few years ago a doctor told me my heart was giving out," he sputtered, tugging on his cravat until it was loosened. "Told me I only had six months or a year to live. I didn't care to believe it then and I don't now. But the lot of you will surely put me in my grave before too long."

Ransom said nothing. His father's temper would rage until it burned itself out, and there was nothing anybody else could do about it in the meantime. Not if they valued their own skin.

"I thought Damon was the *clever* one. I thought he would make the most of his talents and not become distracted." These, at least, were two sentences one could understand, for they were not peppered with various, wildly colorful curses that succeeded in obstructing the English language until it became something else entirely.

"Well, she's gone now, sir, so he can get on with his life, can't he?"

"You know he won't! He didn't believe you when you told him she left London of her own accord. He'll go after her."

Ransom groaned softly. "Yes, but he won't find her."

"Why not? You told him where she'd gone."

"Yes, but I told him she'd gone to Yorkshire."

"And?"

"She's gone to Kent. Other end of the country." He grimaced. "Damon isn't the only one with a brain, sir, even if he is the only one you expect to use his for good." Closing his eyes, he added, "Fret not, the golden boy will recover from this setback. We Deverells are resilient. Like weeds that cannot be eradicated. Isn't that what you like to say?"

He heard his father moving around the room, but nothing was said for a while. There was the clank of an iron poker, the shuffle of coals being stirred up, the squeak of a chair being moved. Finally his father exhaled a gusty sigh.

Ransom opened his eyes. "Still here?" He half expected his father to run out after Damon, but instead he was sitting beside the fire, staring at the flames.

True cleared his throat. "I hope you have not leapt into this marriage idea as recklessly as you leap into most schemes. Miss Ashford appears to be a kind, well-meaning young woman, and she does not deserve her heart broken."

"How can her heart be broken? She's not in love with me. I don't expect her to be. Good lord, there is nothing lovable about me. But I need her. She sees me exactly as I am and yet she is neither afraid nor completely repulsed. It makes me feel as if I could take on the world and possibly win."

"It's purely selfish then, as I thought."

"Not entirely. I can give her some help. I'd like to provide her some business guidance, for instance."

"She's a businesswoman?"

"She has a bookshop, sir."

His father looked askance. "How the devil did you meet her then? She said she is a friend of Raven's, but I assume your sister kept her well away from you. She's not one to share."

"Quite. In typical Raven fashion she wanted to keep Mary all to herself. But I happened upon her by chance and she has not been out of my mind since. So now she'll belong to me and Raven can bloody well put up with it."

His father looked at him sternly. "She's not a toy or a pony."

He would have laughed if it didn't hurt so much. "I know that."

"Are you in love with her?"

"Love? Damn and blast I hope not. That would be dashed inconvenient all around."

His father nodded thoughtfully, then got up and strode to the window, where he stood with both hands behind his back.

"Is that why you began your memoirs, sir?"

"Hmm?"

"Because a doctor told you that your heart is giving out? That you are dying?"

"That was one reason." He gave a loose shrug. "Let's see...it must be eight years ago now when I was given that prognosis. That was when Olivia came to Roscarrock to work as my secretary and help with the memoirs. I hired her for six months. I didn't think it would take that long. But she never left, of course." He smirked, placing a hand to the front of his waistcoat. "My heart started beating with renewed vigor, thanks to Olivia."

"And your memoirs are still not complete."

"How can they be? I'm still living them."

Ransom watched his father's profile in the cool light from outside. "You never told me about that—your heart and what the doctors said."

"I never told anybody. Not even Olivia."

"Why tell me then, sir?"

True turned to look at him. "I wanted you to see how wrong those so-called 'men of medicine' can be." He stretched out his arms. "*I'm* still here, aren't I?"

His father was actually trying to give him hope. For the first time in his life he felt as if his father was on his side. Perhaps even that he cared. A little.

* * * *

Mary scoured the piles of paper on the dresser shelves, searching urgently.

"What is it that you seek, Mary my dear?" Mr.

Speedwell shuffled over to help.

She explained about Ransom Deverell's injured lung and how she wondered if the application of pure air might help.

"You mean *oxygen*, my dear." He looked at her over his spectacles. "That is what they call it now." Proudly he added, "I have some experience of it myself. As a boy I was taken to the Pneumatic Institute in Bristol for treatments to fight the asthma I suffered."

"And was it effective?"

"Indeed. It was rather grim for a little boy who would rather go to the seaside to get his air, but it was effective in improving my condition. I daresay it was that experience which first began my interest in medical science. I might have become a physician myself, if my papa had not seen any future in it and viewed the profession as little more than witchcraft." He chuckled.

Mary prodded his attention back to the matter at hand. "But does this Pneumatic Institute still stand?"

"I think not, my dear. Not as it was then. As far as I recall, it was made over into a hospital at the turn of the century to help accommodate the sufferers of a typhus outbreak. I never went there again once my school days were over." He shook his head. "Fifty years ago. How time dashes by."

Again her heart sank. "There must be somebody here in London who can help. We have a great many doctors and scientists who are customers, do we not?"

"Dr. Woodley was not helpful?"

"I think he was not much in the mood to assist, although he met with considerable resistance from the patient in this case, so I cannot blame him completely."

Thaddeus bent his head to look at her over his spectacles again. "The good doctor is, it must be said, somewhat stuck in his ways."

"I have noticed," she replied grimly.

"And you are very concerned about this young man with the injured lung."

She swallowed. "I am. Perhaps you will understand, if I tell you that he is the gentleman who arranged for all our debtors to come forward and clear their accounts. He is also the benefactor who provided that splendid hamper of Yuletide cheer."

"Ah." His misty eyes grew large and round. "Then we must do what we can for him in return."

Violet came down the staircase, carrying her precious new material— well wrapped against the elements in paper and canvas. "Do let's hurry, or we'll be late for the dressmaker."

There was no more time to discuss Ransom's predicament with Mr. Speedwell at present, but he put a kindly hand on her arm and gave her such a reassuring look that she felt quite tearful again. Without a word more being said, she trusted in his help.

Meanwhile, Violet had stopped sharply in the door of the shop when she saw the carriage waiting.

Mary thought quickly. "Lady Charlotte sent the barouche box for us."

"Gracious! How kind of her. It is very grand, is it not?" Violet bounced gleefully as snowflakes gathered on the brim of her bonnet. "People are sure to stare as we pass."

"Undoubtedly," she replied glumly. Why did she lie? Because having to explain everything to Violet at that moment was beyond her. Almost anything was beyond her, when she could think only of Ransom and his condition. It was as she felt every breath he struggled over. Her own lungs were constricted in empathy and she was in no frame of mind for frivolous shopping. But, having promised her sister a new gown, she could not let her down.

Violet was jolly, of course, knowing nothing of Mary's inner distress. "I shall pretend to be royalty and wave."

"Just step up into the carriage, *Violette*. I thought you were concerned about being late?"

Her sister climbed up and arranged herself on the luxurious padded-leather seat. "You never said Lady Charlotte is so kind a friend. I must say, Mary, I was very surprised. From everything you and Raven ever said I thought she would be older and sharp-tempered. I was quite afraid of her at first. But she is positively delightful."

"You're fortunate, Violet. She took a liking to you— as she does to shiny, decorative things."

And what would Lady Charlotte have to say when she learned that Mary had accepted her son's proposal of marriage? It may never come to pass, of course. This might all be a moment of madness in his mind. But she had accepted him.

Perhaps *she* was the mad one.

Lady Charlotte had once talked of her hopes that Ransom would, eventually, make a "good" marriage.

"After all," she'd remarked while flicking through the pages of a magazine, "my son is, *financially*, most eligible. And has the looks to completely disarm most women."

"You must worry that he could become prey for fortune-hunters," Mary had replied.

"Fortune-hunters?" the lady had laughed, tossing her magazine aside. "My poor, naive Mary, everybody hunts fortune. Both women *and* men. It is the way of the world."

So now she would, inevitably, think Mary a fortune-hunter. As would the rest of society. Lady Charlotte might consider it commonplace, accepted behavior to hunt a man purely for his money, but that was not normal or acceptable to Mary.

She did not care what most of the world thought of her. Just as she'd said to Ransom, she knew herself— felt confident in her choices— and whatever opinion anybody else formed about her was their problem, not hers. But she knew now that she *did* care what Ransom and his family thought of her, most especially what they would think about her reasons for marrying him.

The horses were soon pulling them swiftly across town through the snow and she stared out at the jumble of passing houses, amazed that everything looked much the same as usual. The world ought to look vastly different, surely, after all that had happened that day.

"Where were you all morning, anyway?" Violet asked suddenly. "You still haven't told me."

"There is no time for that now. It is a story of some length, and I'm not much inclined to tell it." Although Mary knew she would have to tell her sister about Ransom soon, she didn't think it wise to let Violet know before Lady Charlotte did.

How to even begin the subject was causing Mary increasing levels of consternation, particularly as Violet did not even know she had ever encountered Ransom Deverell and thought her destined to end her days an old maid, sitting on the dusty shelf with Mr. Speedwell's medical journals.

When they arrived at the dressmaker, they were both startled to find Lady Charlotte waiting for them already. Violet was openly delighted, while Mary's surprise took on a quieter, more anxious tenor. On such a cold, snowy day, the lady seldom slithered out of her suite or far from her fire. Either she had heard some gossip she wanted to investigate, or she was bored.

Fortunately, it turned out to be the latter case.

"I must share my expertise in the design of this dress for you, Violette. Did you think I could leave it all in the hands of a dressmaker with nobody but Mary here to offer her opinion?"

It was apparent that Lady Charlotte still had not heard about the attack on her son. This vexed Mary greatly. Surely the lady had a right to know that he was ill— perhaps would not recover. Yet Ransom had said he didn't want her at the house and his father must have made no effort to get word to her.

Mary felt torn. Having never known anybody else who was divorced, and after hearing many times from Raven about her parents' animosity, she was exceedingly cautious. But there remained the matter of a mother and her son. Mary knew what it was to lose loved ones, of course, and to wish she could have done more, said more, while she still had them. She wanted, desperately, to take the right course, for the good of everybody.

For so long she had been on the perimeter of this family— through her relationship with Raven Deverell— and she felt herself invested in them. Was it because she had so little of her own family left now?

Obviously in the way in that small room, Mary

tucked herself into a chair in the corner, with a book, and tried to read while the discussion about sleeves, pleats and waistlines proceeded. Occasionally her sister called her name to ask what she thought of a frill or a flounce, but only to laugh at Mary's vexed expression— not to actually want her opinion.

"You fight a losing battle in dour Mary's case," said Lady Charlotte, waving a limp hand toward her. "She would not know a gigot sleeve from an *engageante*."

And indeed she did not.

But she was going to marry Ransom Deverell.

If he lived. *Oh, let him live, please!*

"Poor Mary, look at her expression! She is quite hopeless."

They both laughed smugly together, while pretending to feel pity.

Again she looked at her book, but Mary could not concentrate on the printed words.

After a while, Lady Charlotte said, "You are quieter than ever this afternoon, Mary. Are you ill? Your complexion generally has that common swarthy tint, but today there is a ghostly pallor."

"Oh, no, your ladyship. I am very well."

She loved her sister, but with Ransom's health on her mind it was very difficult to show any interest in something as frivolous as a new frock.

At last she could hold it in no longer, and while Violet was being measured in another room, she said to Lady Charlotte, "Have you had word from your son of late, madam?"

"Ransom? Not since last week. As I told you, he never bothers with me until he has to." Her eyes narrowed. "Why do you ask?"

"I wondered, your ladyship...if you had heard...anything. About an accident." Now that she had begun, it was harder than expected, rather than easier.

The woman's eyes were almost black; her eye-lids looked heavy. "To what do you refer?"

"I'm afraid your son had an accident, madam."

"Yes. A few years ago. What about it?"

"No, madam. I meant recently. Very recently. Friday evening to be exact." She took a breath. "I am sorry."

Lady Charlotte raised a hand to her pearl choker. "Sorry?"

"You must forgive me, your ladyship," she exclaimed in a distraught whisper, "but I have struggled with how best to tell you. It has preyed upon me all day and I think that you, as his mother, have a right to know. He was set upon by thugs in the street."

"But I— Friday? And why was I not told until now?"

"I suppose he did not want you to worry." Yes, that sounded tactful enough. "And his father is with him. I have sat here not knowing how to give you this news without alarming you unduly, or over-stepping my bounds, but I would feel dreadful, madam, if you were left in ignorance and... especially later, when you discovered that I had known and kept it from you. Oh, dear." The book almost dropped from her fingers. "I hope I have done right in telling you. That he won't be angry."

"He?"

"Your son." She gripped the book tighter, holding it against her breast.

For several moments, Lady Charlotte simply stared at her, one hand still touching the beads of her necklace, her lips working as if she chewed something that already disagreed with her stomach.

Mary wanted to say so much more, but held it back, unsure how to continue until she had some verbal reaction from the lady.

Finally..."His father is there with him, you say?"

"Yes, madam."

"Then it has been kept from me by *him*. My wretched husband." Her eyes sparked with anger and then she focused on Mary again. "But would you mind telling me how, exactly, you knew of this *accident*, Miss Mary Ashford, and I did not?"

The edge of the book cover was digging into her fingers. "I am engaged to be married, Lady Charlotte. To your son."

Again she heard her heart beating, fluttering wildly. It had to be said and at least she had more tact

314

than Ransom who may not even tell his mother. But how odd it sounded on her lips.

"*You?*" A harsh gasp spat from the lady— almost a laugh, but not quite. "Is this one of Ransom's practical jokes? He talked you into teasing me, did he not?"

She licked her lips. "No, madam. I am quite in earnest. I would not tease you about such a matter."

Lady Charlotte smoothed a hand over the lace ruffle at her shoulder and then inspected the stitching of her calf-skin gloves. "I should have guessed there was something between you. That day when he came back to the suite. You, Miss Mary Ashford, are not nearly so meek as you seem and have been scheming, sneaking about behind my back."

Now she worried that she had spoiled things for Violet, and her sister would never forgive her. "I certainly have not, madam. It only happened this morning."

The lady fluttered her lashes and gave a high, odd laugh that was more of a rattle, like the sharp ring of a bell clapper, snapped off impatiently by the same hand that rang it. "Don't look so distressed, Mary. I didn't think you had it in you to be sly and mercenary. I must admit I'm impressed. I underestimated you, it seems. But this won't last, of course. You're a plaything. Different to most, perhaps, but...ah, wait! I suppose he did this to take you away from Raven. They've always been so competitive. Well, he alters his mind as often as the wind changes direction, so I would advise you to look about before you think to give your heart." She swallowed, blinked, looked as if she might faint. "And I wish someone had warned me the same way, before I—"

The door opened and Violet returned with the dressmaker's assistants. "What happened? What have you both been talking about? Mary looks peculiar."

Silence.

Lady Charlotte stood, recovering her poise with admirable alacrity. She looked down at Mary. "He won't love you, you know. They aren't capable. He's just like his father."

Mary stood too, remembering her Ashford Pride. "Mr. Deverell says that Ransom is just like his mother," she replied in a light, carefree tone.

Rather than meet Mary's eye, the other woman attempted to gain a few inches in height by raising her chin and one elegant eyebrow. "Then he is the worst of both of us. Surely a creature to be pitied, or feared. But not loved."

Violet was still utterly lost, and the dressmaker's assistants were pretending not to hear.

Suddenly feeling quite calm again, Mary said, "Will you come back to the house and see your son?"

"No. I don't believe I shall. Let him send for me, if I am needed. Apparently, for now, I am not." Her lips moved uncertainly, the corners pulling downward. There was something shining in her left eye, but surely it was not a real tear. Mary had heard many complaints and sobbing groans from Lady Charlotte in the past, but she had never seen a genuine, wet tear. It was not the done thing, of course, to show too much emotion. Mary had been raised the same way and struggled often to remind her sister that one's passions should be held out of sight. But Lady Charlotte loved her dramatics, much as "Violette" did. It was simply that her ladyship's were usually empty gestures, extravagant, showy and entirely without depth of feeling. She could change from wailing depression at a rainy day to unbridled, girlish joy at a gift from an admirer, all in the space of two minutes. Often one felt the need to applaud this display and toss flowers at her feet.

The hint of an actual tear, therefore, was new, unexpected. Rare as a blue diamond.

Lady Charlotte swung around to speak with the dressmaker who had just re-entered the room with her book of notes, and the conversation about dresses resumed as if it had never been interrupted. But her expression was fixed, her eyes glassy. Mary had seen that look before on a horse that was about to drop dead in the shafts.

At least it seemed as if Violet would not suffer. Lady Charlotte remained civil to her, graciously extending one hand to her new "protégée" to kiss. "I shall look forward to seeing the dress when it is complete." To Mary she nodded her head slowly and grandly. "I will see you on our usual day, Miss Ashford."

She was back to herself again. As the lady had said, she did not expect her son's engagement to last, so why would anything change?

"You are sure you will not come to your son?" Mary asked her again, hoping the lady would reconsider and avoid any later regret.

But her countenance was a mask now. "Good heavens, Mary, don't whittle at me! What can *I* do for him? The sick-bed is not my province. Better I see him when he is put together again. I doubt he would want guests while in an unsightly state."

Well, Mary had done her best.

"Then Lady Charlotte did not loan us the carriage?" Violet enquired as Mary helped her into her coat. "I thought you said she did."

"No, sister. I told you a bold-faced lie. The carriage belongs to True Deverell."

Violet's eyes had almost sprung out of her head. "But you never lie." Her ringlets trembled.

"I have done several things today that I never did before." Mary took her arm and hurried her out of the dressmaker's premises. "Prepare yourself, sister, for some news." Violet would have to be told, since Mary planned to spend the evening looking after him and it would not be proper under any other circumstances. "I am engaged to Lady Charlotte's son, Ransom Deverell." It did not sound any more likely this time she said it.

"You? Engaged? But how?" It was too much for poor Violet, who stopped, dug in her heels and could not be steered forward. "When?"

"In actual fact he decided it without me. Because I wasn't there at the time to ask."

Violet gripped the carriage door for balance as Mary prodded her speedily up into the carriage. Finally, when the door was closed and the blind lowered for privacy, the carriage moving forward again, all Violet could find to say was, "But if you married anybody, I thought it would be Dr. Woodley."

Sighing heavily, Mary lifted one corner of the blind to peep out. "Luckily for me, the good doctor's gentlemanly manners and reserve kept him from asking in time. Ransom Deverell had no such issues."

Chapter Twenty

The cool, damp cloth swept softly across his brow, down the side of his face and under his chin. Through his lashes he watched the flickering light as her hand moved back and forth, guiding the cloth slowly, gently, chasing away the sticky sweat and the pain.

A drop of water trickled down his cheek, and she caught it with the cloth at the edge of his jaw. Her hand slipped a little, for her finger touched his face and the prickles on his chin must have tickled her. He heard the catch of her breath, like half a hiccup.

Ransom opened his eyes, just in time to see the tip of her tongue slip back from where it had wet her lower lip in concentration. Her pupils were large, velvety black, darkening her gaze until it could be described as sultry, steamy.

After rinsing the cloth in her bowl of water, she raised it once more, dabbing it lightly down the side of his neck. Her sleeves were unbuttoned at the cuff and turned back to keep them out of the water, which gave Ransom an extra few inches of bare arm to admire. Again her fingertips touched his skin, caressing him accidentally, and he suffered the stirring of an intense hunger that had nothing to do with his stomach's needs.

Here he was, dying to breathe, and all he could

think about was holding her in his arms, touching the naked, satiny skin of her back, following the curve downward and rolling her beneath him...kissing that little soft place beneath her ear...licking the sweet, perfumed sheen of perspiration from her skin. Hearing her sigh his name.

Now she wiped the base of his throat, tenderly stroking with that warm, slippery cloth. And he felt her soft, slender wrist moving against the chest hair that curled above the open laces of his nightshirt.

He was having trouble breathing before. If he didn't stop her now, he would forget *how* to breathe.

Reluctantly he raised a hand to his chest and closed his fingers over hers. "Thank you," he managed, his voice taut as a bow about to release its arrow. "That's better."

Mary put her bowl aside and now applied some ointment to his scars and bruises, before wrapping a fresh bandage around his forehead. All this was done without a word from her, so he had no idea what she was thinking or feeling. He'd never known a woman like her.

"Why do you not want to sleep?" she asked.

"If you had dreams like mine, Mary, you wouldn't want to sleep either."

"Tell me about them, then."

"No."

Lips pursed, hands on her waist, she shook her head.

Afraid she might find another excuse to leave, he asked her to continue reading, so she sat in a chair beside the bed and opened her book. As she read aloud, he closed his eyes. Each time she stopped reading, he opened them again and urged her to continue.

"You ought to sleep," she urged again.

"No, thank you, madam. It is a kind thought, but I prefer to keep my wits about me," he replied, aware that he was being oddly polite, but not able to do anything about it. The laudanum did make him sleepy, but he refused to give in just yet. Defiantly he thought he could fight the medicine, much as he once planned to fight Nanny Bond.

But no, he would not think of that harridan tonight. Or of Sally White. They could not get him while Mary sat by his bed.

"You will stay, won't you?"

She gave a wry smile. "Since you told your father that you wouldn't have anybody else, I'll have to, shan't I? I could hardly leave you alone to suffer."

The pain had eased somewhat. Thankfully. "Good." Finally she took pity on him.

He watched her lips move as she read from the book in her lap. The gaslight cast her face in a warm glow, like that of a peach hanging from a tree, not yet ripe enough to be plucked, but soon to be. How lovely she was in her quiet way. Understated, unassuming, and yet not to be missed. Hers was a face that made a man look twice and then a third time. And then he could not stop looking.

It was not the sort of cream-and-roses beauty, instantly recognizable, and used to sell face tonic to the masses. It was timeless, unique, indefinable. He felt as if it was his alone now.

"Where did you go without me, Mary?"

She looked up from her book again. "To the dressmaker with my sister. I told you."

But he meant forever. Where had she been without him for all this time? Where did she go when he had not been there?

His head felt as if it was swaddled in a very soft fleece, and all manner of thoughts wandered through his mind.

"Tell me about your sister."

"I thought you wanted me to read to you."

"I warned you my attention is easily scattered. Now I want to talk." Actually, he feared the gentle lull of her reading voice would put him to sleep too soon. "You said we would not have anything to talk about, but we do."

Placing a bookmark carefully in the page, she closed her book and set it aside. "Violet is very pretty, very young, and very restless."

"You love her."

"Of course. Will you have some water?" She got up and reached for a glass and the jug. He watched her pour.

"I don't love *my* sister," he muttered. "She's a bloody pain in the posterior."

Mary smiled and held the glass, while he sipped. Ah, better. "You love your sister, and she loves you, whether you like it or not. It is the drawback of being family, I fear. The love is inevitable, even if they drive you to madness sometimes. One must accept that many of their faults are also yours."

"My father would disagree with you. He says it's just instinct to protect one's family. Not love. We're all just animals. Surviving."

She held the glass up again, and he took another sip. "Is that so?"

"To help a stranger one needs a motive. Usually mercenary. Wanting something for one's own good."

"Yes," she replied briskly, "I suppose that's all it is." And she set the glass firmly back on the small bedside table, her lips pressed tightly together, the smile gone.

Wanting to make her laugh again, he said suddenly, "Do you know, Mary, I believe you must be the only maiden that ever entered this bedchamber."

She threw him a look over her shoulder. "And I'm certain to be the only one who will leave it in the same state as she came in."

More's the pity, he thought, silently cursing his injuries.

A tap at the door announced the arrival of Smith, who brought a letter. "Pardon me, Miss Ashford, but this just arrived here for you."

Ransom scowled. "Who the devil is it from? Who would write to you here?"

His private nurse primly ignored him to accept the letter and thank Smith. She opened the seal and read quickly. Whatever the news was, it cheered her up again.

"Well?" Ransom demanded. "Who is writing to my fiancée?"

"Mr. Thaddeus Speedwell."

"*Who?*"

Mary refolded the letter. "My business partner at the bookshop. Don't you remember?"

"What the deuce does he want? Does he not know you're busy here with me, damn it? I must have all your attention."

She merely raised her eyes to the ceiling and then shared a quick smile with Smith. The butler, realizing he'd been caught, hastily straightened his lips and then said solemnly, "Sir, I have made up the Chinese bedroom for Mr. Deverell. He informs me that he means to stay."

"It's not necessary. I'm sure he has other things he would rather be doing. Besides, it's Christmas next week, and he should be at Roscarrock with the others."

He heard Mary gasp.

"What?" he demanded, turning his head against the pillow to look at her. "It's only me. No need for the world to stop just because I might die. As long as I have you, I'm content."

She stared in mild disapproval and impatience, just like her portrait on the far wall.

Smith spoke again, "Mr. Deverell is quite certain that he wants to stay, sir. And he says you will need his help overseeing matters at the club while you are indisposed."

"My father must do as he thinks best then. Yes, I suppose he is concerned about the business most of all."

"Very good, sir." Smith hesitated and then added, "When the young Indian lady arrives on Wednesday for your standing appointment, may I take it that she is to be kept separate from your father? And if young Master Rush should call in with one of his letters from the university again?"

Ransom knew Mary was listening, although she pretended to be utterly absorbed in folding a blanket at the foot of the bed.

"Yes." He pressed his head back against the pillow, feeling very tired. "The Indian lady will be here at nine on Wednesday as usual. There is money for her in the desk drawer in my father's study. Top right. And some in my boots, over there, by the fire. But you are quite correct— my father mustn't know about her. For pity's sake keep her out of his sight, will you? And if anything happens to me, you must get word to Captain Justify Deverell, wherever his ship might be."

"Very good, sir."

"As for Rush, if he needs another letter of complaint about his behavior signed off on, put it aside until I can sign it. Best not worry my father on that score either. For now."

"Indeed." Smith turned to Mary and asked whether she required anything, but she replied that she was quite content. The butler bowed and left them alone again.

Ransom waited for her to question him about the Indian lady. Nothing. She moved around his bed, adjusting quilts and blankets, and then returned to her chair. "Are you sure I cannot tempt you to try more of the broth?" she asked.

Earlier she had managed to get him to eat a little, but he was too nauseous for much food and the broth Mrs. Clay had made mostly remained in the bowl.

Finally he prompted, "You must be curious about my Indian lady visitor."

She sighed and smoothed both hands over her lap. "Not particularly."

"You must promise not to mention it to my father."

Her hands stilled, her gaze returned to his face. "Why?"

"She's my brother's wife. But nobody else knows. Justify is planning the perfect moment to share his news. In the meantime, he is at sea, and I am given the task of keeping her safe and provided for, until he returns."

"Why should your father not know? Surely he must, sooner or later."

He groaned sleepily. "You're right, of course, sensible Mary. I wish the folk in my family had your common sense. In any case, she'll be here at nine on Wednesday, if you would like to meet her. Not that she speaks more than a word or two of English. I promised Justify that I would keep his secret, just as I promised Damon to keep his."

"And Rush. He is the youngest of Lady Charlotte's children, is he not? She has mentioned him sometimes. I understand he refuses to visit her."

"In many ways Rush was lucky, for our parents were living apart before he was even born, so he never suffered the worst of the fights, as Raven and I did. It does not seem to have done him much benefit though. He spends a vast deal of his time in one trouble or another."

She tilted her head. "A family trait?"

He smiled, but it was interrupted by a yawn.

Suddenly she reached over and took his hand. "Don't worry about that now. Don't worry about any of that. You must rest." Her thumb moved against his palm, shyly at first, then gaining confidence.

Just like that he forgot it all.

* * * *

At last he seemed to be sleeping. Mary could not move her hand for fear of waking him and seeing those eyes open again. So she sat very still, only her thumb gently stroking his warm palm.

It occurred to her that she had never touched a man's gloveless hand unless he was her father, her uncle, or one of her brothers. At balls, of course, men wore white gloves, as did she. George Stanbury's bare hand had never touched any part of her. He would not have dared try with her brothers always nearby, always in the same room.

Ransom Deverell's hands were infamous for having shot at his father, seduced many women, dealt many winning cards. His knuckles were broad, scabbed and torn, his nails square, not well cared for. No surprise there considering the fight he'd been in.

Three or four leaping upon one man. Thugs. It made her furious.

She thought of everything she had just learned— about how he looked after his brothers. He took on their problems, better than he took on his own. He had even taken on hers.

Yet people called him wicked names, thought him heartless, a man without a conscience.

Ransom's forearm stretched over the quilt, muscular, covered with dark hair the same as his chest. His wrist was strong, thick. Beside hers it looked enormous, and blood still pulsed through it. Mary was determined to keep that blood pumping and all his parts working as they should.

She glanced over at the letter from Thaddeus Speedwell and smiled.

Dr. Woodley could study his ancient manuscripts, keep his leeches, and cling to his old-fashioned ways, manners, and ideas, if that made him comfortable. Like her father. But Mary was a modern woman, forward-thinking. And she was willing to try anything for the ones she loved. No more opportunities would pass her by.

Her gaze returned to the sleeping man — the one she wanted to save, the one who assumed she was there for mercenary reasons.

His eyelids fluttered but did not open, his lashes, dark, fluttering, crescent shadows on his cheeks.

Must be dreaming.

"Sally," he murmured. "*Sally!*"

Sweat broke across his chest, dampening his nightshirt. With her free hand she reached for the washrag again and cooled his face.

Sally? Was that another woman in his life, one he had yet to send on her way?

Clearly, whoever she was, she meant a lot to him. But there was something sinister in his voice.

His body tensed, his fingers rigidly gripping hers. "Sally!"

Mary leaned over and kissed his brow.

He whimpered.

Gently she kissed each eyelid.

His fingers loosened their grasp.

She kissed his lips, and they parted to exhale a light snore.

At last his face was peaceful, his body sunk into the bed with greater ease.

The door opened, and his father came in. Mary hastily straightened her spine and pretended to check Ransom's temperature with one hand to his brow.

"How is the patient?" True Deverell crossed quickly to the bed, although he came no closer than the chaise at the foot of it.

"Suffering bad dreams, I fear. But I think it has passed."

"You ought to take some rest, Miss Ashford. You've been at his side all evening."

"I wouldn't like to leave, sir. What if he wakes? He was very adamant that I stay."

"I'm sure he was. Spoiled boy." He shook his head. "But you can sit a while, eh?" Deverell motioned for her to join him by the fire in one of the chairs that stood on either side of the small hearth.

"I'm glad you came up, sir, as I wanted to tell you that I saw Lady Charlotte this afternoon at the dressmaker's."

He winced, dropping into a lazy sprawl in one of the chairs.

"I thought it only right that she should know

about her son's condition," she added hastily. "I have been acquainted with the lady for some years, and it would have felt deceitful not to tell her."

With the tanned fingers of one hand he scratched his cheek, staring into the fire. "Yes, I suppose she ought to know. Thank you for saving me the onerous task of informing her."

Relieved, Mary sat in the opposite chair.

"Although I doubt Ransom will thank you," he continued. "Doesn't want her here making one of her commotions."

"Well, she said she would not come unless he asked for her. She appeared upset, but thought it best to wait until she is invited."

He looked up, eyes hard and cold suddenly. "Does she know I'm here?"

Mary nodded, biting her lip, hands in her lap.

"Then she'll stay away, if she knows what's good for her."

Across the room, in the bed, Ransom let out a groan, but slept on.

Deverell lowered his voice again. "You will know, I'm sure, about my marriage to his mother and how it ended."

Again she nodded.

He fell further back in the chair, stretching his legs out and crossing them at the ankle. "I often think Ransom had the roughest time of it. Raven too, although she soon learned how to play her mother and I against each other and used that to her advantage. Ransom was closer to his mother, had the fleece pulled over his eyes in regard to her...behavior." With a thin, frustrated sigh, he looked over at his son and added, "Ah, what do I know of these things? Who can say what goes on in any man's mind, eh? We should try to be more cheerful, should we not, for his sake?" But his voice was hoarse and ragged, torn with worry.

"Yes, sir." She hesitated and then decided to plow forward. "Who is Sally, sir?"

His gaze returned to her so swiftly and angrily she felt stung. "Sally?" he demanded.

Oh, dear. Had she pried beyond her boundaries? "Your son mentioned the name as he dreamed."

True Deverell covered his eyes briefly with one hand and then drew his fingers down. He looked more tired than ever then. "I knew he still dwelt on that girl," was all he said.

Mary sat quietly, not knowing what else to say. Clearly, this was a sensitive subject and it was not like her to blunder in carelessly where she might cause pain, so she held her tongue.

Finally he added, "The past is not always a good place to revisit."

She agreed fervently. "I believe in looking to the future, not the past."

"Good." He rested both hands on his thighs and regarded her steadily, intensely. Again he reminded her of his son. The resemblance was very strong, and in the firelight it was almost eerily so. "Then you'd do better not to talk of that," he snapped.

"Of course. I did not mean to—"

"Until he's ready," he added in a kinder tone. "Let him tell you about Sally in his own time. Don't push him." With a self-deprecating grimace, he added, "One thing I have learned in my advanced years, Miss Ashford, is that one must have patience, particularly with one's offspring."

"Of course." In the meantime she would have to contain her imagination before it formed some very dark and bleak ideas.

Mary searched for a brighter subject. "I should tell you, sir, that my business partner has contacted a Professor Faraday at the Royal Institution in Mayfair— a learned gentleman with experience of breathing apparatus and oxygen."

"The Royal Institution? Yes, I know of it. Albemarle Street, is it not? Faraday lectures there, along with other great men of science."

She nodded eagerly. "He cannot see Ransom until tomorrow, but he has agreed to try treatment, for the purposes of scientific research, if...if you are in agreement, sir. The oxygen therapy— as he calls it— can help re-inflate the lung. It has been used with some success for patients with various diseases, such as consumption, asthma, palsy—."

"Miss Ashford, this is wonderful news." His

brows rumpled and then straightened. He sat up. "I thought that sawbones you sent for had no hope of full recovery?"

"Dr. Woodley was of an adverse opinion in regard to any likely success from the treatment, but it does not hurt to try something new, does it? At least," she hesitated, watching his countenance cautiously, "that is what I believe, sir. It may have been forward of me to take these steps without consulting you, but you did say you would leave it in my hands."

His eyes gleamed. "Miss Ashford, I believe you *do* care about my son."

She was relieved that somebody believed it, but darkly amused that he sounded so surprised.

"Yet, you do see the risk in all this?" he asked. "I mean the risk to yourself. You know what I would warn you, surely, for I see you are a woman of intelligence and foresight."

Solemnly she replied, "Yes, sir. I know that once he recovers, there is a chance he will change his mind. Once returned to full function, he could decide that he does not need me at his side after all. I am aware of that risk and of the odds against me. But that is a chance I must take, to get him well again. It is all that matters. I cannot stand idly by and see him suffer. I must be active, and I am sure you feel the same."

"Of course. As my darling wife Olivia would point out to me, my solution is usually to throw money at any problem." He gave her a sheepish grin.

"But in this case I did not know who or what to throw it at."

"And you were frustrated. It made you angry." Hence the pacing, swearing and dropping of knives. "Now, all we need to worry about is getting your recalcitrant son into the special carriage when it arrives to take him to the Royal Institute early tomorrow."

They both looked over at the bed and then at each other.

"He's not going to like it," Deverell muttered.

"No, but I am brave and just as stubborn as he."

He nodded slowly. "Yes, Mary Ashford, I believe you are. How did you say he met you?"

"He bounced off a lamp post."

"Ah. That sounds like him."

Chapter Twenty-One

Mary was not permitted to go in the carriage with him. Professor Faraday's manservant did not consider it proper. She might have protested, because she was Ransom's fiancée and therefore, surely, had a right. But no. Not this time. She stayed silent and let them take him.

They would give him the oxygen therapy for several hours, twice a day, and since it was not convenient to bring him back and forth so many times, he was to be a resident on Albemarle Street with one of the professors, until he showed marked improvement. True Deverell had promised the Institution a large donation. They would take excellent care of him.

Her part was done.

What she had said to his father last night was quite true. Once Ransom regained his full functions, he may, in all likelihood, change his mind and not want to marry her. Or anybody. In his desperate moment he had felt weak, almost a child again, needing...somebody...something to hold.

She was glad she had been there for him. No matter what happened next, she would always remember holding his hand. His kiss. What it felt like to be so needed, to be looked at as someone important and special, a person with opinions, feelings, and ideas that mattered. Especially to be looked at that way by a man of vim and vigor, a man who did not see her as somebody to be pitied at all.

The house was empty without him, grief-stricken.

"Why go back to that bookshop?" his father exclaimed gruffly, when he caught her in the hall, putting on her coat later that morning. "You can keep me company now."

She explained about her sister, and he shrugged. "Why not bring that sister of yours here then? There's plenty of damned room and none of it being used."

But when Mary arrived back at *Beloved Books* she discovered that her sister was already packing a trunk. She had been invited to Lady Charlotte's for the winter. Buzzing about like an addled bumblebee, and without Mary's calming presence, the girl had packed dirty walking boots atop delicate petticoats, crushed her bonnet under several heavy books and — on the verge of closing her trunk—had only just remembered more than half the things she must take.

"You do not mind that I go, do you, Mary? She has offered to let me have Raven's old bedroom, and she will take me to a concert. She has a friend with a box at the Drury Lane Theatre, and he is not in town to use it, so it is entirely at our disposal. I cannot find my better stockings and cannot think what became of them, so I shall take yours. If you do not mind? Mary?"

Belatedly realizing that her sister had paused for her answer, Mary nodded. "Of course. Take anything you need."

How could she stop her sister from indulging in all these promised delights? Her only worry was that once Lady Charlotte's circle returned for the proper social season she might not have so much time for "Violette" and could grow bored of her project, like a little girl casting a doll aside.

"Oh, and she says in her letter that you need not come again now. The weather is so very bad and I daresay...well, she and I will be too busy and you would never find us in when you came." Violet laughed merrily and high in her throat, as people do when they anticipate that what they have said is not particularly funny, but they have already started the sound so they must continue until it peters out, as unnaturally as it began.

So she was being usurped as Lady Charlotte's companion. Punishment, no doubt, for her engagement to Ransom, which must be seen as a betrayal of some kind. Well, she knew it would happen sooner or later, once the lady had better entertainment.

Violet paused again, a petticoat over one arm. "She says her son will never marry you."

Mary turned away, searching through her own drawer to see what she could give her sister.

"She said you are completely unsuited as a

match," Violet added.

"Yes, well, I am only after his money, of course. And he wants my favors in return."

"Mary! Such a thing to say. I know you would never be a mercenary wanton."

"Thank you, sister, for your faith in me."

"You're much too dull, drear, and dignified."

Mary bent her head, reaching further into the drawer, hiding her smile.

"Are you truly engaged to him?"

"I know not, Violet. Perhaps I imagined it. I do sometimes fall prey to flights of fancy."

"You never do!"

"I just hide it better than some people." She offered her sister a fringed shawl which was, quite probably, the prettiest item she had in her possession. Far too nice to be worn, unless a person had somewhere very grand to travel in it. Uncle Hugo had bought it for her birthday, years ago, from one of his trips abroad. "You may take this with you, if you'd like."

Her sister looked at the shawl, wrinkling her delicate nose. "Good lord, no. Nobody young wears shawls like that these days. Unless they feel a draft." Again the laugh, but cut much shorter. Abruptly she gripped Mary by the shoulders. "*You* keep it, dearest," she exclaimed, her eyes big with sympathy.

Clearly, Mary was expected to feel a lot of drafts in her future.

* * * *

That evening she and Thaddeus Speedwell ate dinner in companionable silence, their table set before the fire, he reading a book, holding it in one hand and his fork in the other.

With none of Violet's chatter, the parlor felt even smaller and darker than usual.

"Shall I light more candles, Mr. Speedwell? I wouldn't want you to strain your eyes."

He looked up over his spectacles. "If you wish, my dear Mary. We have plenty now. No need to stretch them."

She got up and lit two more, placing them on the table in brass candlesticks from the mantle.

"I have been thinking, Mr. Speedwell, about the shop."

"What's that, my dear?" He put down his fork to turn a page.

"I have some ideas for the business. A few things I thought we might try, to encourage more customers."

That got his attention. "More customers?" He gazed bleakly through those smeared lenses. "Must we have more?"

Mary smiled. "If we mean to make this a viable, thriving business, we cannot continue to rely on the same few generous, elderly customers...and the occasional unexpected visit from somebody who only stumbles upon us. We must find and encourage new readers. Think of all the people who are missing out on these wonderful books."

"But Mary," his anxious breath pummeled the candle flames, "we manage well enough." Looking around the little room, he shrugged his narrow shoulders. "What more can we want?"

"We can *want* everything and anything, Mr. Speedwell. There are no limits, only possibilities."

"Oh, my dear, I do not like the sound of that."

She reached for the wine jug and poured for them both. "Someone— very successful in business— told me recently that we are not taking advantage of our potential."

"We are not?"

"Indeed. So there are just a few changes I'd like us to make in this bookshop. And if you ever feel it has gone too far, I shall stop."

Thaddeus closed his book. "You must be missing your sister, my dear."

"A little."

"Then that has brought this on?"

Mary chuckled. "No, Mr. Speedwell. A man has brought this on. Or rather, encouraged it out of me. Like a genie from a lamp."

His spectacles slipped down his nose. "I see. Then you must be in love."

"Love?" She sipped her wine. "You read too many novels, Mr. Speedwell."

342

Real life was much too messy, and nothing ever happened the way it did in novels.

* * * *

On Wednesday morning she returned to Deverell's house in time to greet Captain Justify's secret bride, who arrived promptly at the hour of nine. Smith was visibly relieved to hear her tell True Deverell that this visitor was a friend of hers and the gentleman, apparently satisfied with this explanation, returned to his study, leaving the ladies to talk in the drawing room.

Over tea and scones, Mary discovered that the lady's name was Anshula, which meant "Sunny"— a name that she preferred now she was in England, because "it makes people think of hope and summer, and they look less confused when I introduce myself". She was twenty-one years of age, could speak English rather well (but only when she wanted to), and she had been acquired by Captain Deverell at a bride sale.

"The Captain bought me for six pounds. Are you shocked?"

Mary had to admit it was not something she'd ever heard of, but Sunny looked respectable and her manners were polite— more so than those of many people who would consider themselves superior to a woman bought by a man for six pounds. She was well dressed in brilliantly dyed silk taffeta. Rather colorful for a winter's day, but quite beautiful.

343

"Captain Deverell purchased me out of pity. He has a kindness which is rare in men, so I find. But he had to go back to sea, so he asked his brother to look after me. I must come here once a week to let Ransom Deverell know that I am well. I am to tell him if I need anything, because he can then write to my husband for me. I speak the language, but I do not write it well."

"Ransom said you knew only a very few words."

She gave a guilty, but pretty smile. "Yes. I prefer it that way. Especially with the men. The less they know about me, the better."

Mary laughed.

"But this Ransom Deverell is a puzzle to me," Sunny tipped her head as she studied Mary. "I hear he is such a bad man, yet I do not see it."

"Quite. It is something of a riddle."

"And each time I come here, he gives me money." Her beautiful, deep brown eyes flared, the long black lashes sweeping languidly down and up. "It is most curious. Why does he do this?"

"Don't you need it? I thought it was to help pay rent for your lodgings."

"But I have money of my own." She drew back in astonishment. "He does not know this?"

"Apparently not. Neither does the Captain, if he asked his brother to pay your rent."

"I try to tell the little grey fellow who gives it to me." She pointed a gloved finger toward the door

344

through which Smith had left them. "But he will not listen. He insists he has his orders and must follow them. And Ransom Deverell is often not here. Most often he is...away...here and there, I am told. Never in one place. He go here and he go there. But always the money is left for me. That he never forgets."

"Yes. That sounds very much like him."

Again Sunny's head tilted and she put a finger to her lips. "Now you are here, he will stay at home? You can tell him I do not need this money."

But Mary did not know what was going to happen, did she?

"I am glad you are here, Mary Ashford, for now we have met and I have someone to talk with when I come on Wednesday." The other woman leaned over and whispered, "Also you can tell the little grey fellow that he makes the tea too weak and his scones, they are dry."

"Ah, I do not think he is responsible for the tea and scones, he merely brings them to us. The cook is Mrs. Clay and she is usually very—"

"I should bring you *my* scones." she said firmly, nodding her head. "They are very good. The best scones. You will see, Mary Ashford!"

"Yes," she looked down at her tea, "but I don't live here."

"No?"

"I am a visitor. Like you."

Sunny's surprised voice was warm and rich, like a

melting sauce of fudge and syrup, but with the sweetness cut by something hotter and spicier. "It is very strange that you do not live here. You look at home, as if you have always been here."

She thought of her portrait in his bedchamber. "In a way, I have."

* * * *

That bloody interring woman! Is this what happened to a man when he considered marriage to one of them? Suddenly she was taking over, making decisions, having him loaded into carriages and dragged off with complete strangers.

All Mary said to him was, "As you told me once, we must be forward-thinking."

He was furious for about twenty minutes.

Arriving somewhere in Mayfair, he was transferred from a canvas stretcher to a bed in what appeared to be somebody's study, full of wretched books and odd, unidentifiable equipment. He was offered food and drink— both of which he refused, demanding to be taken home again.

"But Mr. Deverell, our good friend Thaddeus Speedwell has asked us to look at your lungs."

"Why?" He seized the front of his nightshirt. "What are you going to do to them?"

He was poked, prodded and experimented upon by a group of fellows in wigs, who did a lot of talking to each other and very little to him. Indeed, when they addressed any remark at him, it was in a loud, hollow voice, as if he might be an idiot.

Oh, Mary Ashford would pay for this when he got his hands on her again.

"Where am I?" he demanded. "This is not a hospital."

One of the gentlemen explained, "We are professors of the Royal Institution, sir, and this is my study where I can administer advantageous *therapia.*"

"I beg your bloody pardon?"

"Medical treatment, sir." He leaned closer and bellowed. "Therapy!"

"I don't want any of that, whatever it is." But when he tried to get up, they shoved him down again.

"Sir, we must auscultate your chest."

"You'll do no such thing. Whatever that is. Get your hands off me."

They calmly proceeded to ignore his protests, open his nightshirt, and listen to his chest through an instrument like an ear trumpet. He had not the strength he could usually rely upon, and some of his bruises felt worse today than they did yesterday, so in the end he lay rigid with anger and allowed these indignities to be committed upon his person.

Mary Ashford needn't think he'd let her get away with this. No indeed. He could imagine her watching over him, like that portrait, smugly enjoying herself with some private joke. At his expense.

There followed considerable discussion between

them all, leaving him utterly out of it.

Eventually a mask was put over his nose and mouth and he was told that he would be inhaling a mixture of pure and common air— whatever the deuce that was— and that he should breathe normally.

Normally. He'd forgotten what that was.

For the past few days he'd been breathing as he would in a thick pea-soup fog. Suddenly now the struggle eased. Blessed peace. Blessed air.

* * * *

Mary spent the next few days cleaning and rearranging the shop, an exhausting task that would have been overwhelming if Sunny did not come to help, bringing some of those scones about which she had boasted. They were, as she'd promised, extremely good and flavored by something delicious but unidentifiable— and apparently a secret that could not be divulged. Mr. Speedwell was soon enamored with them, and with Sunny herself. Making a great fuss of the old man, as if he was a pet, she spent more time talking to him, than she did wielding a broom or dust rag. But she was still far more use than "Violette" would have been.

While Mary washed the small square panes of the bow window one afternoon, she saw that it had begun to snow again. There were very few people walking in the street and it was a peaceful scene, lit by the glow of that single gas lamp by the arch. She often found her gaze wandering to that solitary lamp post lately. This was the post that had caused Ransom Deverell to bump his head and find her that chilly morning just a few weeks ago. Dear lamp post.

Violet would say she must be in love with it, for the amount of time she stood there pining over it.

She ought to decorate it with some pine bowers since they were only a few days from Christmas.

But just as she thought this, a tall figure emerged through the snow and stood in the patch of yellow light cast by her dear lamp.

Mary paused, her wet rag against the window. The man stood there, looking her way. Snow was collecting on his hat and shoulders he stood there so long and so still.

And then he moved, coming toward her shop.

Her pulse picked up from a canter to a gallop. Was it Ransom? Could it be possible that he was well enough to walk out in the snow already?

She had not heard from his father and did not wish to make a pest of herself by going there too often to ask if there was any news. Her one letter to Ransom, care of Professor Faraday at the Royal Institution, had not yet been answered, although she'd made it as harmless as she could, nothing romantic or gushy. Just a letter that one friend might write to another. Mary did not want him to feel trapped, as if she meant to put one of those despised leashes around his throat. And she certainly did not want him to think she'd helped him out of any ulterior motive, or that she waited for thanks.

She had helped him as he'd helped her.

And because...because...

Suddenly the man's face was clearer. He was opening the shop door, making the little bell ring. Mary dropped her rag into the bucket of water at her feet and felt her heart fall likewise.

It was not Ransom.

"Mary. Miss Ashford. So many years it has been." He swept off his snow-laden hat, but did not bow. Instead he stood there inside her shop, looking around with mild disdain. "I had heard you lived here, but did not believe it," he muttered awkwardly. "How are you?"

She smoothed her hands down her sides and then clasped them before her. After eight years and one broken engagement, all he could ask was *How are you?*

"I am well, Lord Stanbury. You have come a long way across town to visit. It must be something very important that brought you out in this weather."

Thank goodness Violet was not there. Mary could not have dealt with him so easily if her sister was there to scowl and make various noises of derision.

"It *is* something important," he agreed, stepping forward rather gingerly, as if he feared stepping on something unpleasant. "The news of your engagement to that cad Ransom Deverell is all over town."

Ah, of course it was.

She waited, watching him warily. George was still handsome, as she had noted in the street outside the haberdasher's, but the ugliness within had begun to take shape in the sagging of jowls that were rarely lifted in a smile, in lips edged with tight, deep lines from the constant expression of condemnation, and in the bulging of a spoiled lower lip. His eyes, once fine, could now be described as "beady", sunken into hollows beneath brows that, from the puckering skin between them, must be frequently drawn together in a scowl.

Once she, a naive, impetuous girl, easily led by the opinions of others, had been prepared to marry George Stanbury. What a blind fool she had been. How lucky she was that he married another. But eight years ago she was devastated by this man and his callous betrayal. Eight years ago she was not forward-thinking and could not see the future.

Why did he come there now? What could he want?

"I know you are all alone in the world now, Mary. You have no male figure to guide and counsel you." He cleared his throat and gestured with his hat. "Abandoned to this place, I'm sure you were desperate to get out. It is...understandable that you might take a wrong path. But I feel— forgive me if I overstep—I feel that I have some responsibility, in the absence of male relatives, to advise you against this terrible mistake you are making."

"You *do* overstep, Lord Stanbury." Passionate outrage was not a very ladylike or British emotion to express out loud, but she was certainly feeling it at that moment. With every fiber of her being. "What makes you think you have any such responsibility?"

"Our families were, at one time, close. I was a friend to both your brothers and a confidant of your father's. And," he looked down, unable then to meet her steady, angry gaze, "you and I were once engaged."

"Thank you for reminding me. I had quite forgotten. As did you, eight years ago."

"I believe your father would expect me to intervene if I saw you being ill-used, making a misstep of this caliber. You must break this off at once before any little bit of reputation you have left is irreparably damaged."

"Why, precisely, is my engagement to Ransom Deverell a misstep?"

He looked up again and there went the gathering of his brows, forming that well-hewn ridge in his brow. "He is a vile seducer. A rogue with every vice—"

"And your proof of that?"

"Proof?" he growled. "Oh, I have my proof, but

I am not at liberty to share all that with you, Mary."

"Why not? You are at liberty to come here and tell me what I *must* do."

"It is a private, intimate matter." His sharp gaze bore down upon her, trying to frighten her.

He never did know her very well, did he?

"Suffice to say, that fiend lures wives into adultery, ruins marriages, and leaves his cuckoos in other men's nests, without the slightest apprehension of a conscience." His gaze tracked across the stained apron she wore over her gown, his mean, pinched eyes simmering with disgust. "To be sure you know of his reputation. How can any woman raised as you were, descend to his depths of sin and debauchery? Think of the honorable Ashford name. Of your proud father, who would surely turn in his grave."

And that was where he went just a step *too* far beyond his bounds.

"How dare you speak to me of the Ashford name and my father?" Her temper rolled and bubbled like a storm cloud about to burst over them. She curled her fingers into fists at her sides. "When was our honor and dignity ever a matter about which you concerned yourself? You never cared for anybody but George Stanbury. But I have forgiven you all these years because I understood why you did it, and I too am practical. You needed a wife with a dowry to maintain your estate. Your selfishness was, at least, understandable, and I could reconcile myself to the humiliation by thinking it was your only sound choice. That you had no other way. But you cannot now come here to me and suddenly pretend to care about *pride and honor.*" The cloud burst, ripping apart at the seams, spilling her fury like hailstones, every word spitting out of her. "You cannot now tell me what *I* should do, when you have always done what was best for you."

He stepped back, knocking into a shelf. "There is no need to raise your voice, madam."

"There is every need. I have been meek and ladylike for far too long. And in the matter of you feeling any responsibility toward me, although I have no inkling of how you might have come by that idea, rest assured I absolve you of it. As far as I recall nobody I know has ever consulted me before *they* married, and I certainly have no plans to consult anybody before *I* take a husband. Whoever he might be."

His eyes narrowed even further. "Then you have not accepted Deverell?"

"I am not at liberty to share all that with you, George," she replied in the same arrogant tone he had used. "Suffice to say he is the most wonderful gentleman I know. And the most honest. At least he does not make promises he cannot or will not keep."

"You are mad, then. The man will not change his ways. I thought to teach him a lesson, but perhaps he needs another. If he comes near my wife again, I will

take more permanent steps to be rid of him." After
that he tried to leave, but, of course, the door stuck.
The handle had been mended again since Ransom
pulled it to pieces, but it remained just as begrudging
as ever when it came to letting customers escape.

Mary watched George fighting with the door
handle. "What do you mean? What lesson?"

He would not answer. Shaking with rage, he
twisted the handle and cursed.

"Did you send those thugs to attack Ransom
Deverell outside his club?" she demanded.

"The devil got what he deserved."

She felt sick. Her head ached.

"Let me out of this godforsaken place," he
shouted. "I should not have come here."

Mary walked over, turned the handle and opened
the door. "No, you should not."

She saw that he was not only enraged, but
embarrassed, his face mottled with white and scarlet
blotches.

"If I told the Deverells what you did, they would
come for you and teach *you* a lesson, Lord Stanbury."
Swinging the door open wider, she waited.

"I did what any other husband would do when
he discovered such an act of treachery committed
against him," he hissed, "with his own property."

Property: that was what he considered his wife.
"And whatever this traitorous act might be, how do
you know Ransom Deverell was responsible?"

He spoke through gritted teeth. "I followed her when she went to his house. I saw her leaving the place after she must have told him. But I'd suspected an affair for some time. So you see, I have *proof*."

But he also had the wrong brother. Mary clasped the door handle tighter. "You have made a great error. The next time you take justice into your own hands— or put it into the hands of your thugs— I suggest you ask your wife for the truth."

"I will not discuss this with Elizabeth. She and I will never talk of it. We will go on as we always have."

"Of course. Why be honest with each other? A great many other unpleasant truths might come out. You're fortunate, Lord Stanbury, that your actions did not cause Mr. Ransom Deverell to be killed. Would you have boasted of it then to me, I wonder?"

"I did not come here to tell you any of that, and certainly not to boast. I came only to warn you against tying your name to that reprehensible family."

"Well, then you have done the service you came to perform. Good evening."

He paused to shake his hat at her and deliver one last piece of advice. "*Think,* madam, what you do. Think on it with care!"

"Yes, indeed." She smiled sweetly. "I must think with great care about whether or not I should tell True Deverell what you did to his son. Whether I would want to be responsible for the consequences of giving him that information."

He did not look at her again, but marched out into the snow. Mary closed the door firmly and then slid the bolt across. Today it felt more satisfying than slamming it.

She knew that, with the threat of True Deverell's retribution hanging over his head, he would never have a moment's peace again. Holding George's fate in her hands was a remarkably fortifying sensation. Quite possibly wicked too. But a long overdue revenge for the time when that circumstance had been reversed.

Chapter Twenty-Two

"Dearest Mary;

My mother wrote to give me some news that has left me in utter despair. You cannot possibly consider marrying my wretched brother! Assure me at once that she has misunderstood in some dreadful way.

You know he is a rake of the highest order and will break your dear, tender heart. He is my brother and I <u>must</u> love him, but no sensible woman would volunteer herself for that duty. My beloved Mary, write back as soon as you can and explain to me how this wicked idea might have come to dwell inside my mother's head. I shall be quite bereft of sleep and comfort until I read, in your own hand, that you are safe from making such a heinous mistake. Your heart was broken once before, and I will not stand by and allow it to happen again in the hands of my brother…"

The story was indeed all over town, as George Stanbury had warned. Wherever Mary went, faces turned to watch and hands covered lips to whisper.

What did she care?

In fact, lurid curiosity brought new customers every day to *Beloved Books,* all of them eager to get a look at the pitiful woman who was engaged to marry the worst rake in London. But they found nobody to pity. Mary, who had experience of keeping up appearances, held her head up and wore a smile upon her face. She even served tea with Sunny's excellent scones and cakes, putting them out on the counter to entice her nosy customers further inside the shop.

As Christmas Eve approached, she put a special display in the bow window, decorating with holly, mistletoe, and two newly purchased oil lamps that kept the window cozily lit even as it grew dark out. That glowing scene drew more folk across the street to look in and browse.

The takings steadily increased.

An old newspaper cutting was sent to her anonymously by some busy body, whose identity she did not care to know. It told her about the fatal curricle accident that had left a woman dead and Ransom Deverell suspected of murder. In lurid detail the article spoke of the young woman's injuries and how she had been left face down in a stream on the Cornish moor.

And her name was Sally White.

Mary had known about the accident before. Raven told her of it, years ago, but she had never known the name of the young woman who was killed.

So now she knew that this was the woman about whom Ransom suffered bad dreams. The reason why he feared sleep and did all he could to avoid it.

Despite the fact that he was cleared of all culpability in Sally White's death, there were still folk who considered him guilty. They had made up their minds about him and he must have given up trying to sway the tide of public opinion. He shrugged it off, laughed and pretended he had no conscience. It was his way of managing and surviving.

* * * *

Sister;

I hope you are well. I am not in the best of health, but you know I never complain.

You will wonder why I have not written this past week, but I have been very busy dashing here and there with Lady Charlotte. At last I have a moment to put pen to paper, although I fear her ladyship will shout for me again presently.

Her ladyship is quite a demanding companion and seldom satisfied. For a lady with everything at her disposal, she is sorely riven with discontent. I am left quite at a loss as how to cheer her spirits.

My feet ache, and I have a blister. Also a sore tooth. I fear I am growing a wart.

I am not so fond of champagne as I imagined I should be.

If you could send me some of your headache powders, I would be grateful. Lady Charlotte does not like me to use hers for fear of running out. She does not like me to use much of anything that is hers.

How is Mr. Speedwell, that dear fellow? I suppose you are huddled together over the fire and imagining all my grand adventures. Of which I am having many, of course, far more than I can tell you about in this letter, for there simply isn't room.

I suppose you miss me dreadfully.

It is quite cold at night, even in Mayfair I wish I had borrowed that shawl you offered, but I daresay you are in need of it more than I, Mary. How warm we used to be in that little bed together.

Yours with great affection,
Violette xxx

The "great affection" had been run through with one bold line of ink and replaced with "love". At the bottom of the paper one final sentence was scrawled in messy haste.

I may come home sooner than planned, if you are desirous of it and ask me to come, for I should not want you to miss my company too long and I know how you both depend upon me.

Absence, it seemed, had indeed made the heart grow fonder. Even an absence of only five days.

On that same morning, Mary received another letter. Also short, it took far fewer attempts to conceal its purpose and required less scratching out to correct erroneous spelling.

The Honorable Miss Mary Ashford;

When I am released into the wild again, I shall expect a full explanation and apology from those infamous lips of yours.

You deserted your post at my side and left me to the care of wigged buffoons, a betrayal of unforgiveable proportions.

You and I have much to discuss.
Prepare yourself.

Annoyed and inconvenienced,
The King of Siam.

* * * *

Mary wrapped the parcel of books and slid them across the counter.

"Thank you, madam." She smiled, hiding a tired yawn for it was Christmas Eve and it had been a very busy day. "Do come again."

The customer agreed that she would and gathered her children to herd them out through the door, which stood open for them already.

A gentleman was holding it for the lady and her family. A gentleman balanced precariously on crutches and pulling faces at the children, who ran, screaming, out of the shop.

She could hear Mr. Speedwell cracking nuts in the parlor while he warmed his feet by the fire. Occasionally there was the chink of glass as he poured himself another sherry. He would not have heard anybody else come in, or even the screaming of the children. Fortunately he couldn't hear her heart beat either.

The man pushed the door shut with one crutch and then made his way down the aisle toward her, cursing under his breath.

Mary finally got her own feet to move and came out from behind the counter. "Mr. Deverell, I did not know you would be out and about so soon. And in this weather."

His face was still a little worse for wear, but much improved from what it had been when she last saw it. Those dark, mischievous eyes were back to their usual arrogant self, taking her in with swift, merciless critique. "Hoped I'd be locked up a while yet, eh?"

"Nobody locked you up! It was for your own good."

His lips curled. "And I am almost my old self again, so although I should like to punish you for defying me and leaving my presence, it seems I cannot. My father informs me I must be polite and thank you for all that you did. It seems I will live after all and it is all due to your persistence. So you only have yourself to blame that I'm still here."

Her heart felt as if it had wings that could not quite raise it off the ground, although they tried hard. Something held it down. Not knowing what to do, she hovered on her toes, hands tightly clasped.

"You've been industrious." His gaze scanned the shop with evident approval and surprise. "I almost did not recognize the place. Two dozen spiders must have been rendered homeless. I could even see through the damned window as I came down the street."

"I took some of your suggestions and put them into practice."

"Then I'm entitled to a share of the profits?"

Mary longed to touch him, to hold his face and kiss him. "I suppose so." Who cared about silly profits? He was well again. He was standing, exuding that commanding aura again, as he did the first time he entered her shop. Whenever he was near he swept all other considerations out of her mind and heart.

"Come here, Miss Ashford," he said crisply, resettling both crutches under one arm.

A part of her felt as if she ought to object to his tone, but the rest of her was too impatient and yearning. She went to him, and he curled his free arm around her waist, drawing her close.

"Don't hurt yourself," she muttered.

"Turn your face up to me. I want to look at you."

So she did. At that moment she would do anything he asked without question.

And then he lowered his mouth to hers and melted a kiss into her lips. It ran like molten silver through her body and caught fire with everything it touched on its way down. She placed her hands on his chest and felt that glorious strength stirring, surrounding her, giving her shelter.

When their lips parted, his eyes searched her face, looking for something with that familiar smoky, smoldering intensity. She would never be able to keep secrets from this man, she realized. He opened her easily, turned her inside out.

"I hope you don't think to back out of this marriage lark, as you called it," he said sternly. "I know you only agreed in the first place to keep me quiet, not expecting me to live long."

She gasped. "That is not the case." But she *had* expected him to change his mind once recovered. Mary hadn't dared hope he'd keep a promise.

His arm gripped her firmer, pressing her tightly to his body. "You belong to me now."

Her struggling heart was off the ground, its little wings succeeding in lifting the weight at last.

"No," she said with a little smile. "*You* belong to *me*."

* * * *

Ransom wanted to carry her out to his father's carriage, but he could not. Soon though, when he was back to full strength and walking without crutches. Then she had better watch out!

"Mary, you look different."

"Do I?"

He squinted. "Younger. Naughtier."

Laughing, she reached up and tweaked his chin with her thumb and forefinger. "Don't flatter me."

"I didn't mean to. Don't want you getting vain." Frustrated by his crutches, he squeezed her even tighter with the one arm he could use. "I came to bring you home with me."

365

Her eyes opened wider, clear and shining like cool water in two silver cups. "Home?"

"I want you back in your nursing duties at my bedside. I do not care to spend another night without you."

She hesitated. "I'll need a moment to pack my things."

"No, you won't. You won't need any things. You need only me."

* * * *

That evening they dined with his father. The mood was merry, as it never had been in that house as far as Ransom could remember. He stayed quiet, letting the others talk, for he was content merely to look at Mary and listen to her voice.

She was very clever, bright, and witty. Not only did she entertain him, but he saw that she pleased his father. No small feat. For once in his thirty years Ransom had a female companion of whom he need not be ashamed or embarrassed, but proud.

That she tolerated him enough to marry was quite remarkable, but he was so grateful for it that he did not care to study her motives any longer.

It would have to be enough for now, and in the future he would hope for more. He would work damned hard to win her heart.

Because he was very much in love with her.

And just like that it happened. Somewhere

between the soup and the oysters, Ransom understood how much trouble he was in. Because he was fiercely in love with Mary Ashford.

Finally he had a name for this feeling that had plagued him. Until that moment he hadn't been able to identify it. Or had not wanted to admit it. He thought it was lust, combined with the need to possess and protect, a desire greater than anything he had ever felt.

But there it was, between the last sip of consommé and the tinkle of a raw oyster shell falling to a plate. Love. A realization as unexpected and sudden as it was deeply felt and undeniable.

How extraordinary.

Ransom Deverell had fallen foul of something he never thought would affect him. It had crept up and taken hold before he knew what was happening. And now he was beset with a new worry, for how could he make her love him in return. How could anybody love him?

Later, just as the dessert was served, another guest arrived and was shown into the drawing room. Smith came to whisper in Ransom's ear.

He got up. "Mary, will you help me?"

Instantly she left her sorbet, and hurried around the table to let him lean on her. He took a sweet breath of her perfume as his arm went around her shoulders. Together they walked across the hall to the drawing room, Mary having no idea who was waiting there for them, but focused on helping Ransom by bearing part of his weight.

At the door he stopped, put his hand under her chin and raised it to see her eyes again. "Mary, I will protect you for every day of my life and yours. Do you know that?"

Her eyes were quizzical, but warm. "Yes. I do."

"I don't care why you're marrying me. I only care that you do marry me. I will never let you be unhappy, not for one day."

She blinked. Her lips parted in surprise. "Why do you think I'm marrying you?"

That was a question for which he had no answer, but could only look down at her, suffering. "When we first met, you pretended not to know me or anything about me. But you do know, don't you? Everything. You must have heard all the rumors."

"Yes."

"You know how I was involved in the death of a young woman. Sally White."

"Yes." Her face was solemn. "But it was an accident."

"It was my fault. I should never have let her take the reins that night. Should never have drunk as much as I did. I was reckless and careless, as a result of which she died. I may not have struck the blow that killed her, but she would not have been wandering on the moor that night, injured and unprotected, if not for me and my stupidity." It had flowed out of him like blood from a wound and she listened, eyes wide, her hand in his.

After a pause she said, "Do you know why you suffer bad dreams about Sally?"

He swallowed. "Because she haunts me."

"No. Sally doesn't haunt you. She knows it wasn't your fault. Ransom Deverell, you have bad dreams because your conscience won't let you rest."

"My conscience?" He frowned.

"Yes, my darling. Despite all opinions to the contrary— your own included— you *do* have a conscience. Which means that you are redeemable, after all, even if you like to believe you're thoroughly wicked." She laughed, rising up to kiss him on the lips. "Don't look so alarmed. Your secret is safe with me."

How simple she made it all seem. There was hope in her face, clear and determined. Nobody else ever looked at him the way she did.

He brought her fingers to his mouth. "Mary, Since I am now being good..."

She looked skeptical.

"... and utterly honest, I have a confession to make."

"Oh, dear."

"Until just a few moments ago I did not realize I was in love with you."

That wiped the smile off her face. She stared, unblinking. "Oh...oh, dear."

"I thought it was lust," he continued, kissing her fingers. "I thought it was ...anything else. I knew I had to keep you with me, next to me for the rest of my life. But somewhere between dinner courses I realized the truth. I'm in love with you, Mary. Completely, utterly, unequivocally." He looked at her, waiting to see if she would run away screaming.

Finally she sighed and shook her head. "You only just decided you love me?"

"That's not what I said." He scowled, gripping her fingers and not letting her pull her hand away. "I didn't know what it was before now. How could I, since I'd never felt it before?"

"Better late than never I suppose."

"Well, I can't expect you to feel the same, of course," he muttered gruffly.

Then she smiled, her eyes shining with amusement. "Don't you know already?"

Ransom sniffed. "Know what?"

"I fell in love with you the very moment you ravaged my door handle."

His first instinct was to celebrate this news, but then the rest of her sentence sank in. Glaring down at her, he demanded, "That's all it took?"

"You left me in as much shambles as you left the pieces of that poor door handle. The first man ever to do so."

"The first ever?"

"Yes. No other man knew quite what to do with

370

it. Or with me."

That was better. He felt a few inches taller now as her words drifted up to him, and he finally let himself believe it was possible.

"I hope you know what you're taking on, Mary," he said, grinning broadly. Couldn't help himself, he was fairly foxed, yet he'd only drunk one glass of wine tonight.

"Yes," came the smug reply. "But do you?"

And with that, she helped him into the drawing room where the hastily acquired Justice of the Peace awaited, forced away from his own supper table by the persuasive efforts of Miggs.

The marriage ceremony took ten minutes and was relatively painless, much to his surprise.

When it was done they toasted with champagne, then Miggs and his father left for the club.

"I suppose you want to go back to your sorbet now," Ransom said to his bride.

"Good lord no, it'll be melted."

"I should have let you finish it, but I couldn't wait any longer. Not even a moment. See what a selfish beast I am?"

"Yes, I heard you always get your own way."

"I did. Until I met you."

She kissed him. "Poor darling. Why don't you sit down now and rest? You must be exhausted."

"No, no, no! I am not in the least tired."

"But you're still recovering and—"

"Newly in possession of a wife, all alone with her in my house at last, and not about to delay the claiming of my marital rights."

Her eyes turned smoky, her lips formed a small, pink circle. "Oh."

He smirked. "Precisely. The sorbet isn't the only thing around here that's melting."

Chapter Twenty-Three

For a man who had suffered a terrible beating eleven days ago, he was remarkably strong and lively. His crutches cast aside, he immediately set about unbuttoning her gown, pulling a few of them loose in his haste.

"Mary," he groaned, kissing the nape of her neck and sending shivers down her spine. "How I have longed for this moment."

"I suppose you haven't had to wait before," she quipped. "I do hope I won't be a disappointment."

"Impossible." His tongue traced her spine downward as her velvet gown fell in ripples from her shoulders, and then he eased each arm from its sleeve, paying diligent attention with his lips, to every newly exposed inch of limb.

"I haven't the slightest idea what to do," she confessed. There were no books on her shelves that dealt with this subject, and romantic novels all ended at the bedroom door.

"Fortunately for you," he nibbled on her earlobe as he began to unlace her corset, "I do."

"Yes, I suppose...there is...some...advantage...to one of us...know...knowing..." and soon after this she forgot what she'd been saying. Mary closed her eyes and leaned back against his body, trusting him completely.

"Don't forget to breathe, Mary my love," he chuckled as his hands loosened the ribbon at her waist, disposing of her petticoats in one deft move. "I thought I was the one who would have to worry about that."

She opened her eyes and caught their reflection in a mirrored wall panel. They were both naked by then, she in only her stockings. He was wildly beautiful. Something about him reminded her of a very fine Friesian horse that she saw once when her brothers took her to a fare. What would he say, Mary wondered, if she told him he reminded her of a horse? His eyes gleamed at her in the reflection, sparking with desire.

"Take down your hair," he whispered.

Quickly she did as he asked, until it fell over her shoulder in a long braid, and then he took over, too impatient to wait.

He lifted her to the bed, kissing her deeply and yet with a gentleness she could never have expected.

"Don't hurt yourself," she urged, concerned again about his injuries. "I'm sure parts of you are still swollen."

He laughed huskily, although she had no idea what was amusing. Until a few minutes later.

There were, Mary discovered that evening, some things one simply couldn't learn from books. But the study was no less satisfying and, she ventured to say, considerably more enjoyable.

* * * *

Several hours later, as they lay entwined in the sheets and each other, warm and sated— for the time being—he kissed Mary's loose, tumbled hair and said drowsily, "Why on earth did you agree to marry me? What were you thinking?" He wanted to keep hearing her say it.

A relaxed feeling had overtaken his body and, for once, made him in no hurry to leave the bed, not even to use the washbasin or fetch a glass of wine. Instead he wanted to go on, holding her there in his arms until somebody came to check that they were still alive.

"You decided it while I wasn't even here," she reminded him.

"But you went along with it."

"Yes. In a moment of sheer madness, I took that reckless chance. A part of me thought you'd change your mind, in any case."

He tangled his fingers in the silky, perfumed ropes of her dark hair, marveling at the softness, the way it curled around him like a living creature, passionate and possessive.

"See, Mary, we managed, despite the lack of shared interests and conversation."

He felt her laughter before he heard it, and then she lifted her head from his chest to look at him. "I believe I discovered one interest we share, sir."

"I'll show you some more in a while," he promised.

"You're not tired? Perhaps you ought to sleep."

He grinned, slipping his hand down to clasp the round, warm, rosy cheek of her bottom. "Plenty of time to sleep, wife, when I'm dead."

* * * *

The next morning he woke very early. While Mary still slept soundly, he left the bed, dressed and took his horse to Curzon Street, where he rang the bell at a very grand house and waited for several moments before the door was opened.

A bored-looking butler appeared to ask what he wanted.

"Is Lord Stanbury at home?" he enquired. "My name is Ransom Deverell, and I have some business with him. I apologize for calling on Christmas morning, but it is a matter of some urgency."

The butler's eyes wrinkled at the corners as he swept Ransom with a slow, careful appraisal from hat to boot and back again. "I shall see if his lordship is at home, sir. Please wait here." Apparently he was not to be offered the comfort of waiting indoors on that chilly morning.

After a considerable time, the butler reappeared. "I'm sorry, sir, but his lordship is not at home after all. Do you possess a card that you can leave?"

"No, I do not." He tipped his hat. "But please tell

his lordship— when he returns— that I will call again. Merry Christmas to you." With that he walked down the steps, mounted his horse and trotted away down the street. He turned the corner and then stopped to dismount again and wait.

Less than five minutes later, Stanbury emerged from the house in some haste, looking warily about, his coat collar turned up against the wind.

Ransom rode after the scurrying figure and then, in the middle of the pavement, cut the fellow off, leaping down from his saddle with only a slight pinch of pain to his chest. Just enough to remind him and keep the anger burning.

"Stanbury. You and I have some business to discuss, do we not?"

The man slipped on some ice, but stayed upright. "I do not know who you are."

"Oh, I think you do. You should, since those were your men that I encountered in the alley behind my club recently. In the dark."

"You mistake me for another. Excuse me. Stand aside."

But Ransom held his ground, feet apart, eyes narrowed. "Of course, a gentleman who believes himself — or his wife—wronged by another man, should call the scoundrel out and propose a duel. Is that not the proper and honorable way these disputes are settled?"

"I do not know you, sir. I suggest you let me pass

or I'll—"

"But you're not a gentleman, are you, Stanbury? You're a bloody milksop coward who can't get his hands dirty, so he sends other men to do the task for him."

The man's face was white. A flicker of terror shot through his eyes as they darted from side to side and he weighed his options in that empty street. "Whoever gave you this information is a liar," he hissed, jowls trembling. "Possibly a woman with an axe to grind against me."

"Nobody gave me any information." Ransom sputtered with harsh laughter. "I'm not as daft as I look, *your lordship*. I can put two and two together, even when my brains been knocked about in my head."

He knew that Stanbury, looking for somebody to pay for his wife's indiscretion, had chosen to blame him. Why not? Ransom Deverell was an easy scapegoat, a safe bet when it came to finding a villain responsible for any indiscretion committed. And Stanbury was the sort of man who only ever chose the "safe" bet.

Ransom was not about to inform the coward that he'd got the wrong Deverell. He'd take a beating for his brother. After all, his head was thicker than most.

He chuckled dourly. "There's not much you do for yourself, is there, Stanbury? Even your wife had to find another man to get your duty done for you."

It was a flash of the old Ransom— the desire to goad the ass into an honest brawl, in broad daylight, one on one, a fair fight. But Stanbury shrank into his own boots. "I'm telling you it had nothing to do with me. I don't know who those men were. They did not act on my command."

That, naturally, would be the excuse he gave to the Peelers if they were ever called upon. And he, a titled knob, would be believed in an instant.

Didn't mean Ransom couldn't serve the man a little punishment of his own.

"Well, I'll let it pass this time. After all, I owe you a debt, don't I, Stanbury?"

The man's jaw twitched angrily. "A debt?" he spat.

Ransom leaned close and whispered. "If you hadn't set Mary Ashford free, she would never have been mine. And I wouldn't be on my way home now to rejoin my beautiful, extremely passionate, and rather naughty wife in bed. The greatest Christmas gift any man could have. Good God, Stanbury, I almost feel sorry for you. If I wasn't such a selfish, wicked, unconscionable scapegallows, I would."

With that he mounted his horse and tipped his hat, before riding away, leaving a speechless, wilted George Stanbury standing in the snow. Quite alone.

* * * *

Mary sat up, clutching the counterpane to her

bosom when he came in. "Where have you been?"
The half empty breakfast tray on the bed proved that
she'd been replenished by a thoughtful Smith while he
was gone.

"My sweet, I just remembered an errand that
called me away."

"On Christmas morning?" she demanded.

"It couldn't wait, I'm afraid. There was no better
time to do it, but today." He grinned smugly, thinking
again of George Stanbury's face.

Raven's letter, received yesterday when he
returned from the Royal Institution, had told him all
about Mary's engagement to the cad and how he
broke her heart. It had been on Ransom's mind since
then and his first order of business, when he woke
that morning, was to serve that ass a long-overdue set
down. He could not get on with his day until he had
done that. For his new wife, as much as for himself.

"But don't pout, Mary, my delectable basket of
cabbages! Your loving husband has returned to
continue the deflowering now that you are awake,
rested and," he took the tray and set it on the floor,
"apparently well fed."

"But I haven't finished! There's cake with
chocolate and cream!"

He took a flying, sideways leap onto the bed,
tugging the covers out of her hands, eager to crawl
into that warm bed with her.

"Ransom! Your boots. Not with them on surely!"

She was right, he realized. In his ungentlemanly haste to get back to business, he'd forgotten his boots. Not the first time he'd kept them on at such a time, of course. But he had absolutely no desire to leave *this* woman's side in haste, and if the house burned down let it. So Ransom removed one boot and she the other, then he tossed them across the room.

"Hurry up then." She snuggled close. "Because I want my lovely cake."

It was then that he noticed something missing from the wall. "Just a moment, madam! What have you done with La Contessa?"

She paused, looked up from beneath a tangle of dark hair and exclaimed hotly, "I couldn't have her glowering down at me so pious and disapproving, could I? It was quite off-putting. What does she, a naive, silly girl, know about men and love?"

Ransom laughed and wrapped his arms around her. "Quite right, darling. We wouldn't want to make her blush."

Besides, he had the real Contessa in his bed now, didn't he?

Epilogue

Dear Mary - and now my SISTER;

It seems you could not heed my advice and married my despicable brother, despite everything! I give up. Why does nobody ever listen to me?

And there I was, always thinking you a moderately sensible woman.

I cannot wait to see you and hear all about it. Do come to Greyledge when you can and, if you must, bring my damnable brother. I suppose I must resolve myself to your utter ruin. At least now I finally have a sister and you had better always be on my side. It's only fair as you were _my_ friend first...

*

Mr. and Mrs. Ransom Deverell;

You are invited by Lady Charlotte Rothsey Deverell to an evening soiree at eight o'clock, on December 31st, 1850, at Mivart's Hotel. RSVP

(I trust, Mary, that you shall continue your visits? Or am I to be tossed aside by you too now? You, at least, always showed me kindness and seemed to appreciate the respect I am due. Your sister, though a sweet girl, makes altogether too much noise and dust. The sooner we get her married the better, but you are right in that a little clerk won't do. We must aim for

greater heights.)

*

My Dear Mrs. Deverell (Mary);

I was so thrilled to hear that Ransom had taken a wife. Please know that you are welcome at Roscarrock whenever you can come, indeed the sooner the better. I look forward to meeting you, as I hear from my husband that you are quite lovely and something of a miracle worker. He returns to us for the new year, and perhaps you could both travel to Cornwall with him then?

Welcome to the family, my dear. We are all delighted and eager to make your acquaintance.

Yours sincerely,
Olivia Westcott Ollerenshaw Pemberton Monday Deverell

* * * *

Mr. and Mrs. R. Deverell;

I saw in the newspaper that congratulations are in order. Best wishes to you both, although I must wonder at Miss Ashford's sanity.

Ransom, I owe you an apology. Although you sent me on a fool's chase to Yorkshire, I understand why you did so, and subsequent events have given me cause to be thankful for the misdirection.

I can divulge nothing more in a letter. Suffice to say, I

may remain in Yorkshire for some time. Fret not.

If you get to my lodgings, would you be so kind as to pack up my better boots, my special dice and my collapsible top hat, and send them off to Darkest Fathoms Hall, near Whitby? Don't tell father. Not that there is anything amiss, you understand. But better he not be concerned for the time being.

D.D.

COMING SOON

The Danger of Desperate Bonnets
(Ladies Most Unlikely - Book Two)

Damon Undone
(The Deverells - Book Five)

Ransom Redeemed

Also from Jayne Fresina and TEP:

Souls Dryft

The Taming of the Tudor Male Series

Seducing the Beast

Once A Rogue

The Savage and the Stiff Upper Lip

The Deverells

True Story

Storm

Chasing Raven

Ransom Redeemed

Ladies Most Unlikely

The Trouble with His Lordship's Trousers

COMING SOON – The Danger in
Desperate Bonnets

A Private Collection

Last Rake Standing

ABOUT THE AUTHOR

Jayne Fresina sprouted up in England, the youngest in a family of four daughters. Entertained by her father's colorful tales of growing up in the countryside, and surrounded by opinionated sisters - all with far more exciting lives than hers - she's always had inspiration for her beleaguered heroes and unstoppable heroines.

Website at:
jaynefresinaromanceauthor.blogspot.com

Twisted E Publishing, Inc.
www.twistederoticapublishing.com

Made in the USA
Middletown, DE
18 August 2016